la courte échelle

W9-BIZ-620

A Kim u 🏳

n'ai pas trop peur!

I ai peur Kim

Les éditions de la courte échelle inc.

24 septembre 1994

Bertrand Gauthier

Bertrand Gauthier est le fondateur des éditions de la courte échelle. Il a publié plusieurs livres pour enfants dont les séries *Zunik, Ani Croche* et *Les frères Bulle.* Il a également publié deux romans dans la collection Roman+. Il a reçu le Prix des clubs de lecture Livromagie pour *La revanche d'Ani Croche.* Plusieurs de ses livres sont traduits en anglais, en chinois, en grec et en espagnol.

Bertrand Gauthier est un adepte de la bonne forme physique. Selon lui, écrire est épuisant et il faut être en grande forme pour arriver à le faire. Mais avant tout, Bertrand Gauthier est un grand paresseux qui aime flâner. Aussi, il a appris à bien s'organiser. Pour avoir beaucoup... beaucoup de temps pour flâner.

Stéphane Jorisch

Stéphane Jorisch est né à Bruxelles en 1956. Il a fait des études en graphisme et en design industriel à Montréal. Depuis une dizaine d'années, il travaille surtout dans le domaine de l'édition et dans celui de la publicité, et il fait de l'illustration éditoriale. En plus de ses illustrations pour des maisons d'édition du Québec, il a également fait des illustrations pour des maisons de l'Ontario. C'est un adepte du roman policier et lui-même avoue qu'il n'a pas peur de grand-chose... mais qu'il a une phobie des prises de sang.

Les griffes de la pleine lune est le deuxième roman qu'il ilustre à la courte échelle. De plus, il a illustré des couvertures de romans de Chrystine Brouillet: *Un jeu dangereux, Une plage trop chaude, Une nuit très longue* et *Un rendez-vous troublant.*

Bertrand Gauthier

LES GRIFFES DE LA PLEINE LUNE

Illustrations
de Stéphane Jorisch

la courte échelle

Les éditions de la courte échelle inc.

Les éditions de la courte échelle inc.
5243, boul. Saint-Laurent
Montréal (Québec) H2T 1S4

Conception graphique:
Derome design inc.

Révision des textes:
Odette Lord

Dépôt légal, 2e trimestre 1993
Bibliothèque nationale du Québec

Données de catalogage avant publication (Canada)

Gauthier, Bertrand, 1945-

    Les griffes de la pleine lune

    (Roman Jeunesse; RJ42)

    ISBN 2-89021-188-6

    I. Jorisch, Stéphane. II. Titre. III. Collection.

PS8563.A847G74 1993   jC843'.54   C92-097332-9
PS9563.A847G74 1993
PZ23.G38Gr 1993

Prologue
Un souvenir
en forme de brrrrrr...!

Depuis bientôt un mois, une folle idée ne cesse de hanter l'esprit de Mélanie Lapierre: elle veut retourner au milieu des pierres tombales. Rien à faire, malgré des efforts soutenus, la jeune fille n'arrive pas à chasser de son esprit ce projet insensé.

Mais d'où vient donc cette véritable obsession?

À la dernière pleine lune, Mélanie Lapierre s'est perdue dans un cimetière. Sans l'aide précieuse de Fabien Tranchant, ce mort vivant aussi courageux que téméraire, Mélanie n'aurait jamais pu s'en sortir indemne.

Non, jamais, au grand jamais, elle ne serait parvenue à se libérer de l'emprise despotique de Justin Macchabée, la plus atroce des créatures mortes vivantes à hanter le cimetière. Et depuis cette nuit fatidique, Mélanie Lapierre juge que c'est maintenant à son tour d'aller libérer Fabien Tranchant de l'odieux Justin Macchabée.

Ce n'est pourtant pas aussi simple.

Jusqu'ici, le souvenir cauchemardesque des morts vivants a toujours réussi à ralentir les ardeurs de Mélanie Lapierre. Elle ne veut pas prendre le risque de se

retrouver entre les griffes de cette meute sanguinaire. Pas plus d'ailleurs qu'elle ne désire redevenir prisonnière de leur chef, l'horrible Justin Macchabée!

Une fois suffit.

Mélanie courageuse? Sans doute!

Mélanie naïve? Sûrement un peu!

Mais tout de même pas au point de nier le danger qui la guette si jamais... si jamais elle décide de retourner au cimetière.

Aussi débrouillarde et valeureuse soit-elle, Mélanie sait bien qu'une jeune fille de douze ans n'est pas de taille à livrer un tel combat. Quand il s'agit d'affronter un bataillon complet de morts vivants abominables, il est évident que le courage ne suffit pas.

Et puis, inutile de le cacher, Mélanie Lapierre est plutôt inquiète du sort qu'on a réservé à Fabien Tranchant.

Ce dernier ne devait-il pas exécuter froidement les ordres qu'on lui avait donnés? N'avait-on pas brutalement commandé à son intrépide sauveur de remettre Mélanie Lapierre à l'ignoble Comité des griffes de la mort? Sa mission n'était-elle pas de livrer ladite jeune fille, pieds et poings liés, au tortionnaire et sadique Justin Macchabée?

Mais n'écoutant que son courage, Fabien Tranchant n'a jamais suivi la moindre de ces instructions. Au contraire, en aidant Mélanie à s'enfuir, il a désobéi à l'implacable Macchabée et à son fidèle Comité de loques putrides et sanguinolentes. Avec raison, Mélanie Lapierre a peur qu'on veuille se venger de Fabien.

Pour ne pas avoir livré sa proie, son brave Fabien devra sûrement payer cher, très cher même...

Sa proie...

À ce mot, Mélanie se met à frissonner.

Après tout, la proie à livrer, c'était bien elle, Lapierre Mélanie, en chair et en os. Elle qui portait le fatidique numéro matricule 1980-1992! Elle dont le nom était déjà gravé dans le marbre froid et veineux d'une pierre tombale!

Même son nouvel habitat était creusé: à quelques mètres sous la terre humide, quelques milliers de vermisseaux se réjouissaient à l'idée de l'accueillir dans leur ventre.

L'affreuse dégustation!

Brrrrrr...!

L'horrible souvenir!

Dans la tête de Mélanie, les idées se bousculent maintenant à un rythme infernal. Elle croit même entendre une voix grave lui crier rageusement:

«Mélanie Lapierre, tu es une vraie lâche, la pire des lâches..., Mélanie Lapierre, tu es la plus grande..., vraiment la plus grande poule mouillée que la terre ait jamais portée...»

Une voix insistante et caverneuse qui ressemble d'ailleurs étrangement à celle de Fabien Tranchant. Mélanie Lapierre souhaiterait tant pouvoir tout expliquer à son audacieux sauveur.

«Fabien, je ne peux pas, tu comprends... Je ne me sens pas de taille à affronter... cette meute sanguinaire qui veut sûrement se venger de toi... Je suis peinée, vraiment peinée..., mais même si j'essayais, je n'y arriverais pas, c'est au-delà de mes forces... Tu comprends, Fabien... J'espère que tu vas comprendre... Tu dois me comprendre..., comprendre..., comprend...»

— ... Mélanie, peux-tu répondre à cette question?

En entendant ainsi son nom, Mélanie Lapierre sursaute.

— Comprendre..., comprendre..., pardon..., pardon, monsieur..., la quoi...? La question...? Mais quelle question au juste, monsieur...?

— Encore distraite, Mélanie...? Je ne sais pas ce qui t'arrive, mais il me semble que depuis quelque temps, tu es très souvent dans la lune. Mélanie, peux-tu bien me dire ce qui se passe?

Mélanie Lapierre n'ose pas répondre, car ce serait trop difficile à expliquer. Et puis elle sait bien que M. Moreau-Guerrier a raison. Au cours des dernières semaines, elle a été profondément distraite. Ce n'est cependant pas par manque d'intérêt, c'est plutôt le contraire. Mélanie adore le jeu des capitales que son professeur aime bien leur proposer de temps en temps.

— Bon, je vais répéter ma question, reprend alors M. Moreau-Guerrier, ce passionné de géographie. De quels pays Oslo, Quito, Tōkyō, Mexico et Togo sont-elles les capitales?

Il a à peine le temps de finir sa question que la cloche se fait entendre. Dans un indescriptible brouhaha, toute la classe est debout.

Mélanie Lapierre aurait donc pu se

14

contenter d'être sauvée par la cloche. Mais elle ne tient pas à remporter ce genre de victoires trop faciles. Pendant que les élèves se précipitent vers la sortie, Mélanie crie donc à son professeur:

— De la Norvège, de l'Équateur, du Japon et du Mexique. Pour ce qui est du Togo, monsieur Moreau-Guerrier, ne comptez pas sur moi pour tomber dans le panneau.

Tout le monde est maintenant dehors.

Y compris Mélanie Lapierre!

L'école est bien finie.

Du moins pour aujourd'hui!

Chapitre I
Adieu, Mélanie!

Dix-sept heures!

Mélanie est maintenant devant la porte de chez elle.

Inutile de sonner!

Elle voit bien que la maison est déserte. Ses parents ne sont pas encore rentrés de leur travail. D'ailleurs, ils reviennent rarement à la maison avant dix-huit heures.

Après avoir déposé son sac d'école, Mélanie Lapierre ramasse le courrier près de la porte d'entrée.

Enfin!

Dans la pile, il y une lettre pour elle! Mélanie songe alors à sa correspondante de France.

— Il est temps qu'elle me donne des nouvelles, s'écrie Mélanie, en se dirigeant vers le réfrigérateur. En tout cas, on peut dire qu'elle porte bien son nom, cette Marie-Claire Latortue, ajoute Mélanie en se versant un grand verre de lait.

Il y a déjà plus d'un mois que Mélanie Lapierre a écrit à Marie-Claire Latortue. Ce projet d'échange de lettres est une idée de Mlle Lison Dumolong, sa professeure de français. Et, depuis trois semaines et demie, Mélanie attend impatiemment une réponse à sa lettre.

Une fois dans le salon, Mélanie Lapierre ouvre le téléviseur en appuyant mécaniquement sur la télécommande. Tout en croquant dans un biscuit à la farine d'avoine — de loin, sa sorte préférée — et en buvant son verre de lait, Mélanie commence à décacheter l'enveloppe qui lui est adressée.

Fébrilement, elle se met à lire ce que sa nouvelle correspondante d'outre-Atlantique peut bien lui raconter.

Chère Lapierre Mélanie,

Si je t'écris, ce n'est pas pour te demander de venir à ma rescousse. Non, surtout pas! Mélanie, je veux simplement te prévenir que tu ne dois plus mettre les pieds dans ce cimetière infect.

Mais je tenais à tout prix à te dire qu'à la prochaine pleine lune, mon sort en sera jeté. Ainsi va ma destinée, Mélanie, et personne ne peut s'aviser de la détourner sans avoir à subir de terribles châtiments.

De toute façon, ma pauvre Mélanie, même si tu voulais m'aider, tu n'aurais aucune chance de vaincre l'horrible Comité des griffes de la mort. Alors, il faut te faire à cette idée: pense à toi, pense à ton avenir et oublie au plus vite que tu m'as déjà connu.

Impossible, ce ne peut pas être lui!
Vraiment incroyable et inimaginable!
Trop intriguée, Mélanie ne peut s'empêcher de continuer sa lecture.

Tout ce qui m'arrive est de ma faute, j'aurais bien dû être plus prudent. Il aurait fallu brûler le bout de papier sur lequel était dessiné le plan du cimetière. Au lieu de ça, je t'ai simplement dit de le déchirer et de le lancer aux quatre vents.

Justin Macchabée a alors vite fait appel à tous les morts vivants de la terre. Il a pu recoller tous les morceaux du plan et l'abominable a pu ainsi continuer son oeuvre de destruction.

Mélanie en est tout abasourdie!
Elle se souvient bien d'avoir déchiré le plan qui lui a servi à retrouver son che-

min, mais elle l'a déchiré en quatre morceaux seulement. Un par point cardinal. Elle comprend maintenant qu'elle aurait dû déchirer ce plan en mille morceaux avant de le lancer aux quatre vents. Ainsi, les morts vivants n'auraient pas pu le reconstituer.

Non, jamais!

Et elle continue de lire.

Je saisis l'occasion pour te souhaiter une vie heureuse et douce. Tu dois savoir que si c'était à refaire, je n'hésiterais pas une seule seconde à agir de la même manière que je l'ai fait. Oui, Mélanie, je te protégerais encore de l'effroyable Comité des griffes de la mort.

Longue vie à toi, Mélanie!

Et, encore une fois, s'il te plaît, tiens-toi loin de ce cimetière maudit, tu pourrais le regretter amèrement. Oui, amèrement!

N'oublie pas, Mélanie Lapierre, que je ne serai plus là pour t'aider. Je vais bientôt disparaître, victime d'une éclipse permanente. Disparaître à jamais, n'oublie surtout pas ça, Mélanie!

Ne l'oublie jamais, s'il te plaît, ma chère Mélanie!

Disparaître à jamais!

Depuis un mois, Mélanie Lapierre se doutait bien que son brave sauveur était dans une fâcheuse position.

De plus, elle est convaincue que dans sa lettre, Fabien ne lui raconte pas toute la vérité. Elle est persuadée qu'il a voulu lui cacher les horribles tortures qu'on lui réserve.

Avant de le condamner à la réclusion perpétuelle, l'abominable Justin Macchabée va sûrement s'amuser à faire souffrir Fabien Tranchant.

Pour satisfaire tous ces esprits tordus du Comité des griffes de la mort, il est évident que faire disparaître Fabien Tranchant ne sera pas suffisant.

Dans l'esprit de Mélanie, pas le moindre doute là-dessus!

Fabien Tranchant est encore dans de plus mauvais draps que Mélanie aurait même osé l'imaginer. Les pires appréhensions de la pauvre jeune fille étaient donc parfaitement justifiées.

Avant de poursuivre sa lecture, Mélanie Lapierre doit essuyer une larme. Une larme qui a le temps de descendre sur sa joue et d'aller humecter ses lèvres.

Chère Mélanie,
c'est bien fini.
Heureuse Mélanie,
pour moi, c'est bien fini.
Adieu, Mélanie,
bel et bien fini.
Et je signe Fabien
qui ne vaut plus rien.

Pauvre Fabien!

Il se juge bien sévèrement. Pour penser qu'il ne vaut plus rien, il doit être profondément déprimé, mais Mélanie le comprend de réagir de cette manière. Les perspectives d'avenir de son sauveur ne sont pas très roses.

La révolte commence donc à germer dans le coeur de Mélanie. Elle prend conscience, encore une fois, qu'elle ne peut pas abandonner Fabien Tranchant à son triste sort. Malgré ses nombreux et constants efforts des dernières semaines, elle n'arrive pas à l'oublier.

Et puis non, bel et bien fini, il n'est pas question d'accepter ça!

Mais que peut-elle faire?

À la seconde même, fort peu.

Pourtant, en analysant la situation, en

restant calme et en s'armant de courage et de ruse, elle peut faire de grandes choses. Elle l'a déjà prouvé en affrontant avec sang-froid l'horrible menace du Comité des griffes de la mort.

Aidée de Fabien Tranchant, bien sûr!

Mais seule, pourra-t-elle vaincre?

C'est à voir...

Non, rien à faire, elle ne peut pas, Mélanie Lapierre ne veut pas abandonner son sauveur. Elle trouve qu'il serait trop injuste que cet infâme Justin Macchabée finisse par l'emporter. Non, elle doit croire en ses forces..., il le faut, elle doit prendre son courage à deux mains, elle se doit d'affronter une nouvelle fois le Comité des griffes de la mort...

Son esprit est d'attaque.

«Gare à toi, Justin Macchabée, on va voir ce qu'on va voir! Qui a dit que Mélanie Lapierre te laissera réaliser ton horrible projet d'éliminer aussi facilement Fabien Tranchant?»

— Tiens bon, Fabien Tranchant, mon sauveur, j'arrive... C'est à mon tour de te sauver, crie tout à coup Mélanie dans la maison toujours remplie du bruit du téléviseur.

C'est bien beau de crier son indignation et de manifester son enthousiasme, mais il faut aussi passer à l'action.

Et vite!

Le calendrier!

L'urgence de la situation semble évidente. En effet, le calendrier indique que dans quelques heures à peine, la pleine lune apparaîtra dans le ciel. Pour établir un plan d'attaque, il n'y a donc pas une minute à perdre.

Heureusement pour Fabien Tranchant, Mélanie Lapierre n'a pas encore dit son dernier mot.

Et sûrement pas vécu, non plus, ses derniers frissons!

Chapitre II
En route vers sa destinée!

Quelques heures plus tard, d'un pas déterminé, Mélanie Lapierre atteint l'intersection de l'avenue Lever-Croquet et de la rue Ravi-Dlavie. Armée de son sac à dos, la jeune fille s'engage aussitôt sur l'avenue Lever-Croquet, celle-là même qui longe le cimetière.

Quand Mélanie parvient à la porte d'entrée du territoire des morts vivants, elle voit que la lourde grille est fermée à double tour. Rien de plus normal à cette heure tardive! Mais ce n'est sûrement pas ce détail qui va l'arrêter. Mélanie Lapierre a maintenant une mission à accomplir et elle n'a pas l'intention de s'y dérober.

À quelques centaines de mètres de l'entrée officielle, Mélanie connaît un endroit où l'on peut se glisser sous la clôture qui entoure le cimetière. Elle s'y rend aussitôt. Pour arriver à passer, elle doit retirer son sac à dos, car la brèche est infime. Aussi agile qu'une gymnaste, elle réussit à se faufiler dans le territoire des morts vivants.

Depuis peu, à l'horizon, le soleil s'est couché. Et du même coup, il a cédé sa place à une magnifique pleine lune.

Toutefois, aussi magnifique soit-elle, la pleine lune arrive difficilement à percer les nuages. Afin de mieux repérer ses ennemis, Mélanie Lapierre aurait préféré une nuit sans le moindre nuage.

C'est l'évidence même!

Pour lutter adéquatement, elle aurait bien besoin de toute cette lumière lunaire, de ce miraculeux reflet du soleil au milieu de la nuit. Contrairement aux morts vivants qui sont des créatures essentiellement nocturnes, Mélanie Lapierre est une vivante qui a besoin de lumière.

Dans sa lutte pour la libération de Fabien Tranchant, Mélanie Lapierre part donc désavantagée. Mais comme elle a déjà vécu une première expérience au cimetière, elle a pris ses précautions. Sachant trop bien que ses ennemis jurés sont armés jusqu'aux griffes, Mélanie ne se présente pas les mains vides devant eux.

Au bout de quelques centaines de mètres de marche, Mélanie s'arrête pour fouiller dans son sac à dos. Elle en retire quelques cailloux qui semblent briller dans la nuit noire. Prudemment, elle continue ensuite d'avancer vers le coeur du cimetière, là où elle risque le plus de retrouver la bande à Justin Macchabée.

Et, bien sûr, Justin Macchabée lui-même!

Tous les dix mètres environ, Mélanie se penche et dépose par terre un caillou fluorescent. Elle ne tient pas à s'égarer bêtement comme la dernière fois. Avec ces cailloux déjà enduits de teinture jaune fluo, elle prend soin d'indiquer le chemin parcouru.

De temps en temps, Mélanie jette un regard derrière elle. Son stratagème fonctionne parfaitement bien. Les cailloux sont très visibles dans la nuit. Ainsi, prise

au dépourvu, elle saura dans quelle direction courir pour échapper à la meute sanguinaire qui voudrait l'attaquer.

Mélanie sait qu'elle a un avantage certain — le seul peut-être — sur ses ennemis. En effet, les morts vivants se déplacent lentement. Mélanie Lapierre, par contre, est en pleine forme et elle court vite.

Peut-être est-ce le seul avantage qu'elle ait! Mais il est de taille! Cette pensée rassure Mélanie et lui donne le courage nécessaire pour continuer sa progression en territoire ennemi.

Mélanie Lapierre s'aperçoit maintenant qu'elle est entourée de pierres tombales. En son for intérieur, elle sait bien qu'elle vient d'atteindre la partie la plus habitée du cimetière et, par le fait même, la plus dangereuse.

L'inévitable territoire du Comité des griffes de la mort!

À partir de ce point, il est essentiel que Mélanie Lapierre réussisse à se concentrer encore plus. Tout en scrutant le décor, elle tend l'oreille. Malheureusement, elle voit peu de choses, car les nuages ont complètement caché la pleine lune. Par contre, le moindre bruit apparaît aussitôt à Mélanie comme une ultime menace à affronter.

Urgence oblige, elle s'arrête donc et se glisse derrière une pierre tombale afin de réfléchir à sa situation.

«Non, ce n'est pas comme ça que tu vas réussir à sauver ce pauvre Fabien. Au contraire, si tu continues à paniquer au moindre bruit de branche séchée que tu écrases, tu n'y arriveras jamais. Au lieu d'aider Fabien, tu risques de te retrouver dans d'aussi mauvais draps que lui. Du courage, oui, c'est sûr qu'il en faut. Mais surtout, c'est de calme et de ruse que tu dois faire preuve.»

Pour garder son calme, Mélanie Lapierre observe ses cailloux qui brillent dans la nuit. Une idée germe alors dans son esprit.

Patience et ruse dans la nuit!

Le principe est simple: elle doit laisser l'ennemi dévoiler son jeu. Les morts vivants, qui n'ont aucune raison de se méfier d'elle, finiront bien par se trahir.

Il suffit donc d'attendre qu'un mort vivant sorte de sa tombe pour le prendre en filature. Mélanie a raison de croire que la plupart d'entre eux se rendront assister au procès du pauvre Fabien Tranchant. Ensuite, ils fêteront sûrement la victoire de la mort sur la vie.

Leur victoire sordide et immonde!

Subitement, le ciel s'illumine.

Quelques secondes plus tard, un coup de tonnerre se fait entendre. Un violent orage éclate aussitôt.

Vite, Mélanie fouille dans son sac à dos et en retire un petit paquet. Elle se glisse entre deux pierres tombales et déroule l'imperméable noir qu'elle place au-dessus de sa tête. Sous cette tente improvisée, Mélanie Lapierre arrive tant bien que mal à se protéger de la pluie violente qui s'abat maintenant sur le cimetière.

Heureusement, l'orage dure à peine cinq minutes.

Mais c'est tout de même assez pour que des flaques d'eau se forment un peu partout. Et pour que Mélanie ait les pieds mouillés et pleins de boue.

À première vue, rien de grave!

Au cas où la pluie recommencerait à tomber, Mélanie décide de porter son imper. Elle retourne vers le sentier avec l'intention de se trouver un endroit moins détrempé. Si elle doit faire le guet pendant des heures, aussi bien le faire dans les meilleures conditions possibles.

En effet, ce sera peut-être long avant d'apercevoir un de ces spectres macabres sortir des entrailles de la terre. Comme elle cherche des indices de leur présence, Mélanie regarde derrière elle.

Non, impossible!

Mélanie se frotte les yeux. Elle se dit qu'elle rêve sûrement, que c'est sûrement une erreur de sa part, qu'elle est sûrement victime d'un affreux cauchemar.

Non, rien de tout ça!

La pauvre Mélanie doit se rendre à l'évidence: derrière elle, la réalité dépasse la fiction. Dans les yeux horrifiés de Mélanie Lapierre, on peut maintenant lire toute sa détresse.

Il y a de quoi!

Les cailloux fluo ne sont plus du tout fluo. Ils se sont fondus dans le paysage terne des pierres tombales. Sous la pluie intense, la teinture a dû disparaître.

Mélanie trouve que c'est injuste.

Et plutôt décourageant!

En plus d'avoir à combattre une horrible bande de morts vivants, elle doit aussi affronter les éléments d'une nature qui lui est hostile. Si tout doit se déchaîner contre elle, il ne lui reste plus beaucoup d'espoir d'arriver à compléter sa mission.

Une mission devenue maintenant encore plus délicate et périlleuse.

Rebrousser chemin?

Non, jamais!

De toute façon, il est un peu tard pour songer à ça. Mélanie ne s'y retrouverait plus, ayant perdu tous ses précieux points de repère.

«Fabien, comme j'ai été téméraire de vouloir voler à ton secours. Maintenant, je suis dans le même pétrin que toi», songe Mélanie en avançant lentement sur le sentier sinueux qui la mène vers sa destinée.

Son implacable destinée!

Fort probablement!

Chapitre III
La terre tremble

Depuis bientôt une heure, Mélanie Lapierre fait le guet.

Malgré la malchance qui s'acharne sur elle, Mélanie a su éviter de sombrer dans une panique aussi paralysante qu'inutile. Sagement, elle s'est plutôt résignée à attendre le plus patiemment possible que l'ennemi se manifeste.

Après tout, un des spectres de la bande à Justin Macchabée finira bien par se montrer le bout du crâne.

Inévitablement!

En effet, les morts vivants n'ont pas la réputation de résister longtemps à l'appel de la pleine lune.

Surtout que cette nuit, on leur promet

une prime alléchante: l'immolation sadique de Fabien Tranchant, celui-là même qui a trahi les idéaux pourtant dégoûtants des morts vivants.

Penser ainsi à Fabien, le voir prisonnier, l'imaginer souffrir, l'entendre gémir: toutes ces images redonnent le courage voulu à Mélanie Lapierre.

Tel un animal sauvage, entre deux grosses pierres tombales, Mélanie reste sur le qui-vive. Elle est à l'affût du plus léger bruissement, elle demeure aux aguets du moindre brin d'herbe qui se mettrait à bouger.

On a beau dire, ce n'est pas facile de pourchasser de tels ennemis. Les morts vivants ont un comportement tellement imprévisible.

Une bonne nouvelle, cependant!

Depuis au moins une dizaine de minutes, le ciel s'est complètement dégagé et la pleine lune éclaire maintenant le cimetière de tout son éclat.

Tout à coup, sans le moindre avertissement, la terre se met à trembler. Et très violemment, au point où Mélanie Lapierre en perd l'équilibre.

La pauvre Mélanie n'arrive pas à croire

qu'une autre catastrophe naturelle est en train de se produire. Après l'orage qui s'est abattu sur elle, il ne manquerait plus qu'un tremblement de terre. Sous les yeux de Mélanie, la pelouse se soulève et la terre continue à se fendiller. Pas le moindre doute, c'est un vrai tremblement de terre!

Mélanie Lapierre décampe, car elle ne tient pas à disparaître dans une fissure terrestre. À la télévision ou au cinéma, elle a déjà pu voir les terribles effets des tremblements de terre: des humains, des animaux et des arbres sont aspirés instantanément et s'enfoncent à jamais dans le ventre de la terre.

Même si elle adore sa planète, Mélanie ne veut pas finir tout de suite dans ses entrailles.

En continuant sa course, elle voit pourtant que le sol reste bien solide sous ses pas.

Dans l'esprit de Mélanie, l'hypothèse du tremblement de terre commence à s'effriter. Intriguée, elle se penche pour observer l'asphalte de plus près.

Elle ne détecte pas de fissures majeures.

Mélanie reprend son souffle et elle jette un regard derrière elle: ce qu'elle aperçoit alors la laisse complètement médusée.

Tout près d'elle, Mélanie voit la terre se soulever. Elle croit même déceler une forme étrange, à moitié sortie du sol. Elle s'approche prudemment et elle continue à observer.

Rendue à proximité de la scène, Mélanie se faufile lentement derrière un arbre. Elle a maintenant une place de choix pour observer cette masse informe qui surgit de la terre.

Mélanie Lapierre est à la fois contente et inquiète.

Contente de voir que sa patience est enfin récompensée. Inquiète d'imaginer ce qui l'attend si vraiment cette masse bizarre est bien ce qu'elle pense.

Inutile de se leurrer, plus le moindre doute possible!

À une vingtaine de mètres devant Mélanie Lapierre, c'est un mort vivant qui est en train de s'extraire de la terre. Mais il n'est pas seul. Pourtant, ce ne sont pas tous les habitants du cimetière que Mélanie Lapierre a sous les yeux.

Non, ils sont deux...

Plutôt trois...

Ou, finalement, quatre.

Côte à côte, quatre morts vivants marchent maintenant en direction de la pleine lune. Ils avancent lentement et lourdement, selon une habitude qui vient de leurs ancêtres.

À une distance respectable, Mélanie Lapierre entreprend donc de suivre ce quatuor plutôt morbide. Si elle veut sauver Fabien Tranchant, elle doit entreprendre cette filature.

Mission Sauvefachant!

Sauver Fabien Tranchant!

Mélanie Lapierre met donc de côté ses craintes pour se consacrer uniquement à sa filature. Elle est maintenant convaincue que ces carcasses ambulantes la mèneront tout droit là où l'on séquestre Fabien Tranchant.

Trop concentrée, Mélanie en oublie de placer des cailloux fluo le long de sa route. Au moment où elle s'en rend compte, elle trouve qu'il est un peu tard pour commencer. Comme les morts vivants marchent très lentement, Mélanie a le temps de réfléchir à la situation.

«De toute façon, à la fin de l'orage, mes repères fluo étaient effacés. J'étais donc déjà perdue. Quand on est perdu, on ne peut pas l'être à moitié. On l'est ou on ne l'est pas. Et puis, je dois me fier à ma bonne étoile, elle finira bien par me montrer le chemin, celle-là.»

Un espoir se dessine dans la nuit.

À cause de sa filature, il n'est pas question pour Mélanie de lever le nez et de quitter la terre des yeux. Pourtant, juste au-dessus de sa tête, une étoile traverse le ciel.

Trop tard, Mélanie Lapierre vient de rater le bolide lumineux.

Elle n'a donc pas pu faire un voeu comme elle le fait habituellement lors du passage d'une étoile filante.

Malheureusement!

Chapitre IV
Les pissenlits par la racine

Mélanie Lapierre commence à s'impatienter.

Au rythme où se déplace le quatuor des morts vivants, elle trouve qu'elle ne rejoindra pas Fabien Tranchant avant au moins un siècle. Et il sera alors trop tard. Autant pour le pauvre Fabien que pour elle!

Pourtant, Mélanie sait qu'elle doit garder son calme.

Elle essaie de se convaincre qu'on ne commencera pas à torturer Fabien avant que tous les invités ne soient arrivés. Et les quatre zombis qu'elle suit à la trace font sûrement partie des personnalités choisies par Justin Macchabée lui-même.

Avant de lancer son signal fatidique, il est évident que l'infâme Macchabée s'assurera que tous les participants à la fête soient bien là.

Que le carnage commence!

Son horrible cri de ralliement!

Tout à coup, Mélanie ne sait trop pourquoi, mais elle a la sensation bizarre d'être épiée. Elle veut se retourner pour vérifier ce qui se passe derrière son dos. Elle n'a pas le temps de bouger qu'on vient déjà de la happer.

D'un coup sec, on tire sur son sac à dos. Brutalement, on tente de le lui arracher. Mélanie résiste, car elle ne peut se permettre de voir s'envoler son précieux sac. À coups de coude et de pied, elle se débat. En sautillant nerveusement sur place, elle sent que l'emprise se relâche.

Elle s'est enfin libérée.

Courageusement, elle se retourne aussitôt.

À son grand étonnement, Mélanie ne voit rien. Rien de louche, du moins, dans le style des affreuses carcasses de la meute à Macchabée. De toute façon, Mélanie est sûre que ce ne sont pas ses ennemis jurés qui ont fait le coup. Les coupables ont disparu trop vite et les morts vivants n'ont pas l'habitude de voyager à la vitesse de l'éclair.

En observant plus calmement les lieux, Mélanie Lapierre se met alors à sourire. Elle peut maintenant se détendre, car elle vient de comprendre ce qui est arrivé.

Afin d'exercer une filature efficace, il n'est pas question pour Mélanie d'emprunter les grands sentiers qui arpentent le cimetière. Elle risquerait trop d'être rapidement démasquée.

Elle choisit plutôt de longer tous ces chemins étroits et sinueux, plus propices au camouflage. Bien involontairement, elle effleure souvent les arbres et les arbustes qui ornent la bordure de ces petits sentiers.

Cette fois, une des courroies de son sac à dos s'est accrochée à une branche d'arbre. La pression a été tellement forte sur les épaules de Mélanie qu'elle s'est aussitôt sentie agressée.

Comme une véritable déchaînée, elle s'est alors débattue. C'était légitime de sa part de réagir ainsi: elle pensait vraiment avoir affaire à ses coriaces et sournois ennemis.

Heureusement que ce n'était pas le cas!

Non, présentement, ses seuls et uniques ennemis visibles sont à une centaine de mètres devant elle.

Tout ce temps-là, le quatuor n'a ni ralenti ni accentué sa marche. De véritables robots téléguidés, moins alertes, cependant! Et, il faut bien le reconnaître, beaucoup plus répugnants!

Dans la nuit, Mélanie continue donc sa filature.

Soudain, le quatuor s'arrête. Pour se camoufler, Mélanie Lapierre plonge aussitôt sous un tas d'arbustes. Elle aperçoit alors les morts vivants qui pivotent lentement sur eux-mêmes. De leurs regards globuleux et insistants, ils scrutent impitoyablement le décor.

Puis, de leur même pas lourd, les froides créatures reprennent leur marche. Mais cette fois, le quatuor quitte le sentier et semble se diriger vers un amas de pierres tombales de très haute taille. En les voyant ainsi tourner à gauche, Mélanie Lapierre se met à espérer. Elle s'approche du but, elle le sent bien.

Bientôt, elle va revoir Fabien Tranchant.

Mais dans quel état sera-t-il?

Pour combattre ses appréhensions, elle murmure intérieurement.

Courage, Fabien,
tu as bien de la veine.
Courage, cher Fabien,
et cesse ta peine.
Courage, brave Fabien,
car je viens te sauver.
Courage, pauvre Fabien,
oui, je viens te sauver
de cette meute assoiffée...

Mélanie Lapierre voudrait bien croire qu'elle arrivera à réussir sa mission.

Elle veut y croire.

Mélanie doit y croire.

Mélanie Lapierre y croit.

Malgré tous ses efforts pour dominer sa peur, Mélanie demeure anxieuse. Elle se rapproche du but, mais elle peut difficilement contrôler sa fébrilité. Les mains moites et le coeur serré, elle essaie pourtant de se convaincre que son bel exercice de courage sera bientôt récompensé.

Récompensé...

Là, Mélanie Lapierre se trouve bien

présomptueuse de passer aussi vite aux conclusions. C'est vrai qu'elle lutte férocement pour dominer sa peur et pour tenter de délivrer Fabien Tranchant. L'effort y est, mais malheureusement, ça ne suffit pas.

Pour vaincre le Comité des griffes de la mort, il faut compter sur une bonne dose de chance. Mélanie Lapierre ne doit pas se laisser leurrer. En suivant ses mousquetaires ambulants, elle n'est même pas certaine d'être sur la bonne piste.

Sournoisement, des doutes l'assaillent.

«Tu vois des morts vivants sortir de la terre et tu les prends en filature, car tu es sûre qu'ils vont te conduire à Fabien Tranchant», songe-t-elle. «Ça, c'est une hypothèse, une belle fantaisie sortie tout droit de ton imagination. Tu es tellement naïve, ma pauvre Mélanie Lapierre, que je désespère de toi, si tu veux savoir toute la vérité.»

Encore une fois, la confiance de Mélanie est affaiblie.

En effet, comment a-t-elle pu présumer aussi rapidement que ce quatuor se rendait bien au banquet sanguinaire organisé pour immoler Fabien?

Depuis le début, toute cette mise en scène est fort probablement un piège. Un piège astucieux pour livrer Mélanie Lapierre sur un plateau d'argent à ses ennemis. Un piège comme seul l'infâme Justin Macchabée sait en tendre. Un ignoble piège pour pousser Mélanie Lapierre dans les griffes de ce sinistre déchiqueteur de chairs humaines!

Pour la jeter dans la gueule avide de la mort!

Alors, avant qu'il ne soit trop tard...

«Non, non et non!» s'écrie intérieurement Mélanie Lapierre.

Aux yeux de la courageuse jeune fille, pas question d'abandonner sa filature! Si elle a parcouru tout ce chemin, ce n'est pas pour reculer à la dernière minute. Même ébranlée, Mélanie n'a pas l'intention de se laisser envahir par ces vagues d'inquiétudes.

Une longue et profonde respiration la ramène les deux pieds sur terre, une terre à la fois ferme et boueuse. Bien se concentrer, continuer sa filature et oublier tout le reste!

Pour l'instant, uniquement *Mission Sauvefachant!*

Assaillie par ces doutes aussi soudains que tenaces, Mélanie Lapierre a été distraite de sa filature et l'a ainsi négligée. Si bien que les quatre morts vivants ont maintenant disparu.

Le coeur battant à un rythme affolant, Mélanie Lapierre se met aussitôt à courir. Elle laisse de côté ses dernières craintes, car elle doit rattraper le sinistre quatuor. Après tout, cette piste n'est peut-être pas la bonne, mais elle reste tout de même la seule valable.

Alors, il faut foncer!

Quand elle songe à la vitesse à laquelle les morts vivants se déplacent, Mélanie se sent rassurée. Ils ne doivent sûrement pas être très loin. En quelques bonnes enjambées, elle finira bien par retrouver leur trace.

Brusquement, Mélanie s'arrête.

Elle croit entendre des bruits confus sortir de la terre. Elle s'approche du lieu suspect et aperçoit alors ses mousquetaires. Les quatre créatures descendent lentement un long escalier qui les mène dans les entrailles de la terre.

Au milieu des clameurs, Mélanie entend une voix crier:

— Le voilà, le quatuor *Les pissenlits par la racine* vient d'arriver. On peut maintenant commencer.

Le quatuor *Les pissenlits par la racine*...

Des musiciens?

Commencer?

Commencer quoi, au juste?

L'immolation de Fabien?

Sûrement!

Pour le savoir, rien de plus simple: il faut aller voir ce qui se passe là-dessous. Pour faire progresser sa mission, Mélanie Lapierre doit atteindre ce caveau humide. Même si elle imagine ce trou infect complètement envahi par des tas de créatures répugnantes, elle doit descendre.

Il ne faut pas flancher.

Surtout pas si près du but!

Chapitre V
Incognito

Bercée par le doux espoir de venir bientôt en aide à son sauveur, Mélanie Lapierre fouille fébrilement dans son sac à dos.

Opération Déguisemépierre pour accomplir *Mission Sauvefachant!*

En quelques minutes, Mélanie Lapierre est métamorphosée en un véritable squelette ambulant. Puis elle prend bien soin d'aller se rouler dans la boue. Deux fois plutôt qu'une. Après tout, les morts vivants vivent dans la terre boueuse. Si on veut leur ressembler, on n'a donc pas le choix.

Heureusement pour Mélanie, à cause de la pluie qui est tombée, la boue ne manque pas.

Maintenant devenue aussi sale qu'elle

le pouvait, elle est prête à rendre visite à ses semblables.

Ouf, ses semblables!

Grâce à la magie de son déguisement, elle espère réussir à se confondre aux morts vivants.

Après tout, en n'étant plus qu'un squelette recouvert de boue, n'est-elle pas devenue une véritable morte vivante? N'est-elle pas prête à s'intégrer parfaitement à cette fidèle meute sanguinaire de Justin Macchabée?

Au-dessus des clameurs peu invitantes du caveau, Mélanie Lapierre prend de longues et profondes respirations. Ses narines sont aussitôt envahies par une odeur nauséabonde.

«Normal, se dit-elle, qu'avec ce mélange d'humidité et de morts vivants, ça ne sente pas le jardin de roses.»

Mélanie Lapierre entreprend maintenant sa descente vers le tréfonds de la terre.

Courageusement et, bien sûr, fort lentement.

Fort, fort lentttttteeeeeemennnnnnt!

La gorge serrée, Mélanie se rend compte qu'elle se rapproche de plus en plus du flot des clameurs.

À ce moment précis, Mélanie Lapierre ne souhaite qu'une chose: demeurer incognito.

Sinon..., sinon...

De toutes ses forces, Mélanie lutte.

En effet, ce n'est pas le temps de se laisser envahir par les mauvais présages. Au rythme de sa lente descente, elle se laisse plutôt bercer par son désir de sauver Fabien.

Son inébranlable désir!

Patience, Fabien
si je viens de si loin
patience, cher Fabien
c'est pour prendre bien soin
patience, brave Fabien
de toi, le magnifique
patience, pauvre Fabien
aux prises avec ce maléfique,
ce spectre trépassé,
ce monstre aux griffes d'acier,
ce tortionnaire sadique,
ce Justin dit le Macchabée...

Plus rien ne semble vouloir arrêter Mélanie Lapierre: pas plus les griffes d'acier du maléfique que les gueules d'hyènes de son troupeau d'ardents fidèles. Même le risque de souffrir ou de mourir aux mains du tortionnaire sadique n'arrive plus à diminuer les ardeurs de Mélanie.

Depuis quelques instants, Mélanie Lapierre est alimentée par une nouvelle énergie. Propulsée par son désir de sauver Fabien Tranchant, elle en oublie tout le reste. Elle est maintenant sûre de pouvoir surmonter les derniers obstacles qui la séparent de Fabien. Et elle est certaine de la réussite de sa noble mission.

Mission noble mais difficile et pleine d'embûches, oui!
Mais impossible, non!

Mélanie Lapierre vient d'atteindre le bout de l'escalier. Elle est bien consciente d'entreprendre maintenant la portion la plus délicate de sa folle odyssée.

À la porte d'entrée, pas le moindre contrôle de routine! Comme la plupart des invités sont arrivés, on a probablement cru bon de relâcher la surveillance.

Sans être importunée par qui que ce soit, Mélanie se faufile dans la grande salle humide où sont réunis des centaines de morts vivants. En retenant son souffle, elle peut alors se fondre dans cette foule compacte.

— S'il vous plaît, s'il vous plaît..., j'aurais besoin d'un peu de silence... Un peu de silence, s'il vous plaît...

Ne tenant pas à rester trop longtemps immobile au milieu de toutes ces créatures, Mélanie se glisse aussitôt vers l'endroit d'où proviennent ces paroles.

— Merci d'être venus en si grand nombre et bienvenue à cette nuit de festivités qui promet déjà d'être des plus excitantes. Je me présente: Yvon Souterre, votre maître de cérémonie. Pour l'instant, je n'en dis pas plus. J'inviterais tout de suite notre distingué et...

Pas possible!

À ce moment précis, Mélanie est fière d'elle. Elle comprend qu'elle ne s'est pas trompée en suivant à la trace le quatuor de morts vivants. Les mousquetaires ambulants l'ont menée là où elle devait se rendre.

Face à face avec le plus tenace de ses cauchemars!

Mélanie Lapierre reconnaît celui qui s'approche maintenant de la tombe fermée qui sert de podium.

Avec l'aide de quelques disciples, Justin Macchabée se hisse sur ce macabre podium.

Après s'être bien solidement ancré les deux pieds, il entreprend de livrer son discours.

— Je vous remercie d'avoir répondu à mon invitation personnelle, commence-t-il sur un ton plutôt calme. Et je vous promets une très agréable nuit. Pas une nuit terne où vous vous endormirez comme ces pauvres vivants qui manquent d'imagination! Non, moi, je vous promets une vraie nuit faite sur mesure pour ceux qui savent apprécier la valeur des plaisirs délicieusement inattendus.

Dans la foule, les murmures de satisfaction commencent à fuser de partout. L'orateur, aussi habile que sournois, continue son envolée.

— En somme, une nuit digne de la magnifique pleine lune qui nous fait l'honneur de sa présence. À vous tous et à vous toutes, mes chers complices de toujours, je souhaite donc la plus horrible et la plus juteuse nuit de toute votre vie de mort vivant.

En mordant dans le mot horrible, Mélanie Lapierre s'aperçoit que Justin Macchabée a commencé à s'enflammer.

— Oui..., oui..., une vraie nuit où justice sera rendue, continue-t-il. Oui..., oui..., car il sera puni. Oui..., oui..., l'immonde traître que vous verrez bientôt apparaître, puis disparaître à jamais. Je vous le promets, mes amis, ce vil rat d'égout sera traité comme il le mérite.

Mélanie voit que le discours de Justin Macchabée prend de plus en plus les allures d'une oraison funèbre. Dans cette grotte humide et macabre, Mélanie Lapierre se sent bien seule. Autour d'elle, toutes ces infâmes créatures murmurent maintenant des oui, oui d'approbation à l'endroit de leur chef vénéré.

Tout à coup, Mélanie Lapierre a la nette impression qu'on l'observe. De son regard plutôt sinistre, son voisin de gauche est même en train de paralyser la pauvre Mélanie.

Heureusement, elle se ressaisit très vite.

En bonne morte vivante docile et fidèle, elle décide donc d'entrer à son tour dans la ronde des murmures de satisfaction. Rassuré, le mort vivant détourne alors lentement son crâne décharné, non sans avoir esquissé son plus beau sourire cadavérique à l'endroit de Mélanie.

Par mesure de prudence, Mélanie Lapierre décide aussitôt de s'esquiver. Le corps frissonnant, elle part à la recherche de nouveaux voisins qu'elle souhaiterait moins communicatifs.

Entre-temps, Justin Macchabée a cessé de parler à son troupeau. Toujours sur le podium, il regarde lentement à droite, puis à gauche. Silencieusement, la foule observe le grand manitou. On entend les mouches voler et on peut même voir quelques vermisseaux se régaler. Un vrai silence de mort comme les aime sans doute Justin Macchabée!

Brusquement, dans un geste théâtral, l'habile orateur soulève ses bras décharnés vers la foule. Puis il lance un cri tellement déchirant que Mélanie cesse de respirer.

— Trrrrrraîtrrrrrre...

Peu à peu, il baisse les bras et il semble se calmer. Illusion, profonde illusion!

— Infâme traître, prépare-toi à payer ton dû, reprend-il de plus belle. Et vous, larves et vermisseaux, régalez-vous par anticipation. Bientôt, nous serons débarrassés de ce chien galeux qui nous a tous trahis. Car trahir Justin Macchabée, c'est nous trahir tous..., tous autant que nous sommes.

D'autres murmures approbateurs accueillent ces déclarations terrifiantes du chef incontesté du Comité des griffes de la mort. En voyant cette masse de fidèles l'idolâtrer, le cynique Justin Macchabée jubile.

— Que l'on traîne le vil traître à mes pieds, lance-t-il fermement à ses troupes. Place à la réunion extraordinaire du C.G.M. pour que justice soit rendue! La justice, notre justice, la seule, l'unique, la vraie. Pas la stupide justice des pauvres humains qui ne comprennent jamais rien, qui n'ont jamais rien compris et qui ne comprendront d'ailleurs jamais rien...

Même si ce n'est pas facile, Mélanie tente de garder son sang-froid. Ce n'est pas le temps de se trahir par des réactions trop émotives. Elle se doit de continuer à réagir comme une morte vivante. Si elle a réussi à se rendre jusqu'à ses ennemis sans être repérée, ce serait vraiment trop bête de se faire démasquer aussi près du but.

Malheureusement, depuis quelques instants, Mélanie Lapierre a l'impression d'être de plus en plus vivante. Vivante et fébrile, dans chaque pore de sa peau! Mais prudence et retenue sont les consignes qu'elle ne cesse de se répéter intérieurement. En proie à de vives émotions, elle parvient quand même à se maîtriser.

Alors, Mélanie Lapierre est aussitôt récompensée.

Elle voit apparaître Fabien Tranchant.

Titubant, le pauvre Fabien semble trop faible pour marcher. On le traîne sans ménagement vers le podium où est juché Justin Macchabée.

À tout prix, Mélanie doit retenir ses larmes. Elle sait qu'il lui serait fatal de donner un tel indice sur sa véritable nature. Humaine jusqu'au bout d'une larme. Une larme au goût de sel. Beaucoup trop humaine!

Non, il ne faut pas.

Mélanie se permet donc d'être triste, mais elle ne versera pas la moindre larme traîtresse.

Traîtresse et fatale!

Et puis, à ce moment-ci, tristesse ne rime pas avec courage. Dans courage, il y a plutôt rage. La rage de vaincre l'odieux Comité des griffes de la mort. La rage de sauver Fabien. La rage de vaincre la mort. La rage de vivre.

Au moment jugé opportun, à la vitesse de l'éclair, il faudra frapper.

Avec vigueur!

Et avec cette rage de vivre au coeur!

Si profonde et tellement vivante!

Chapitre VI
Un macabre requiem

Fabien Tranchant gît maintenant aux pieds de Justin Macchabée. Dans la foule hostile, les injures pleuvent de partout à l'endroit de Fabien. Et les cris aigus du *brave* Justin Macchabée encouragent la foule. Sans le moindre répit, l'immonde dictateur ne cesse de bombarder le pauvre Fabien Tranchant des pires invectives.

— ... Lève-toi, épave ambulante... Allez, vil traître, affronte ceux que tu as si lâchement trahis... Pour une fois, chien galeux, fais preuve d'un peu de courage... Allez, debout, qu'on puisse cracher notre venin à la face du miteux rat d'égout que tu es...

La terrible infamie!

Pour ne pas répliquer, Mélanie Lapierre doit se mordre les lèvres. Elle a
une chose plus importante à faire que de
crier sa profonde indignation.

Il faut à tout prix trouver une astuce
pour se rapprocher de Fabien. Il doit savoir que Mélanie est là pour le libérer des
griffes du morbide Justin Macchabée.

Tout près, tout près de lui, prête à
bondir.

— Regardez-le, le vil crapaud, il ne
peut même pas se lever, continue le sadique orateur. Le pauvre petit Fabien
Tranchant aime mieux croupir dans la
boue que de rendre grâce à son maître.

Plutôt mourir que de rendre grâce à
Justin Macchabée!

Mais ne pas bondir tout de suite!

Pas encore!

— Allez, *Les pissenlits par la racine,*
au travail! Jouez-nous au plus vite le *Requiem en sol majeur pour quatuor à
cordes* du grand Macchabée. Une pièce
sublime composée par un célèbre vir-
tuose. Un classique, quoi! Je suis assuré
qu'on va tous vibrer à l'unisson.

Sous un tollé de gémissements approbateurs, le quatuor *Les pissenlits par la*

racine s'approche alors de la scène improvisée. On apporte aussitôt des fouets aux quatre morts vivants.

Des instruments de musique ou de torture?

Mélanie n'ose pas répondre à cette question.

Mais elle arrive encore moins à écouter ce diabolique *Requiem* de Macchabée.

À tour de rôle, les fouets sifflent aux oreilles de Fabien Tranchant. Sans le moindre répit, tous ces claquements se font entendre dans ce caveau qui devient de plus en plus sinistre.

De temps en temps, un de ces fouets risque même de s'abattre sur le dos du courageux sauveur de Mélanie. Le choeur improvisé des morts vivants en profite alors pour manifester sa joie. En effet, les abominables créatures s'amusent à ridiculiser les lamentations pourtant légitimes du pauvre Fabien Tranchant, maintenant terrorisé.

Bien triste et désolant spectacle!

Et beaucoup plus ignoble que Mélanie n'aurait pu l'imaginer!

Le bruit des coups de fouet et les cris de

Fabien arrachent littéralement le coeur à Mélanie.

Après tout, Mélanie Lapierre est descendue dans ce lieu sordide pour sauver Fabien Tranchant.

Et non pour devenir prisonnière d'un tel cauchemar! Et encore moins pour assister aux atroces souffrances de son cher sauveur!

Finalement, au bout d'une dizaine de minutes, le sinistre *Requiem* s'achève.

— Bravo, bravo au quatuor *Les pissenlits par la racine,* lance Yvon Souterre venu remplacer Justin Macchabée. Il y aura un court entracte afin de permettre aux dévoués organisateurs de bien se préparer. Le prochain numéro sera *Traîtrise fatale.* Un numéro unique et sans lendemain. Parole d'Yvon Souterre et garantie de Justin Macchabée, ajoute le maître de cérémonie au rire sardonique.

Mélanie juge que c'est le temps de profiter de ce brouhaha pour s'approcher de Fabien. Mine de rien, elle se faufile donc tout près de la scène improvisée. Rendue là, elle fait semblant de glisser dans la boue et elle réussit à tomber à quelques pas de Fabien Tranchant. Elle en profite aussitôt pour remettre un message à son sauveur qui semble en bien piteux état.

Mélanie n'a cependant pas le temps d'attendre sa réaction.

En effet, s'attarder serait trop louche. Déjà, quelques créatures s'approchent pour vérifier ce qui se passe. Mais trop tard, il n'y a plus rien à voir!

Prudemment, Mélanie Lapierre s'est de nouveau confondue dans la meute informe des morts vivants.

La face contre la terre boueuse, Fabien Tranchant semble toujours inconscient.

A-t-il compris?

Oui, car il vient de refermer lentement sa main.

Cinq minutes plus tard, un timide sourire se dessine sur les lèvres de Fabien. Mais lui aussi doit maintenant être prudent.

Même si dans cet océan de souffrances, un grand message d'espoir vient de lui être lancé, Fabien Tranchant doit néanmoins continuer à se lamenter.

Moi, Mélanie Lapierre, je viens te sauver. Attends mon signal. Tu vas bientôt t'enfuir de ce cimetière maudit, sois-en sûr.

Un message d'espoir insensé et inespéré dans l'esprit de Fabien Tranchant!

Mais tout de même bien réel dans le coeur de Mélanie Lapierre!

Chapitre VII

Deux ombres dans la nuit

Traîtrise fatale.

Tout semble maintenant prêt pour ce numéro fort attendu.

On sent de l'effervescence dans la meute sanguinaire. Mélanie constate avec étonnement que même ces créatures, habituellement froides et cyniques, n'arrivent pas toujours à garder leur calme.

Le retour de Justin Macchabée est accueilli par un flot continu de lamentations. Chez ces créatures nocturnes, c'est la routine habituelle, quoi!

«Contents ou pas, les morts vivants ont toujours l'air de se lamenter», pense Mélanie, tout en prenant soin de murmurer quelques gémissements de son cru.

Les cruels plaignards dévorent maintenant de leurs yeux globuleux le grand manitou du cimetière. Mélanie en profite pour se glisser derrière la tombe fermée servant de podium aux orateurs.

— Maintenant, nous y sommes, commence Justin Macchabée. Mais malgré tout, le traître a droit de faire un voeu, un tout dernier, comme le veut la tradition millénaire. Fabien Tranchant, avant de disparaître à jamais sous la bienfaisante caresse de nos tendres griffes, exprime-moi ton ultime désir.

La bienfaisante caresse de nos tendres griffes!

L'affreuse image!

Non, il n'est pas question de se rendre jusque-là. Mélanie a l'intention d'arrêter cette petite fête macabre bien avant que Fabien n'ait à subir d'autres outrages.

— Alors, réponds, qu'aimerais-tu faire de tes dernières secondes, vil chien galeux?

Péniblement, Fabien Tranchant se soulève de terre. Il cherche à s'approcher de l'orateur, mais les gardes du *brave* Justin Macchabée le repoussent brutalement.

— Maître incontesté des morts vivants..., gémit alors Fabien, mon voeu le plus cher serait de monter sur le podium pour m'excuser devant tous mes frères... Ainsi, je pourrai vous quitter en paix... Sinon..., sinon..., je serai hanté par trop de remords. Je t'implore de m'accorder cette ultime faveur.

Fabien a réussi à attendrir quelque peu la foule. Mais pas Justin Macchabée qui crie de rage.

— Maintenant que tu as exprimé ton voeu, place à la *Traîtrise fatale!* Si tu pensais vraiment que j'allais t'exaucer, Fabien Tranchant, tu es bien naïf. Exprimer, c'est suffisant! Exaucer, ce serait trop injuste pour tous les autres qui ont toujours été loyaux et francs!

Un affreux simulacre de justice!

— Qu'on tranche cette tête de chien galeux et qu'on dévore ce coeur de vil traître!

Là, c'est trop!

Plus une seconde à perdre!

Prête, pas prête, il faut foncer!

Les poings serrés, Mélanie Lapierre se prépare à intervenir. Par derrière, elle va sauter sur le podium et pousser Justin

Macchabée dans la foule. Profitant de la confusion qui va suivre, Mélanie pourra alors lancer à Fabien la fiole qu'elle a préparée à son intention.

Un mélange explosif de jus de bette-rave, d'extrait de fraise et de toutes les vitamines en poudre qu'elle a pu trouver. De quoi remettre rapidement sur pied le pauvre Fabien!

Du moins, c'est à souhaiter!

Le temps de le boire!

À la vitesse de l'éclair, Mélanie bondit. L'effet de surprise aidant, elle réussit à faire perdre l'équilibre à Justin Macchabée. Il tombe rapidement par terre, au milieu de ses gardes du corps complètement médusés.

Profitant du brouhaha, Mélanie lance aussitôt la fiole à Fabien en lui criant de boire rapidement cette racine de vie.

Aussitôt attrapée, aussitôt bue d'un trait!

Grâce aux encouragements de Mélanie, Fabien reprend peu à peu une certaine vigueur. Après avoir entendu siffler autant de fouets, même un mort vivant est amoché.

Mais le plus difficile reste à faire: il faut maintenant arriver à s'échapper de ce lieu infect.

Mélanie sait bien que toutes ces griffes inquiétantes qui l'entourent ne demandent pas mieux que de plonger avidement dans sa chair.

N'écoutant cependant que son courage, Mélanie Lapierre fonce vers Fabien Tranchant. Heureusement, ce dernier s'est relevé. C'est maintenant évident, Fabien semble avoir été ragaillardi par la racine de vie.

— Mélanie, je t'avais pourtant écrit de...

— Fabien, ce n'est pas le temps de parler de ça, le coupe aussitôt Mélanie. On a autre chose à faire que de s'expliquer. Vite, avant que la trappe du caveau se referme.

Deux ombres dans la nuit!

Deux ombres qui courent à corps perdu vers la liberté!

— Merci, Mélanie, mille fois merci, arrive à dire Fabien au beau milieu de sa course.

— Je te rends la monnaie de ta pièce, Fabien. Une fois, tu m'as sauvée. Maintenant, c'est moi qui te sauve. Alors, tope là, on est simplement quittes.

Au loin, la clôture métallique est en vue.

Heureusement, Fabien Tranchant connaissait les sentiers du cimetière par coeur. En apercevant la sortie, les deux fuyards piaffent d'impatience à l'idée de pouvoir enfin quitter ce lieu sinistre.

Mais Mélanie sait bien que, durant la

nuit, la porte du cimetière est toujours fermée à double tour.

— Maintenant, Fabien, tu me suis, lance Mélanie à son compagnon.

Elle se dirige vers la droite. Quand elle aperçoit la brèche sous la clôture de fer, elle n'arrive plus à contenir sa joie. Vivement, Mélanie Lapierre se faufile par la fissure et franchit la clôture qui protège le cimetière de tous les indésirables.

Mission Sauvefachant accomplie!

Et liberté enfin retrouvée!

Derrière elle, Mélanie entend brusquement un cri déchirant.

Quelques mètres seulement avant la brèche de la clôture, Fabien Tranchant semble soudain immobilisé. Pourquoi n'avance-t-il plus? Mélanie s'approche et aperçoit des dizaines de mains squelettiques qui retiennent Fabien. Ces mains qui sont tout à coup sorties de la terre empêchent Fabien Tranchant d'avancer.

D'ignobles et effroyables mains!

— Va-t'en, Mélanie, sauve-toi... Il n'y a rien à faire, je t'avais pourtant prévenue, ils finiront toujours par m'attraper... Tu sais, Mélanie, c'est plus facile d'entrer dans un cimetière que d'en sortir.

Au loin, Mélanie voit maintenant s'approcher la meute de morts vivants. Ils ont dû prendre un raccourci. Et à leur tête, elle reconnaît la démarche et la longue silhouette décharnée de Justin Macchabée.

Si près du but!

Dans la nuit, le rire diabolique de Justin Macchabée se fait entendre, suivi de son horrible voix caverneuse!

— Fabien Tranchant, tu croyais nous échapper avec l'aide de cette jeune emmerdeuse. Mais tu avais oublié qu'on ne quitte pas aussi facilement le pays des morts vivants. Surtout quand on est le pire des traîtres.

Désemparée, Mélanie Lapierre ne sait trop comment réagir.

— Va-t'en, Mélanie, je t'implore de partir, lui lance alors un Fabien Tranchant résigné. Tu vois bien que Macchabée et sa bande s'approchent de plus en plus... Tu les vois bien aussi ces dizaines de mains qui m'empêchent d'avancer... Il n'y a plus rien à faire, non, vraiment plus rien, tous ces obstacles sont devenus insurmontables... Et cette fois, Mélanie, oublie-moi pour de bon. Adieu, Mélanie, adieu...

Quelques instants plus tard, Mélanie

aperçoit les morts vivants qui commencent à enchaîner Fabien. Par les mains, par le cou et par les chevilles si bien que le pauvre Fabien peut à peine bouger. Par la suite, le cortège funèbre se met en marche. Au plus vite, on veut ramener Fabien Tranchant au milieu du cimetière, dans le caveau fatidique qui l'attend.

En voyant cette horrible scène, Mélanie Lapierre ne peut s'empêcher de verser une larme... Puis une deuxième.

Mélanie Lapierre sait qu'elle n'a maintenant plus le choix: elle doit abandonner Fabien Tranchant à son impitoyable destin.

Mélanie pose ensuite un dernier regard vers son courageux sauveur, un regard embué de larmes. Un ultime regard hanté par toutes les tristesses du monde!

«Justin Macchabée, sois sûr que je reviendrai», ne peut s'empêcher de crier Mélanie Lapierre à l'ignoble tyran du cimetière, avant de s'éloigner.

La gorge pleine de sanglots!

Et le coeur débordant de rage!

Fin

Épilogue
Lima, Sofia, Ouganda, Brasília et Addis-Abeba

Le générique du film défile maintenant sur l'écran géant du cinéma Au Vilain Croque-Mort. On y apprend que c'est Emma Lerouge-Sang qui a porté à l'écran *Les griffes de la pleine lune,* le dernier roman de Blanche Dépouvante. Et que la musique lugubre est de Hiboud Ripa-Souvenh.

Emma, Hiboud et Blanche, toute une équipe! Mais à inviter seulement si on a le goût de faire des cauchemars.

— Stéphanie, il est temps de rentrer à la maison.

— Un instant, papa...

Stéphanie Perrault veut savourer jus-qu'aux dernières images de ce film. Elle n'aurait jamais voulu rater cette adaptation cinématographique du dernier roman de Blanche Dépouvante, elle adore tellement cette auteure.

— Bon, je vais t'attendre à la porte du cinéma, s'impatiente quelque peu son père en se levant et en se dirigeant vers la sortie.

Le père de Stéphanie Perrault est bien nerveux et semble même inquiet. Aussitôt qu'il voit apparaître sa fille, il ne peut s'empêcher de l'interroger.

— Réponds-moi franchement, Stéphanie, serais-tu capable de faire la même chose que Mélanie Lapierre? Pourrais-tu partir de la maison en pleine nuit sans me prévenir?

— Ça dépend, répond Stéphanie, le sourire aux lèvres.

— Comment ça, ça dépend?

— Voyons, papa, qu'est-ce qui te prend de t'inquiéter ainsi? Ta fille sait faire la différence entre un film et la réalité, pas toi?

Le père de Stéphanie comprend bien les arguments de sa fille. Mais il voudrait tellement la protéger, lui éviter le pire, ne lui offrir que le meilleur. D'ailleurs, s'il

arrivait malheur à sa Stéphanie, il ne sait pas comment il pourrait surmonter cette épreuve.

— Papa, si tu veux absolument te casser la tête avec quelque chose, on va jouer au jeu des capitales. À ce jeu-là, je suis aussi bonne que Mélanie Lapierre. Et meilleure que toi, mon cher papa.

— C'est ce qu'on va voir, répond malicieusement le père de Stéphanie qui est maintenant plus détendu.

— Tu commences, papa?

C'est parti.

— Lima, Sofia, Ouganda, Brasília et Addis-Abeba, ça te dit quelque chose?

La réponse de Stéphanie Perrault ne tarde pas.

— Le Pérou, la Bulgarie, ha, ha, ha! tu ne m'auras pas, avec ton Ouganda, mon petit papa, le Brésil et finalement l'Éthiopie.

Stéphanie Perrault sourit à son père, puis continue ses explications.

— Ma foi, tu te prends pour le prof de Mélanie Lapierre. L'Ouganda c'est comme le Togo au début du film, les deux sont des pays, pas des capitales. Tu vois, Mélanie Lapierre et moi, on n'est pas tombées dans le panneau.

Rempli de fierté, le père de Stéphanie sourit à sa fille. Stéphanie aime bien sentir la complicité qui existe entre son père et elle.

Durant quelques instants, elle a ainsi pu oublier la grande question qu'elle ne cesse de se poser: un jour, Mélanie Lapierre arrivera-t-elle à sauver Fabien Tranchant?

Stéphanie Perrault le souhaite, mais elle en doute.

Pourtant, avec l'intrépide Mélanie Lapierre, on ne sait jamais!

Pas plus d'ailleurs qu'avec l'imprévisible Blanche Dépouvante!

Table des matières

Prologue
Un souvenir en forme de brrrrrr...! 9

Chapitre I
Adieu, Mélanie! 17

Chapitre II
En route vers sa destinée! 27

Chapitre III
La terre tremble 37

Chapitre IV
Les pissenlits par la racine 45

Chapitre V
Incognito 55

Chapitre VI
Un macabre requiem 67

Chapitre VII
Deux ombres dans la nuit 75

Épilogue
Lima, Sofia, Ouganda,
Brasília et Addis-Abeba 85

"Good morning, what can I get–"
The waitress's mouth dropped open.

So much for no one noticing him. The woman's cheeks filled with color and her hand moved protectively over her heavily rounded stomach. "C-c-coffee?"

Joe's neck prickled from the multitudes of stares brought on by her behavior, but he ignored them as best he could and nodded. The pot shook wildly as coffee splashed into his cup. The pregnant waitress hurriedly waddled away with an audible sigh of relief.

Comments came to him then, the whispers getting louder and easier to hear. The words *baby killer* and *murderer* at the forefront.

Let them talk all they wanted. Threaten. He wasn't going anywhere, except to see his dad at the nursing home, and then–

Then he'd have to do what he'd done for the past ten years—keep his head down and figure out how to survive in a place where everyone hated him.

Dear Reader,

We've all made mistakes, but have you ever been accused of something you didn't do? Ever had to piece together the remaining shreds of dignity while trying to go about your business and live your life when you're surrounded by people you'd thought of as friends when the reality is they never believed in you?

Man with a Past is about family and community, but more important, it's about relationships and all the little idiosyncrasies that come with living in a small town where everybody supposedly knows your business better than you. It's also about hope, faith and all the emotions that surround the loss of a child.

Joe's story was one I found intriguing, one that had to be told. When I researched Shaken Baby Syndrome, I found it nearly impossible to fathom why, better yet *how,* someone would shake a child to death. But even more unfathomable to me were the lesser-known, and admittedly rare, stories of men convicted of murdering their children by SBS, men who'd served time, who were then released many years later when new evidence was brought to light that proved their innocence. By that time many had lost the support of marriages, family and friends on top of the loss of their child.

I hope you enjoy *Man with a Past.* I love to hear from readers, so please write to me at P.O. Box 232, Minford, OH 45653, or e-mail me at kaystockham@aol.com. To sign up for my e-newsletter, check out my Web site at www.kaystockham.com. I can't wait to hear from you!

Enjoy Joe's story,

Kay Stockham

MAN WITH A PAST
Kay Stockham

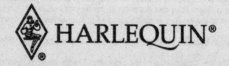

TORONTO • NEW YORK • LONDON
AMSTERDAM • PARIS • SYDNEY • HAMBURG
STOCKHOLM • ATHENS • TOKYO • MILAN • MADRID
PRAGUE • WARSAW • BUDAPEST • AUCKLAND

ISBN 0-373-71347-9

MAN WITH A PAST

Books by Kay Stockham

HARLEQUIN SUPERROMANCE
1307–MONTANA SECRETS

As always to my husband, Chad,
for being the kind of man to walk beside me,
not in front of or behind me. Fifteen years is a long time,
but I'm looking forward to *at least* thirty-five more!

To Karen Solem for being so excited about my stories, and
to all the Harlequin Superromance authors—what a welcome
you gave me and the other newbies. Thank you.

To Bill and Ryan, who want so badly to be
on my covers—will this do? ;)

And to family, friends and everyone who has ever
mourned the loss of a child. My heart is with you.
I hope you'll hold them again one day.

CHAPTER ONE

"I AIN'T HIRIN' no baby killer to work in my store."

Joe Brody ground his teeth together at Mr. Thompson's words and reminded himself he needed a job more than he needed his pride. "Your ad says you need—"

"I don't need somebody like you." Short and squatty, the middle-aged man rocked up on the balls of his feet as though trying to impress. Or intimidate. Either way it didn't work because the hardware store owner refused to meet his gaze.

Since he'd stepped off the bus this morning everyone in town, the women especially, had avoided looking Joe in the eyes. Glancing at him frightfully as though one glance would taint them for life.

"Look, Mr. Thompson, I served time I didn't—"

"*I said no.* Now git before somebody sees you." The heavy man's chins bounced as he did that rocking thing again and jerked a thumb toward the door. "Business is bad enough without you scarin' off customers."

The bell attached to the door jangled loudly and footsteps clicked against the cheap tile floor. Joe glared at Thompson even though he'd focused his attention on the newcomer.

"Ah, hell, what do *you* want?"

Surprised someone besides himself warranted such a response, Joe glanced at Thompson's customer then did a quick double take at the woman presently returning the man's baleful glower with one of her own.

She slammed a box on the counter. "This didn't work."

Her voice was rich and husky and laced with sheer fury. Thompson remained by the cash register, and as the two faced off, Joe used the moment of invisibility to his advantage.

Thin but stacked, the woman was a sight to behold after his ten years in prison. He guessed her to be in her mid to late twenties, a few years younger than his twenty-nine.

Her jet-black hair was pulled away from her angular face and the dark hue tinging her cheeks hinted at the temper she barely held in check. If Thompson held true to form after all these years, he typically responded more favorably to women willing to flirt with him. Obviously she didn't know that.

"No returns."

She flattened her palms along the top of the

counter and leaned forward, her height giving her a distinct advantage over Thompson. "You *deliberately* sold me the wrong product."

Thompson didn't acknowledge her accusation. "No returns if the box's been opened."

Long, straight tendrils teased the length of her jaw and she brushed them away in irritation. That's when Joe noted the presence of a plain silver wedding band.

"Of course I opened it—*you* said it would work."

"Did I? Can't remember."

Her gaze narrowed, and Joe had a hard time holding back a chuckle. Not many people had ever stood up to Thompson's dictatorial ways, but this woman was the exception.

"Look, I know you're still mad at me for buying the house—"

"Damned straight."

"But you can't change the fact it *wasn't* for sale to you."

"Shouldn't have been for sale to outsiders, either. You city folk think you can move in here and buy up whatever you want. You tricked that old fool, but you ain't gonna trick me!"

"You have no *idea* what I want, and I didn't trick anyone. Now, you guaranteed this part would fit that old sink—"

Thompson waved her toward the door. "Go bother somebody else."

"You'd like that, wouldn't you? But I'm not budging until you give me my fifty dollars back."

Joe eyed the box. Fifty dollars? He gave a small cough.

Thompson glared. "Why ain't you left yet?"

"Mighty pricey part," he drawled, shooting Thompson a look that stated clearly he was on to his game. "Can't help but wonder how business would suffer if folks thought your prices had a tendency to *fluctuate* depending on who was doing the buying."

The woman frowned as she caught on to what he implied. Then she flashed Thompson a quelling smile. "Oh, really? Fluctuate, huh? Maybe I need to call the local paper instead? *Or* the Better Business Bureau?" Her tone left no doubt that she would do just that and relish every minute.

The little man sputtered a moment. He fumed at Joe, his bushy brows nearly obscuring his eyes they pulled so low. "You stay out of this," Thompson grumbled.

The woman leaned over the counter and grabbed the phone receiver off its base.

"Hey, now—"

Eyes wide, her expression changed to one of innocence. "Would you like to call the BBB yourself?" She glanced around the otherwise empty hardware store before she gave Thompson a shrug. "Looks pretty dead in here, but I imagine it'll only get worse once word gets out."

The threat of losing money darkened the man's complexion to a dull maroon. Mouth pursed, Thompson made a noise deep in his throat and stomped his way around the counter.

"Man can't make a decent living. Folks always whining and complaining and not willing to abide by the law. Sign says no returns and it means no returns." He pointed a finger at her. "Don't you be tellin' folks I done this now, you hear me? I'll have all sorts of kooks in here wantin' money."

She made a face at the word *kooks* but nodded as Thompson stalked by. "I won't say a word…so long as you don't try this again. I want the right part at the right price."

The man complained some more as he waddled a wide path around Joe and headed toward the plumbing supplies.

Joe turned back to the woman, figuring it was about time for her to recognize him and go running like all the others. She dropped the handset back on the base, her gaze sparkling with amusement and lingering irritation, the almond-shaped eyes completely without fear or condemnation.

"Thanks for the backup."

Hesitant, still waiting for her to call him names, Joe tried for a smile. "No problem."

The woman took a step in Thompson's direction but hesitated, one hand on the counter. "So… exactly how much does 'fluctuate' mean?" Almost as soon as the words were out of her mouth, she stuck her hand up in the air. "No, never mind. Forget I asked. I don't think I want to know how badly he took advantage, but I'll watch him in future. *If* I come back at all."

Joe glanced over his shoulder at Thompson and saw the guy still muttering to himself as he sorted through plumbing fixtures. "Demand store credit if he tries to charge you more than thirty bucks."

Her full lips parted in shock at the price difference, and after a deep inhalation that caused his attention to stray south, the fire reappeared in her eyes.

"O-kay," she said slowly. "Well, I see how he works." She nodded again. "Live and learn, right?"

That motto he knew well. "Right," he agreed, watching as she squared her shoulders and headed toward Thompson. The sway of her jean-clad hips forced him to remember the silver band on her finger.

Exhaling a breath he didn't know he held, Joe shook his head and grabbed his duffel from the floor. Time was wasting away.

Outside, the muggy morning air latched on to his skin despite the shade covering the storefront. August was a hot, hot month in southern Ohio. The humidity nearly unbearable as it was trapped between the valleys and hills. Days like this were best spent on the water, boating, swimming. Picnicking somewhere private with a beautiful girl in a bikini top and Daisy Duke shorts.

All in good time. After all, he'd served his and at least he wasn't on a job site somewhere with an armed guard ready to fire should anyone try to make a run for it. Still, as he walked down the sidewalk and people scattered into shops or crossed the street to avoid passing him, he wondered how well some of the other guys would do when they made it home. Not many people liked the state releasing inmates for time served due to statute reorganizations. Especially not those convicted of killing a child.

Joe glanced at the clock in the town square and grimaced. Eleven-ten. Thompson's Hardware had been the fourth job listed in the Help Wanted section of the paper. Four of four, and after pounding the pavement walking the distances between locations, he'd been turned down by each and every one of them.

On the corner of Main and Elm, he hesitated outside Pat's Diner. Back in high school it was the popular place to hang out, and pretty much the only place to eat downtown.

Through the glass door he spotted an empty bar stool well away from the patrons who occupied the booths, and he grabbed the handle before he could change his mind. If he kept his head down maybe no one would notice him.

"Good morning, what can I get—" The waitress's mouth dropped open. "Oh. My. God."

So much for no one noticing him. The woman's cheeks filled with color and her hand moved protectively over her heavily rounded stomach. She looked familiar, but he couldn't put her face with a name.

"C-c-coffee?"

His neck prickled from the multitude of stares brought on by her behavior, but he ignored them as best he could and nodded. The pot shook wildly as coffee splashed into his cup.

"C-cream?"

She still hadn't let go of her belly.

"Black's fine, thank you."

His thanks seemed to throw her. She bit her lip and then said, "You, um, want something to eat?"

Joe shook his head and stared down into the murky depths of the rich-smelling brew. The pregnant waitress hurriedly waddled away with an audible sigh of relief, meeting up with another waitress at the end of the counter.

Comments came to him then, the whispers getting louder and easier to hear. The words *baby killer* and *murderer* at the forefront. Josie's name. *Josie's killer*. His manslaughter charge and how he'd gotten off easy when an eye for an eye would've been better.

The diner door opened behind him and Joe immediately shifted his back to the wall on his left. Old habits were hard to break even though he'd been in a workhouse most of the last ten years.

Still, once the other inmates had discovered what he'd been convicted of, things had a tendency to happen. So-called accidents. If not for his height and build he probably wouldn't have lived long, but as it was he'd gotten used to putting his back to the wall for protection.

Head down, Joe took a sip of coffee, but just when he thought his morning couldn't get any worse, Taylorsville's police chief took a seat two stools down from his.

"Mary, can I get a cup to go?"

Mary. Mary Bishop. That was her name. She was John Bishop's little sister, and that explained the familiarity. She looked like John, who'd been one of his buddies in high school, but was a good bit younger. Seven or eight when he'd been convicted, which put her around eighteen now.

Like magic Mary reappeared out of nowhere and handed the lawman a plastic-capped cup as though she'd already had it ready and waiting. Known he was coming as though he'd been called.

"Here ya go, Hal."

"Thanks, hon, I appreciate it. That baby doin' okay?"

Joe watched as her gaze darted nervously to him before she placed both hands over her front.

"Fine now. The doc says I'm okay so long as nothing more goes wrong."

Silence.

It was almost comical how quiet the diner was compared to when he'd walked in. Not even the normal sound of banging and clanging pots and pans could be heard from the kitchen. The proverbial pin could've dropped and the most hard-of-hearing would have flinched from the noise.

"Nothing's going to happen," the chief stated firmly as he pulled the perforated tab off the top of his coffee, giving the task more care than it needed. Casually, his leather holster creaking as his badge flashed beneath the lights overhead, Hal York turned to face him.

"Isn't that right, Joe? Nothing's going to happen because as soon as you drink your coffee, you're going to leave town."

Joe didn't move. "I heard about Melissa," he murmured softly, acutely aware their audience listened to every word. "I'm sorry—"

"Don't," Hal ordered, his voice gruff. "Don't you even say her name. Maybe one day God'll forgive you, but I won't and neither will my daughter." He leaned toward Joe. "Leave town and don't ever come back. Do it, or I'll make you wish you'd stayed in prison."

Several people in the diner seconded the chief's sentiment, and Joe tried to ignore the slight tremor in his hand as he lifted the cup and finished off his coffee before reaching behind him. More than one person gasped as the occupants of the diner waited to see what he was reaching for, and bitterness filled him. It took some doing to ignore them all as he pulled a few bills from his wallet and tossed them onto the countertop, leaving Mary a tip he couldn't afford.

Joe told himself it was to prove a point, but he couldn't lie to himself. She reminded him too much of Melissa's overwhelming panic when she'd found out she was pregnant. Pregnant and unwed, and having to face her father the cop.

Without a word to Hal, he grabbed his duffel and left, wincing when the diner erupted into a small roar of voices just before the door swung closed behind him.

Let them talk all they wanted. Threaten. He wasn't going anywhere except to see his dad at the nursing home and then—

Then he'd have to do what he'd done for the last ten years–keep his head down and figure out how to survive in a place where everyone hated him.

ASHLEY CADE decided that when she had a bad day, she *really* had a bad day. She'd been up nearly all night with her teething toddler and finally settled him only to see her chance at getting any sleep disappear with the rising sun.

Downstairs she'd discovered the coffeepot had chosen today of all days to die, and then she'd been so distracted by Mr. Thompson's two-faced, childish prank of deliberately selling her the wrong item, she'd forgotten to stop by the diner to splurge on her much needed caffeine jump.

Now as she parked the truck beneath the shaded carport in an attempt to keep the already torn seats from drying up and cracking more, she had a headache that pounded like a jackhammer.

Should she have stayed in the city?

No. The cost of living would've eaten up her savings and she wanted a career that would allow her to stay home with Max. No way could she have bought a house anywhere near as nice as this one, much less owned her own business.

She'd made the right decision. It was just days like this that made her wish she'd never gotten out of bed. Made her ache with loneliness and want someone to lean on, just for a little while. Companionship and Mac's husky belly laugh beside her.

The door of Wilson's battered old truck squeaked when she opened it, but the pain streaking through her head was nothing compared to the start she got when she realized a large dog stood two feet away, teeth showing.

What now, a dog bite?

"Go on, get out of here." She tried to shoo the dog away but the dirty brown animal stared at her, unmoving, a mix between a lab and a retriever. "Go on. Go."

The stupid dog wagged his tail. Uh-huh, like

she'd fall for that. "Get out of here. Go!" When he still didn't move she swallowed her unease. "You'd better go home, dog. Your owner might find another and ship you off to the pound."

Its skinny butt wriggled back and forth, tail flying. What was it with people who got a pet and then didn't take care of it?

She eyed the dog's thin frame and wondered briefly if it was hungry enough to make a snack of her. That's when she noted the way it froze and tilted its head to one side. Seconds later she understood the cause.

Her son's angry cries filtered from the open windows of the house and she groaned. So much for him sleeping long enough for her to get something done.

"Oh, Max." She kept an eye on the dog as she leaned in the truck and searched for the bag with the sink piece inside. Holding it in one hand, her keys in the other and ready to swing if she needed to, she edged out from behind the protection of the door and shut it.

The dog stepped forward.

"Forget it, mutt. Go home." She pointed to the hill behind the garage and carport, since the closest house was on the far side. "Go on, go!"

At her tone the dog scampered back a couple steps as though waiting for her to throw something at it. Ashley refused the niggle of guilt she felt at the sight. How many people had run him off? Should she toss him some scraps?

If you do that you'll never get rid of him.

The dog loped several feet in the opposite direction before turning back to look at her again. Max's ongoing cries reminded her that Wilson was on his own inside. She ignored the mutt as best she could and quickly walked toward the house, all the while checking over her shoulder every couple seconds to see if she was being followed, or better yet, chased. No sign of the mutt now.

Ashley pressed a hand to her temple to ease the throbbing as she let herself into the kitchen. She tossed the plastic bag in the general direction of the table only to hear it clatter when it slid off the top, hit the seat of a chair and land on the floor with a crash.

Great. The way her luck was going the stupid *thirty-dollar* part was now broken.

"'Bout time you got back, missy." Wilson stood next to the crib in the living room, a befuddled frown on his wrinkled face. "Thought I heard you, but then you didn't come in—"

"Sorry, Wilson. Hey, you know you can't pick him up and use the walker at the same time," she chided.

"Just hate to hear the boy cry. Thought if I got closer he might hush."

She smiled at Wilson's comment. When the old

man had stopped by the road that night months ago to offer help, she hadn't known what to make of him. Too many years living in the city and in a group home for kids past their prime adoption age had taken a toll. Somehow, though, she'd wound up staying with Wilson, not only accepting his help but his grandfatherly presence as well.

"I was gone twenty minutes. Half an hour tops. After being up all night he should've stayed asleep." Ashley lifted Max into her arms and snuggled his little body close. "Shhh, Max, it's all right. Mommy's here. It's all right," she crooned. She bounced him and talked nonsense to calm him down. "Oh, honey, why won't you sleep? You've got to be tired. I know I am."

Red-rimmed eyes blinked up at her, his lower lip stuck out and quivered. She smoothed her hand over the downy blond hair that was such a contrast to her own, and kissed his forehead. It always amazed her how he had her hazel eyes, but nothing else.

"Oh, you. Stubborn just like your daddy. You know that?"

Max waved a fist in the air before he brought it close to his mouth and sucked on it. He lowered his head to her shoulder and exhaled with a shudder.

"Max okay?"

She shifted her son to get a better grip and turned. "He's fine, but between him not sleeping and Mr. Thompson's tricks, I'm going to lose my mind. Do you have any idea how much he over-charged me for that part he guaranteed would work? Twenty dollars! I picked up some tarps and stuff for the roof because the weatherman said there would be thunderstorms later, but next time I'm making the drive to Baxter."

Old Spice lingered in the air as Wilson made his way to his chair. Because of the pain in his hips, he'd moved downstairs several years ago into what had been the servant's quarters. A small sitting room, bedroom and bath located off the kitchen, there was plenty of room for Wilson without him getting in the way of her plans for turning the large house into a B&B.

"Might not be havin' such a hard time if you'd warm up to one of the local boys."

She groaned. How many times had she heard this lecture? And how many times had she consid-ered it of late? Just thinking about dating again made her feel disloyal.

"Wilson, please. I've got too much to think about and do before next spring to even consider dating."

Chicken.

"Max needs a father."

She closed her eyes and rested her cheek on Max's head. Her son *had* a father. One of the few good guys she'd ever known. What were the odds of finding another one?

"Max's father hasn't been gone that long," she reminded him with a murmur. "And not everyone wants or appreciates an instant family."

"It's been long enough, missy. Almost two years now," Wilson countered. "And you said he was in training almost a full year before that. Nobody would blame you for gettin' lonely for someone your own age, but suit yourself. You'll change your mind soon as the boy is old enough to want friends an' comes home crying 'cause he don't have none."

Ashley carried her son with her across the room, but paused inside the doorway. She wanted to keep going, to ignore Wilson's comment, but her curiosity wouldn't let her.

"What does my dating a local man got to do with Max having friends?"

Wilson released his walker one hand at a time to grip the worn arms of his green recliner. Watching him balance always made her nervous so she looked down at Max and smiled as she waited for Wilson to seat himself.

"This ain't the city, missy," he said with a relieved sigh. "You want Max to have friends then you got to be accepted as one of the town. To do that, you got to be kin whether it's by blood or marriage."

He didn't have to tell her that. Being related, or rather, her *not* being related to anyone in town other than Max, was a fact she knew well. But what did she know about family? Roots? In the group home the mantra was every kid for herself.

She was so out of her element here.

"Might not be right, but it's the way it is and if you ain't gonna get married, then you've got to go out and get involved in things. Make friends."

"How? What *things?*" Exasperation sharpened her tone. Lack of caffeine, lack of sleep and the unpleasant memories of her difficult childhood made the thought of putting herself out there iffy at best, and disastrous at worst. She wasn't a "get involved" kind of person. Especially not when gaining attention usually meant inviting trouble and getting picked on.

How could she fit into this small, close-knit town when she never seemed to fit in anywhere else, including the base where Mac had been stationed? The military wives had pulled together after shipping their husbands off to war, but she'd never felt a part of that. And while she'd dated her share of guys as a stupid teenager, they were casual relationships that only lasted as long as the fun. She didn't want to go back to that, couldn't now that she'd known Mac's love. Where did that leave her in Taylorsville?

"Are you telling me I have to join the quilting circle and PTA just to buy plumbing supplies without getting ripped off?"

"Wouldn't hurt."

She rolled her eyes and instantly regretted the movement when pain shot through her skull. "Wilson, I want Max to have a home, roots, to grow up somewhere safe and nice—"

"Like you didn't have," he said, nodding.

"So what happened to small towns being open and friendly? You know...*Mayberry?*"

"You been up watchin' reruns again? There's too many weirdos in the world now, that's what happened. People's got to get to know you first and with you always holed up workin' on this house, nobody don't know what to make of you. You've got to be the one to get out there. Ain't a soul going to bring a cake to your door these days. You've gotta go to them."

Go to them?

Ashley rubbed her nose against Max's. "Yeah, well, I can't deal with that now. I've got a sink to fix if we want water. Don't I, Max?"

"Be better off hirin' a plumber since I cain't get under the sink to help you. Bobby Butcher's son's a plumber. Think he got divorced a year or so ago, too. Then again," he said with a frown, "I think his wife caught him cheatin' with Don Boyle's girl. Maybe you could call—"

"Wilson?" She pasted a smile on her face, more than a little overwhelmed and slightly panicky. "Thanks for the advice, and when I'm ready to date you can fill me in on all the Billy Bobs out there—I'll listen to every word—but in the meantime, all I can concentrate on is Max and fixing the sink. It isn't rocket science. I've read the book, I've got the right part now... I'll have it repaired before lunch."

"Uh-huh."

"I can do this," she insisted. "I don't need a plumber."

Wilson chuckled and slowly shook his head back and forth. "Just remember us *Billy Bobs* sometimes know a thing or two," he called as she walked into the kitchen carrying Max. "And I say you'd be better off callin' a plumber!"

CHAPTER TWO

THE DOORS OF the nursing home swooshed as they opened. Inside, patterned, coffee-stained carpeting led Joe forward in blessedly cool air until he came to a desk manned by a gray-haired lady wearing a red hat. She looked up at him, squinted over the broad, black rims of her glasses and frowned.

He remembered that frown. He remembered those glasses. The hat was new. "Mrs. H.?"

Her lips firmed and showcased the lipstick that had leaked out into the multitude of lines around her mouth. But other than grayer hair and a lot more wrinkles, she hadn't changed a bit since high school English.

"Mr. Brody," she said, carefully enunciating each syllable like always. "You're back."

"Yes, ma'am."

She pushed herself away from the desk and stood. Holding the handle of an elegantly carved cane, she limped around the desk. "Follow me. We don't allow just anyone to roam the halls amongst our dear patients. When you're ready to leave, use the phone in your father's room to contact the desk and someone will escort you to the door."

Jaw locked, Joe stared at the red bow bouncing atop the hat before giving in and following her fairly quick pace. "Is that normal? Escorting the visitors to and from the rooms?" he asked, even though he already knew the answer.

She slid him a sideways glance. "For some, Mr. Brody."

Joe shook his head but didn't say anything else as he shadowed Mrs. H. down the hall and to the right, down another hall past a cafeteria where a smock-clad woman led a bingo game and two men in wheelchairs played checkers.

She stopped at room 209. *Ted Brody.*

Joe stared at the numbers, at his father's name written in black marker on a small white message board attached to the door, and a sudden case of nerves racked him. He'd always thought of his father as being invincible. The kind of man who'd go out with a bang instead of slow and painful as his body wore out.

He shoved his hands into his pockets and looked at the teacher who'd been so brusque and demanding in high school. She'd been hated by some of the students because she'd made them strive to be better. Always reminded them to do their best, be their best, whether anyone watched or not.

"Thanks, Mrs. H."

The old woman's faded blue eyes narrowed on him from behind the thick glasses. "You always were a nice young man, Mr. Brody," she stated as she turned to walk back the way they'd come. "Too bad you weren't when it mattered most."

Joe stared after her, futile anger knotting his stomach. Everyone believed him guilty. And maybe he was. He certainly hadn't known what he was doing as an eighteen-year-old kid turned father. Maybe if he had, Josie would still be alive.

"Who's out there? Murray? I'm awake so just come on in! The board's a waitin'!"

His father's voice brought back a flood of memories. Joe pushed Mrs. H.'s cold reception and the incident at the diner to the back of his mind and stepped inside the room. The cloying smell of antiseptic and bleach tackled his nose as he dropped his duffel to the floor and smiled.

"*Joe?*"

He swallowed the lump in his throat and rushed forward, leaning over the hospital bed to wrap his arms around a frail body that couldn't possibly belong to his larger-than-life pop.

Thin arms surrounded him and hugged his neck, weak and shaking now that they weren't separated by glass and guards. "Ah, Joe. My boy's finally home, eh?"

"How ya doin', Pop? Flirtin' with the nurses?"

A gruff laugh rumbled out of his chest as his

father pushed him back to arm's length and patted him roughly. Gnarled fingers slid up his arms to cup his face. "Let me look at you. Ah, Joe, you look good. You still growin'?"

Joe nodded, straining to hold back his tears. "We got a new guy at the home a month or so ago. He's a chef in training and he fed us well. Think I'll actually miss his cooking."

Him being in prison had taken a toll on his father. At seventy-four, his pop looked eighty-four, maybe older. Deep lines creased his face, and his hair had turned a blinding shade of white. Dark circles shadowed his eyes and he'd lost weight. At least twenty or thirty pounds since he'd last seen him in person two years ago.

"I can't believe it's been so long." He squeezed Joe's forearm. "I'm so sorry I couldn't make it up there."

"It's all right, Pop, I understand."

"Had that stroke and just learned how to walk again when I fell and broke my hip. Been here ever since."

Joe nodded. He'd heard the apologetic story in every letter and call his father had made to the halfway house where he'd been moved before being released. And he'd gotten angrier and angrier because his brother, Jack, should've been there for him since Joe couldn't. Shouldn't have taken off and left their pop to face the town alone.

"I know you would've come if you could. I'm just glad you're healing up. I'll go home and get things ready for when you're released and then we'll… Pop?"

Something was wrong. His father looked away, a deep, ruddy color in his cheeks.

"There's nowhere to go, Joe."

He leaned against the bed rails, but stopped when the frame rolled a bit and forced him to lock his knees. "What happened?"

A tear trickled down his father's cheek. "Shameful. Man my age behaving like this."

"Just tell me what happened."

He rubbed his hands together repeatedly, the movement creating a sandpapery sound. "I couldn't make it, Joe. I tried to hold on, but I had to sell out to pay all the bills. The hospital and the home here. I—I lied to you in my letters about the insurance. Didn't want you to worry none."

Shocked, Joe looked around the room at the cold metal utilitarian chairs and trays instead of the antique rocker and quilt rack his great-grandmother had brought from Ireland.

A lone picture of him and his mother was on the table opposite, another one of the four of them, taken before his mom died, topped the television. Joe stared at Jack's face, wondering why his brother couldn't have believed in him the way his dad did.

"You needed what little money you made, Joe.

I wasn't going to take that from you. Would've only dragged things out longer and ended the same way regardless."

His old man reached beneath his pajama shirt and pulled out a length of string with several keys on it. "Got a little cash in a safe-deposit box from the sale. It's not much, but you go get it and find a place to stay."

"I can't take what you've got left, Pop."

His father's mouth trembled. "It's all I got to give you with the house gone. I did keep some of your mama's things. Gave 'em to a friend to keep for me."

"Where?" he rasped. Surely his father hadn't sold everything?

"Willow Wood. Remember that big house up on the hill outside town? Met him once or twice through the years, but never really knew the man before I had to share a hospital room with him. You go on there and Wilson will give everything to you."

"Where's Jack? Has he been here to visit? To help?"

"Haven't seen or heard from your brother since the day he left." He wiped a hand under his nose. "Don't expect to anymore. I tried to stop him but he made his choice. Maybe one day he'll come home, or maybe he won't."

The warm metal of the safe deposit key bit into his calloused palm. Joe squeezed it tight. Four years younger, Jack hadn't been able to handle the talk and speculation surrounding Josie's death. Hadn't been able to handle being a murderer's brother. The day he'd graduated high school, he'd hopped on the back of his bike and roared off without a backward glance. Maybe he didn't believe in Joe's innocence, but Pop deserved better.

"How soon will you be released?" Joe asked, shoving the memories and pain aside. He needed to know what he was dealing with. How much time he had to find a job, a place to live. Somewhere decent where he could take care of his old man. It was his fault his family was so divided.

His pop's chin firmed, the tears dried up and Joe was glad to note some starch reappeared in his shoulders. "Docs say it'll be another few months at least. But I'll show them, you just wait. After all this time without you, I'm going to get out of here. I won't burden either one of us with paying the bill for this place."

"Don't push too hard or you'll injure yourself again," Joe said.

He acknowledged Joe's words with a nod. "Town's growing fast. Lots of work to be had. Saw jobs in the paper yesterday morning. You check those out. Promise me you'll find something close by. I want to see you every bit I can."

Joe forced a smile to his lips and nodded. "Sure thing, Pop. I'll have a job in no time."

"YOU JUST GOING to stand there and watch it gush?"

Ashley turned toward the sound of Wilson's voice. He hovered outside the kitchen doorway, and for the first time since she'd bought the house from him, she was absurdly thankful the floor slanted. At least the living room wouldn't flood.

You hope.

But as she presently stood ankle deep in water in the middle of her antique wood floor, she figured it was only a matter of time.

"Well?"

Ashley swore under her breath and grabbed a wrench from the toolbox she'd left on the table. She fell to her knees and gasped as water hit her in the face and surged up her nose.

"Gonna have to get down there under it."

She ignored Wilson and attempted to maintain her position and turn the wrench at the same time, but no matter what she did, she couldn't get a good enough grip to stop the flow. Mainly because she couldn't see what she was doing.

A frustrated growl escaped her as she flipped over onto her rear, banged her head against the cabinet on the way down and lay in the water collected in the bottom of the sink cabinet.

"I'll go turn the water off at the pump outside."

"I'll get it here! You go down those steps with your walker and you'll need another hip replaced."

Ashley let her head fall back to ease the strain in

her shoulders, and sucked in a sharp breath as the icy fluid swamped her hair. Tears threatened, but she determinedly held them back even though a part of her mind wondered why the sink should be the only thing leaking.

She shrieked at the sink and did the only thing she felt like doing at the moment—she hit the pipe for all she was worth.

Amazingly, the gush slowed, sputtered, then peetered out with irregular drips. What the—

She was still lying there, staring up into the underbelly of the cabinet at the stupid pipe and the stupid leak now dripping on her chin, when she heard Wilson greeting someone.

Great. Just great. No doubt the mailman delivering yet another bill. She threw her arm over her face, the wrench still in her hand.

The house she'd thought a godsend, the one that had been such an unbelievably good deal and came complete with a built-in grandfather for Max, could now be described only as a money pit. Pretty to look at, but a disaster where it mattered most. What was she going to do?

A deep murmur reached her ears, low and rich. Strong. Her mind had to be playing tricks on her because if she wasn't mistaken, she recognized that voice even though she didn't know anyone in town.

And whose fault is that?

"She ain't movin'. Think she drowned?" Wilson asked, his tone half serious, half amused.

She frowned at Wilson's comment and shifted onto her side when their visitor spoke again. She couldn't make out his words, but at the moment she honestly didn't care, either. There wasn't a single part of her body that wasn't cold and wet.

Distracted, she banged her head on the cabinet on the way up and gasped out a curse.

"I heard that. Makes two now, don't it?"

Talk about discriminative hearing. Wilson only heard the things he wanted to hear and nothing else.

"Don't forget to pay up. And it's about time for you to make a trip to the store," he added from somewhere on her left. Near the back door.

Ah. So whoever it was, maybe Wilson hadn't let them in to see the damage, not that water running out onto the porch from *beneath* the screen door wasn't a dead giveaway that she had one heck of a problem on her hands.

She eyed the belly of the cabinet and was tempted to crawl back in and shut the doors. Instead she wiggled the rest of the way out and glared up at Wilson, but someone's jean-clad knees got in the way.

Her gaze traveled up, all the way up, until she had to tilt her head back, since she still sat on the floor. She finally got a look at their visitor.

The man from the hardware store?

Amusement softened his rough features. "Looks like you could use some more help."

Bite me. He might have put her on to the fact the hardware store owner had ripped her off, but she'd handled the man. Sort of.

She just couldn't handle the house.

Ashley glared up at her visitor while he surveyed the damage her attempt at do-it-yourself home improvement had wrought. Broad hands settled on his hips, fingers splayed, and his smile rapidly turned into a disgruntled frown.

If he opened his mouth and said a *word,* so help her, she'd—she'd—

Splash him?

She shook with frustration and embarrassment. She didn't need any more I-told-you-so's. She'd get plenty of those from better-hire-a-plumber Wilson.

Ashley shoved herself to her feet and attempted to ignore the way gravity took effect when water ran from her clothes in an undignified surge.

Wilson snickered, the man smirked, but she forced her chin high anyway. *Attitude is everything.* How many times had Mac told her that?

She spared a glance at Wilson only to note with no small amount of irritation he looked relieved, as though the cavalry had come to the rescue.

Chauvinistic old geezer.

She'd read the book on how to repair the sink. Done everything the so-called expert said. It wasn't her fault the pipe had sprung a leak when she'd gone to check on Max.

"Are you all right? You banged your head pretty hard."

"What do you want?"

The man's expression tightened at her rudeness and given his help earlier in the day and his supposed concern now, her guilty conscience forced a mostly sincere apology from her lips.

"Sorry." She indicated the mess around her. "It's been a bad day."

"Yeah." The man hesitated before he stuck out his hand. "I'm Joe Brody."

She transferred the wrench to her left hand so she could shake his right and noted how his gaze darted away from her. "Ashley Cade."

"Joe turned off the water and saved the day," Wilson informed her, a gleam in his rheumy eyes.

"Right place, right time. I, uh, saw the flyer posted at Meenick's Garage. You still looking for a handyman?"

"Are we ever."

Ashley glared at Wilson and wondered for the millionth time how wise she'd been to agree to Wilson's stipulations for selling her his house. Despite the hugely discounted price—and it was huge—she'd agreed to let him live there for as long as he was able to take care of himself. She'd felt sorry for him, alone, no family. She knew what that felt like and now she couldn't imagine life without the old man.

Except on occasions such as this.

"Ashley cain't fix a darn thing and with my new hip, I cain't, either. Whole house'll fall in soon if we ain't careful."

Their visitor acknowledged Wilson's words with a slow nod. "We'd better get these plank floors cleaned up before they turn and warp."

"We?" Did she want a complete stranger walking into her house and immediately making himself at home? After she checked his references, maybe, but—

Hellllo? What is a B and B, if not strangers coming in and making themselves at home?

She fought off a wave of unease. Doing this with her husband at her side was one thing—Mac was one of those guys who'd never met a stranger—but…could she *do* this?

"I, uh, came to pick up the things my father left with you," the man murmured, his blue eyes focused intently on Wilson.

So intently Ashley got the feeling she was being deliberately ignored.

"But I'm also looking for a job and I'm good at work like this."

She tried not to be irritated by the fact he obviously thought Wilson still owned the house and was responsible for contracting the work.

Ashley's hands settled on her hips and the independent woman in her bristled as she took in his all-male appearance of scuffed work boots, old, well-worn jeans that molded his long legs and thighs with indecent familiarity and an equally faded black T-shirt that stretched across impossibly broad shoulders and arms any bodybuilder would envy.

The man's nose had taken a beating and appeared to have been broken multiple times, a small scar lined the right side of his mouth and chin while another, more prominent scar cut across a good three inches of his neck before it disappeared beneath the band of his shirt. He'd been in his share of fights. But had he won them?

"We're certainly lookin' to hire—"

"But we need references." She shot Wilson a pointed glare she hoped would remind him whose name was now on the deed. "And pay is mostly room and board, very little cash."

Joe Brody looked around at the dated seventies kitchen. She could practically see his mind working.

"How little?"

She wet her lips and stated the figure that had made the last guy laugh so hard, he'd left the house wiping his eyes and short of breath.

Mr. Brody didn't look happy about it, either.

"I'll take it," he murmured with a slow nod.

She stared, unsure she'd heard him correctly. "You acc—"

Halle-lu-jah!

The man nodded again. His gaze flicked about the room rapidly, but paused on her for a few seconds before he looked away. "My father's in Ridgewood, the nursing home," he clarified, voice husky. "I need to stick close until he's released."

Ashley frowned at his behavior, not sure she liked how he wouldn't hold her gaze. "So when your father's released you'll quit? Getting this house ready to open as a bed-and-breakfast at the end of next spring is a long-term job, Mr. Brody, and—"

"Joe." His Adam's apple bobbed as he swallowed and shifted his weight from foot to foot. The water at their feet rippled. "Call me Joe. And we can, uh, discuss this later." He rubbed a hand over his mouth and jaw.

"Why later?"

He swallowed again, the sound audible. A groan?

"Just thought you might want to change into dry clothes, that's all."

Mortification deluged her. Could she really have forgotten she stood there soaking wet?

She lunged by the wanna-be handyman, each step a humiliating splash as she crossed the flooded floor. "I'll be back," she muttered, absurdly upset her statement wasn't more Schwarzeneggerish.

"I'll get him started on the cleanup, missy. No problem."

No problem? Yeah, right. The first man to agree to take on the job of repairing her house and she'd just given him an impromptu peep show.

Ashley pulled the T-shirt away from her body as she stomped her way up the stairs. Her pace lightened to a tiptoe when she passed Max's room and entered her own, but once her door closed with a *snick* of the antique latch, she sagged against its frame and covered her face with her hands.

What had she done to deserve this?

A shiver racked her despite the heat of the day and she grabbed the fabric clinging at her waist, yanked it over her head and shivered again when water trickled down her back. She ignored the goose pimples, and stalked into the bathroom between her room and the nursery.

Her last freshly laundered towel awaited in the linen closet but her hand froze over the cloth. She wouldn't have time to do laundry today the way things were going so if she wanted a fresh towel tonight after her bath, well—

"This is what you get for thinking a hundred-year-old Victorian would make a great fixer-upper."

Changing directions, she grabbed the already damp towel hanging on a hook by the tub and dried off. When she finished, she wrapped it around her dripping hair and stalked back into her bedroom for underwear and a change of clothes.

The warmth of the shower called to her and she

wished she could jump in and stay there until Joe Brody gave up and left. But hiding equaled defeat.

No, no way. She relegated the coward within her to a firmly locked closet in her mind, yanked on fresh jeans and grabbed her favorite T-shirt, which was black with "Bite Me" in bold white letters on the front. She needed that sassy attitude now.

In her haste she forgot the towel wrapped on her head and wound up fighting with it before she managed to pull it off through the neck hole of the T-shirt. Finally dressed, she glared at the offending towel and ground it under her heel as she stalked back into the bathroom.

She had work to do. A house to fix up, a son to raise. Stupid, archaic *countrified* rules to figure out so Max would have friends. She didn't have time to worry about anything else.

Attitude *was* everything and in this case, her attitude was the only thing that could get her through going back downstairs where she had to present herself as the man's potential boss all the while aware he'd seen her at her absolute worst and virtually topless thanks to the wet T-shirt.

References.

Ashley lifted her chin, determination stiffening her spine. What were the odds his references would check out? Did she actually want them not to? Just because of a stupid incident?

She had to prove to Joe Brody—and herself—

that she was capable of doing what a man would do given a similar situation. Go down there and be strong, confident and capable, the personification of a take-charge, kick-butt, streetwise woman.

Not an orphan who never belonged anywhere, or a somewhat desperate widow running out of time.

She nodded firmly. She could do this. After all, it wasn't like the man had never seen a woman's breasts before.

CHAPTER THREE

"CLOSE YOUR MOUTH, BOY. Gonna choke on a fly gaping after her."

Joe snapped his mouth shut and turned toward the old man. He hoped he had his body well enough under control that he didn't embarrass himself any more than he had already by not being able to keep his eyes off her and the T-shirt stuck to her like a second skin.

Ten years in prison and then to see something like that—

"She's—" He indicated the stairs off the kitchen where Ashley had disappeared.

"In my day we called girls like that top heavy," Wilson acknowledged with a grin. "And, yup, that she is. Now mind your manners and open the door on your right. Grab that big broom and make yourself useful."

Joe followed orders, grateful to have something to occupy his hands and take his thoughts off the woman upstairs.

"How's your dad? He doin' any better?"

Joe nodded. "Mad at himself for falling and looking forward to getting out of there."

"Can't blame him. In places like that it's hard to avoid the vampires always out to suck your blood."

He chuckled at the description of the nurses, but didn't comment. Instead he grabbed the broom and used the thick bristles and his excess sexual energy to shove the water toward the back door, all the while conscious the old man hovered behind him.

Out of the corner of his eye Joe saw his father's friend lean against the peeling, chipped woodwork with a grunt, his face screwed up in a grimace as he settled himself.

"We need somebody who'll work hard and get the job done on time. No shoddy work or slacking off."

Joe glanced over his shoulder, surprised he was still in the running since the old man appeared to know so much about him. "I've got a good work history. No complaints."

"You know how to plumb?"

"Yes, sir."

"Carpenter?"

"Yes."

"What about roofin'?"

"That, too."

"Don't suppose you can provide references for Ashley? She's a stickler for those. Comes from reading all those how-to books."

References he had, but they were through the

work release program and from the teachers the state hired to come to the penitentiary. He nodded once more. "Yes, sir, I do have references, but—"

"Been about ten years now hasn't it?"

Joe paused long enough to meet the old man's gaze. "Yes, sir. I served ten years of a fifteen year sentence. Under the statute change, the review judge released me with time served due to good behavior."

Wilson nodded again. "Your daddy talked about the letters you sent him. Proud of you, he was."

Proud? Joe lowered his head and swivelled the broom around to shove some more water out the door.

No, not proud. His father couldn't be proud to have a son convicted of manslaughter.

"Said you'd turned a tragedy into something good. Tried to make something of yourself instead of sitting there rotting your brain or joining a prison gang. Bragged on what good grades you made taking all those courses. From the sound of it, you've done good."

"Thank you, sir, but—"

"Wilson. Wilson Woodrow." The old man laughed. "My father thought it'd be funny since they always call a person's name out last name first."

"Wilson," Joe said, smiling at the comment. "Nice to finally meet you. I'm one of the many who've always admired this house from town."

Wilson accepted his words with a grin. "That

so? Well, the way I see it, it'll take some time for people to get used to havin' you around again. You'll prob'ly need to lay low for a while and this job would help you do it. Keep you mighty busy earnin' your keep, but it'd sure be a good way to show folks things."

Joe paused again. "The chief has made it clear he doesn't want me around. I already had a run-in with him in town."

Wilson glanced at the staircase. "He's a tough one, Hal is. But a good man. Person's gotta keep in mind people change when they lose so much at once like he did. But Hal will come along and get used to seeing you if you do things right. Take things nice and slow. And like I said, a big old house like this will take a while to repair. Shouldn't have let it get so bad, but I couldn't keep up with it once my Maddy got sick."

Joe tightened his grip on the broom. "Mrs. Cade isn't from around here, is she?"

"Nope."

"Then she probably doesn't know what happened. Once she finds out she won't want an ex-con under her roof. Not many people would." He couldn't blame her, either. Wouldn't blame anyone when, ten years ago, he'd have felt the same way himself.

Wilson straightened and Joe found himself ensnared by the old man's unblinking scrutiny as he used his walker to cross the wet floor.

"Be careful you don't f—"

"Ted said you didn't do it," Wilson murmured, cutting him off. "Now if that's the case, I don't see no need to go telling Ashley unless your daddy's wrong and you did."

Was he actually asking? Joe couldn't believe it. Once a person's accused of something—especially something like murder—everyone assumes him guilty until proven innocent. Even his own brother. Having been convicted *and* imprisoned had written his guilt in stone.

"Come on, boy, this is your chance to speak up. Did you?"

The words stuck in Joe's throat as memories overwhelmed him. Holding his baby girl in his arms, her tiny little body so still, then trembling uncontrollably as seizure after seizure racked her. He'd been so scared. Didn't know what to do.

Footsteps and the low murmur of Ashley's voice pulled his thoughts from the past. Joe turned, and in an instant, shock and nausea battled for control.

He stared at the sleepy-eyed baby boy on Ashley Cade's hip, all the while conscious that Wilson took in his every blink and reaction.

"Did you do what?"

ASHLEY WASN'T SURE what she'd walked into, but the tension in the air led her to believe it was more serious than the condition of her aging kitchen pipes.

"Did you do what?" she repeated.

"Lock the wrench I left outside by the pump. If it's not tight and comes loose off that valve, it'll leak again." Wilson nodded firmly and jerked his head in Joe Brody's direction. "My Maddy knew Joe's mother, God rest their souls. And I got to know Ted in the hospital. You know that?"

"No, I—"

"Told Joe that was good enough for me. And he can carpenter, plumb and roof. Cain't turn away a man who can do all that."

Irritated that Wilson had promised Joe the job without her permission, she frowned. "What about electrical work?"

"Now you cain't expect a man to—"

"I'm a certified electrician."

Wilson's brows rose as though he were impressed by that bit of news, and she had a hard time curbing her own desire to jump up and down.

Joe Brody was too good to be true. A gift sent straight from above. *But if he's so well-trained, why was he willing to work for a pittance?*

"References," she blurted suddenly. "I need references. Do you have people who'll vouch for you? Places I could maybe go to see your work?"

"Now I done told you, Ashley, I know his parents. There's no call for pesterin' people. I've already warned him there'll be no slackin' off. Besides, Joe here's not like those contractors that take your money and leave you high and dry. He's good stock."

Her arms stiffened protectively around Max. Living with Wilson the last six months, she'd grown to trust him and he'd yet to steer her wrong, but by referring to Joe as *good stock,* Wilson had hit a sore spot.

An outsider to Taylorsville, she knew exactly what the term meant to the townspeople as far as whether or not they'd claim a person as one of their own. And with her big-city license tags, *good stock* she wasn't. Nor was she related through blood or marriage as Wilson had already pointed out once today.

"How's my boy?" Wilson continued, wagging a finger in Max's direction. "You gotta stop keepin' your mama up at night, youngun. She's gonna fall asleep in her cereal one of these days."

Ashley used Max as an excuse to distance herself. She smoothed her hand over her son's sleep-flushed cheek and kissed his forehead as she moved farther into the kitchen.

Once she'd securely buckled Max inside his high chair and adjusted the tray into place, she added his favorite toys looped together with hard plastic rings and attached them to the chair so they wouldn't fall to the floor.

That done, she turned her attention back to the room. Joe stood broom in hand, stock-still, staring at Max like he'd never seen a baby before in his life.

"This is my son," she said by way of introduction. "Max, short for Maxwell Allen Cade, the second."

"Named after his father," Wilson supplied needlessly.

"And this, little man, is Joe. Can you say 'Joe'?"

In response, Max blew a slobber bubble and shook two chubby fists in the air, his mouth wide as he drooled. Ashley laughed softly, captivated as always by her baby's every action, and grateful for the distraction where her new employee was concerned.

She faced Joe, prepared to get down to business, then laughed again. Her earlier embarrassment receded when she noted his discomfort. "Relax, I don't expect you to babysit or change diapers. Now, you ready to talk terms while we clean this up?"

HAL YORK ENTERED his home and quietly shut the door behind him, the weight of the world on his shoulders.

Ever since he'd walked into the diner this morning after a call from the manager, he'd been in a surly mood. Snapped at his officers and barked out orders that had reduced more than one of his civilian help to tears.

But seeing Joe Brody sitting there at the diner's bar drinking coffee had pissed him off like nothing ever had. How could he not be mad when the justice system he'd spent his life serving had let him down?

Time served. In his opinion Joe had deserved the death penalty.

A life for a life.

Instead he'd gotten three meals a day and satellite television. An exercise yard where the tall, scrawny kid he'd known had turned into a formidable man, stronger than before thanks to the workout equipment provided. Where was the justice in that?

He dropped his hat onto the kitchen table and made his way down the hall. He paused at Melissa's room and peered inside to find his daughter's eyes open but unseeing as she stared blankly at the television.

Hal rapped softly on the door and forced a smile when she turned her head and caught sight of him. She looked like hell.

"How are you feeling today?"

"Fine. Been a rough morning?" Melissa asked, her voice raspy from lack of use.

He stepped into her bedroom and ambled over to the side of her bed. "Just hectic."

Her brow raised, or at least what would have been her brow had the hair covering the muscle and skin still been there. Thanks to chemo and steroids, Melissa's face was smooth and more rounded than usual.

"Mrs. Morris brought over chicken and dumplings for lunch. They're in the fridge."

"You eat?"

She inhaled and sighed. "I'm not really hungry today."

"So you were sick again? Mel, you've got to keep some food down or else—"

"When were you going to tell me, Dad?"

He tried to pretend he didn't know what she meant. "Tell you what?"

Melissa frowned at him. "Mrs. Morris couldn't wait to tell me Joe was back in town. Did you know he was coming?"

"Nosy busybody." He stalked away from the bed to the window overlooking the backyard. "No, I didn't know."

"But he is here? In town?"

Hal could still picture her out there. His baby girl, pigtails flying as she pumped her legs to swing higher, faster.

"Not anymore. I ordered him to leave. Last I saw of him he was headed out with his duffel over his shoulder. My boys are keeping an eye out for him."

"Why?"

Incredulous, he turned to face her. "You're asking me why I ran a murderer out of my town? Away from the people I've sworn to protect?"

Melissa flinched at his tone. She managed to keep her tears at bay although he could tell by the redness rimming her eyes and coloring the tip of her nose, they were close. Tears were the norm these days. Expected and understandable. He knew the routine well, having been through breast cancer with her mother before she'd lost the battle.

He shoved the helplessness away. God's will be done. He had to remember that. It just didn't make it any easier.

"What…did he say?"

He ran a hand over the muscles beginning to spasm in his neck. "Don't you worry—"

"Dad, what did he say? I have every right to know, now tell me."

He stared out at the empty yard. How he wished Melissa's mother was alive and she and Mel were *both* healthy. Wished his little girl had never fallen in love with Joe.

"He didn't say much," he answered honestly. "Just drank his cup of coffee at the diner and got up and left like I told him. Heard from George Thompson he'd been in looking for a job. A few others said the same thing. Everybody in town turned him down."

"Poor Joe—"

"*Poor Joe?*" Hal cursed. He closed his eyes and pictured the little girl he'd held within moments of her birth. "She'd be ten, Mel. *Ten.* I can't pass the school when it's being dismissed because seeing those girls makes me wonder what she would've looked like. Who would've been her friend."

A sob brought him out of his rant and he turned to find Melissa's face buried in her hands, shoulders quaking. He moved back over to her bed and sat on the edge. "I'm sorry. I shouldn't have said— Mel, don't cry."

She shook her head firmly. "No, *I'm* sorry. I'm just so sorry. If I could only change—"

"What?" he murmured. "None of us knew. I'm a lawman and didn't suspect Joe could do something like that. But it'll be all right. *Everything* will be all right," he soothed, even though they both knew good and well it could go either way. Just like it had with her mother.

Please, God, please don't take her, too.

Hal pulled his daughter into his arms and held her for a while, rocked her back and forth on the bed like he had when she was little and she'd had a bad dream.

After a bit Mel pulled herself together and he kissed the top of her head, then gently pushed her away from him with his hands at her shoulders. Once she relaxed against her pillow, he grabbed a tissue from the box by her bed and handed it to her.

"Dry your eyes and blow your nose. I'm going to go heat up some of those dumplings for us."

She did as she was told, sniffling. Silent. But he could see her mind working. See her remembering. "No more worries, Mel. I'll take care of Joe Brody."

Because if he ever comes near you again, I'll kill him myself.

ONCE THE WORST of the water was off the floor, Ashley continued to mop and dry the aged wood while Joe got to work under the sink. He welcomed the task since it gave him the opportunity to distance himself from his memories of Josie.

He knew he should speak up then and there, tell Ashley the truth before she found out some other way, but something held him back. Maybe it was the expression on the old man's face that warned him to remain quiet until they could finish their conversation. Maybe it was the fear of losing the only job someone had been willing to give him.

Or maybe it was Max himself.

Joe shifted beneath the sink, the damp towels beneath his back bunching at his neck as Max's and Josie's faces blended.

Josie had been younger than Max when she died. Only two months, and so tiny since she'd been born premature, but in Max's face he saw his little girl. Big, soulful eyes surrounded by a sweetness and innocence that drew him in and reminded him of all the good in the world.

"Do you, um, need anything?"

The wrench slipped from his fingers and landed in the center of his chest with a painful thud.

"Sorry. I didn't mean to startle you."

Joe angled his head until he could see Ashley's anxious face outside the cabinet. "No problem. It's hard to keep a good grip when it's wet."

He thought he heard her mutter "Don't I know it" under her breath. She hesitated, then squatted down next to his hips as he lay with his head and upper body under the sink. His blood heated, began to pool where it had no business, but her nearness and the image of her in the wet T-shirt flashed through his mind and obliterated all attempt at control. Where was her husband?

She must be the one in charge of restoring the house, but he wouldn't be having such a difficult time if he could see them together.

"You look like you know what you're doing."

"No." He caught himself, and smiled wryly. "I mean, yes, I do—and no, thanks, I don't need anything."

Her tongue swept out over her full lower lip and drew his gaze there. Wet, moist, she had lips made to be kissed. Sort of like that actress Angel or Angeline. What was her name?

"It's past lunch time. Nearly two-thirty. You want to take a break and eat a sandwich?"

His stomach rumbled at the suggestion, but that reaction was nothing compared to what he felt when she smiled at his loud response.

Get a grip, Brody. Don't screw this up by fantasizing about your boss. Your married boss.

"Mayonnaise or mustard?"

"Mustard."

"You makin' lunch, missy?" Wilson called from

the room located off the kitchen. "Gonna starve that boy, if not."

"Lunch is coming, Wilson, just be patient."

Joe returned her smile with a tense one of his own. "He's a hoot."

"Yeah, he is. He sort of came with the house, and now I don't know what I'd do without him."

Joe took the opening she presented. "He's related to your husband?"

Another small shake of her head. "No."

Ashley Cade didn't offer up any more information than asked, much the same as he'd learned to do while behind bars. But the comparison made him question her past and wonder what experiences had created the need to keep to herself.

"Wilson's sort of an adopted grandfather. We broke down as we drove through town and Wilson helped us out. Long story short, he found out I wanted to open a B and B and we've been here ever since."

"But…he's still living here."

She shrugged. "Yeah, he is. That was part of the deal. In exchange for selling us the house dirt cheap, we agreed to let him stay as long as he was able to care for himself."

He raised a brow. "And when he got hurt?"

"You mean his hip?" She waved a hand in the general direction of the living room. "Oh, that's no big deal. He'll be back to normal in a few weeks."

He stared at her, curious. No big deal? It certainly was to some. How many people would care for an elderly man who wasn't a relative? She might keep to herself, but Ashley Cade had a soft heart.

He shifted beneath the cabinet, guilt plaguing him. "What about your other plans? Where were you going when you broke down?"

Another shrug. "Mac and I always wanted to get out of the city and raise a family someplace quiet. Taylorsville is as good as any other Mayberry."

Mayberry. The remark alone said a lot. She obviously had preconceived notions of small towns. A lot of people did. Small towns were great. Filled with folks with big hearts and generous souls.

But small towns were also filled with problems, and it was hard to start a life, or rebuild one, when everybody thought they knew your business better than you.

"I'll go get those sandwiches."

She stood and from his position beneath the cabinet, Joe watched as she walked away. Unable to help himself, he stared, appreciating the slow sway of her hips until she left his line of vision.

Where was her husband?

Joe clenched his jaw. It was none of his business. Ashley's T-shirt said it all. She wasn't a clingy woman who depended on her husband to take care of things at the house.

He shook his head at his wandering thoughts,

and got back to work gluing and reattaching the pipes. Once everything was in place, he got out from beneath the cabinet.

"I'll let that set for a bit while I eat and then test it," he informed her as he got to his feet.

Ashley whirled around, her eyes widening comically as she took in the kitchen's now spotlessly clean and dry floor.

A smile tugged at his lips. "Don't worry. I'll keep the pressure low until I know for sure it'll hold. That way there'll be no more floods."

"Oh."

A guilty expression played across her face and made him wonder if she'd caused the flood by blasting the pressure.

"Oh, yeah, of course. I knew that." She hesitated briefly before she returned to making the sandwiches, waving the mustard-covered butter knife in his direction. "You can use the baby wipes over there to wash up since there's no water. And there's antibacterial gel, too, if you can't get the gunk off."

Her words prompted a glance down at his hands. Grime and glue coated his fingers and despite his unwillingness to use the items, he walked over to the container and opened the lid.

Memories bombarded him as the scent of baby powder filled the air. Lost in thought, he pulled out several wipes, his mind spiraling back in time to impossibly soft skin and sweet baby noises. The papery sound of diapers. Gurgles and trusting little eyes.

God help him, he missed her. And he hated himself for letting Josie down. For not being the father he should've been when she needed him most.

"Here you go."

Joe punched the pop-up lid closed with a snap and tossed the now shredded towelettes in the wastebasket sitting on the counter out of flood range. He inhaled the baby-scented air and found Ashley holding a loaded plate with two sandwiches, chips and a slice of pickle on the side. He stared at it, his appetite gone even though he'd been starving minutes earlier.

"I hope turkey is all right. I'll make you something else if you like, but I've got to warn you all I have at the moment is bologna."

"Turkey's fine." He reached for the plate.

"Iced tea?"

He nodded again and she hurried to pull a glass from a nearby cabinet.

"Wilson, you want a tray?"

"No, missy, I'm a-coming." Wilson appeared in the doorway, his knuckles white as he gripped his walker for the next step. Distracted, Ashley poured the tea and handed the nearly full glass to Joe, frowning as she watched the old man's progress. "You've been up a lot today. Better take it easy or you'll pay for it tomorrow."

Wilson ignored her and continued on into the room. "Max is playing with a chew thing and drooling all over hisself. Never seen a youngun water so much. He's gettin' fussy, too."

"I hope that tooth comes in soon," she said as she quickly loaded a second plate with food. "And it's his lunchtime. Maybe he'll settle down with a bottle and take a nice long nap."

She hurried around Wilson and placed the plate on the kitchen table before pulling out the closest chair for the old man to sit down. That done, she hurried back to get another glass of tea.

"Here's your iced tea and, please, go easy on the sugar. I've already warmed a bottle, so I'll feed Max and try to get him to sleep while you two eat." Ashley grabbed a bottle from the counter next to the stove and disappeared into the living room as her son's fussy whimpers turned into full-fledged cries.

"Always running somewhere, that one. Get that sink done?"

Joe pulled out the chair next to Wilson and sat down. "It's drying. Should be set by the time I finish this," he said, picking up one of his sandwiches. "What's next on the list of repairs?"

Wilson shrugged. "Gotta ask Ashley that. She's got a list a mile long."

Joe glanced at the empty doorway and cleared his throat, careful to keep his voice low. "Look, I don't mind helping out, but as far as this job goes…I don't like keeping secrets. Especially one as big as my record."

Wilson pursed his lips and nodded sadly. "Guess the evidence was right then," he drawled. "You killed that baby girl."

CHAPTER FOUR

"I DIDN'T," JOE countered forcefully.

Wilson pointed a gnarled finger at him as he nodded. "That's what I wanted to hear. And I never said you couldn't tell her, boy. But I'd wait and let her get to know you and have something else to go by before you go spillin' your guts about why you were behind bars."

Joe stared down at his plate.

"Got some friends left in town, you know. Buried more than I care to think about, but a friend called to check on me while you were under that sink. Heard all about you getting turned down when you went looking for a job this mornin'. You tell Ashley now and you'll be out of here so fast your head'll spin." His rheumy eyes narrowed. "Whether I believe you or not."

Joe took a drink of tea only to find it bitter. He set the glass down and watched as Wilson scooped spoon after spoon of sugar into his.

"I know I'm the topic of conversation today," Joe murmured, "so Ashley will know soon enough.

I'd rather it came from me. What's going to happen when her husband shows up for dinner and finds me here after hearing the news in town when he stops for gas or something?"

Wilson dipped his spoon into the tea and began to stir the syrupy liquid, giving Joe his chance at adding a little sugar to his own glass.

"Well, now, if he did show up, it'd be as an angel."

He stilled. "Come again?"

"Her husband's dead. Got killed before she found out she was pregnant. One of our first boys to go join his Maker in Iraq."

Joe's empathy for her loss warred with a surge of relief and protectiveness. She wasn't married.

But she still wore her wedding band.

Which meant…what? That she still loved her husband? Wasn't finished mourning him? Wasn't interested in anything but finishing her house?

It didn't matter. Regardless of who told her the truth, Ashley would know about his record eventually and then he'd be out of her life. Long before he ever got the chance to get to know her. He cursed softly.

"Every swear word costs money in this house," Wilson informed him. "Ashley don't want Max repeating 'em since he's startin' to talk so she came up with something called a swear jar." He leaned forward. "I say plenty when the boy ain't around to hear 'cause it pays for the good stuff."

Almost afraid to ask, Joe frowned. "Good stuff?"

The old man glanced behind him to the room beyond, his gray head cocked to an angle. From within the living room, he heard Ashley talk to her son as though reading him a story.

The husky, happy sound touched a place in him long buried.

Wilson waved a hand and motioned Joe closer. "You know—good stuff. Cookies, ice cream. Popcorn. Once a month she empties the jar and buys treats with it, but when they're gone they're gone and we don't get no more until next time." Wilson shook his head and shot Joe an nettled look. "She's a stubborn one. Says junk food rots the innards."

Joe sat back in his chair with a chuckle. He finished off one sandwich and picked up the other. "I'll remember that."

"Anything you partial to? Oreos? Little Debbies? I like ginger snaps myself. With vanilla ice cream and caramel syrup on top."

Still smiling, Joe shook his head as he finished off his second sandwich and drank the last of his tea. He gathered up his dirty dishes and carried them to the sink. "Whatever you like is fine. Anything's good when you haven't had it for such a long time."

Anything *was* good after being confined so long. New and different. Everything tasted better, had more color. Smelled good. Things had changed while he'd been incarcerated and the limited access with the outside world he'd had at the halfway house and working on the various job sites hadn't prepared him for everything.

Like the grocery store where he'd tried to get a job to help stock. It was huge, one of those new super stores versus the little mom-and-pop places that had been around when he'd been sentenced.

And the latest style of clothes? He'd seen teenagers in belly-revealing shirts that gave new meaning to the word skimpy. Piercings in places he cringed just thinking about.

Then there was Ashley Cade and her son.

Absolutely nothing could have prepared him for being out of prison a day and suddenly finding himself under the same roof as the mother and child.

ASHLEY SMOOTHED her fingers over her baby's soft forehead and simply enjoyed the peace that came with holding her son in her arms.

"What do you think, Max? Think we might've finally found someone to help us?"

Max blinked up at her, his little hand tapping the bottle.

"Guess we'll see, huh? We'd be pretty silly if we didn't give him a shot, but don't worry, I won't take any chances. No, I won't. Because this is our future and your daddy paid a high price for it."

Max latched on to her finger where it held the bottle up for him and squeezed as though he understood her words, her sadness.

"I miss him, Max. He always knew how to make me smile, you know that?" She laughed, her memories sliding backward in time faster than she could adjust. She closed her eyes and rested her head against the back of the rocker as she moved them to and fro. "Hmm, I stopped our story not long after your daddy came to the home to live, didn't I?

"Well, there was this girl. Her name was Sarah Peters and she was pretty and blond with pasty white skin and big blue eyes. Everyone talked about how quickly she'd be adopted in spite of her age. A family was coming who wanted to meet all the girls so they paired us up and took us into a room two at a time." She made a face. "Yeah, *I* got Sarah. Lucky me, huh? So we were waiting outside when Sarah went on and on about how nobody would ever want me after they saw her. I got so mad and so upset I forgot all about the people wanting a little girl and pushed her down. Sarah made a ruckus and I knew I'd get in trouble so I left, which was exactly what she wanted.

"You know what happened next? Well, your daddy came after me. He looked right at me and said, 'Get your butt back in there before you lose your chance at getting out of here.'" She smiled down at Max and earned a smile in return. Formula leaked out of the side of his mouth and she caught it with the burp cloth covering his chest. She began rocking again.

"Then he wrapped his grubby, scrawny arm around me and kept yelling at me while he pulled me back inside. Boy, was he mad. Not because I'd pushed Sarah down but because I'd let her cause me to miss out on a chance at being adopted. Attitude is everything," she said, mimicking Mac's tone. "Attitude is everything."

She smoothed her forefinger over Max's dimpled knuckles. "I didn't know it then but now I think about that day and realize your daddy liked me. Because he cared enough to want me to be adopted even though he'd have been sad if I'd left."

Max stared up at her, blinked drowsily in response.

"And even though your daddy's not here now to help us," she continued as she pulled the now empty bottle out of his mouth and sat him up on her lap to burp, "we're going to succeed because that's what he'd want for us. That's right. He loved us so much and he'd want us to be happy, Max, so—"

A prickling sensation slid over her and she turned her head, startled to discover Joe stood in the doorway watching her, one shoulder propped against the casing. How long had he been there?

"Sorry. I didn't want to speak up and chance waking him," he murmured.

"He's not asleep yet."

Obviously uncomfortable, Joe glanced over his shoulder into the kitchen behind him. "Wilson ordered me in here because he said time was wasting and you'd want to be the one to show me around."

Max let out a burp that rivaled a volcanic eruption, but more surprising was the sound of Joe's deep chuckle. What was it with guys and bodily functions?

"Good one, Max." She kissed his cheek and neck a couple times as she carried him over to the crib. "Hopefully a full tummy and no sleep will make for a long nap."

She lowered Max to the mattress and snuggled him up with his favorite stuffed toy and a light blanket, aware of Joe behind her in the doorway.

"There you go. Go to sleep, bugaboo." She smoothed her hand over his head. "Behave for Grandpa Wilson and have good dreams."

Ashley turned and faced her handyman with a self-conscious sigh. Back to business. "Okay, well," she said, forcibly pulling herself from the past and her memories of Mac and focusing on the overwhelming job at hand, "the most important thing needing fixed is the roof. I'm sure you noticed the water spots in the kitchen? Once the roof's taken care of, the damage from the leaks needs to be repaired. I already know some of the Sheetrock will have to come down and I thought while we're at it, the pipes and wiring should be checked out just to be safe. The other major job is updating the kitchen, but the rest of the house mostly needs only minor repairs. I've got a list already made up."

With one last glance down at a sleepy Max, she crossed the room and ignored the way Joe seemed to jump back a step to get out of her path. In the kitchen she asked Wilson to keep an eye on Max and grabbed her ongoing list from a drawer.

"Thought maybe you might've at least fixed some pudding for dessert."

She shook her head. "Sorry, Wilson. Maybe to-night." She read over the list to remind herself of what all needed to be done while the old man grumbled about not getting his sweet tooth appeased.

She turned and reentered the living room. "Here's the list," she said softly, noting Joe now stood over the crib. "I'm not sure where to start after the roof's fixed though. Maybe you can figure out a better order of things."

When Joe didn't respond or step near, she looked up. "Joe?"

No response. Frowning, she edged a step or two to one side to get a better view of his face and gasped. He looked...pained. *Devastated?*

She crossed the room in an instant and after seeing for certain Max was okay, she laid her hand on Joe's arm. He flinched.

"Is something wrong?"

He shrugged, his face pale. "No. Nothing."

"Are you sure?" she pressed. "You're staring at Max like—"

The expression on Joe's face hardened to one of careful indifference. "Where did you get that crib?"

She looked down at where Max lay. His little mouth now moved rapidly in a sucking motion, his eyes closed. Just above him, on the head of the wooden crib, someone had painted an angel hovering over a sleeping baby, protecting and loving. Guarding. She liked to think the angel was Mac, watching over his son.

"I took it from one of the rooms," she whispered. "The books said it's best if children have normalcy in their routine and with me working so much, I put Max in the crib here during the day so Wilson can keep an eye on him, and in his crib in the nursery at night."

"The crib was part of my father's things. He made it for…me."

"*Oh.*" She swallowed, uneasy. "I'm sorry. I thought it was Wilson's. He sold me the furnishings with the house and I didn't realize— He never said a word when I brought it in."

"Forget it, it's fine. It's a beautiful piece of woodwork and it should be used."

"Maybe with permission, but when you saw it you probably thought—"

"Forget it," he repeated, his voice rough. "I was surprised, that's all. Where's that list?"

She held the paper out and without a word, Joe took it and walked away. He continued on into the kitchen and passed Wilson along the way. Ashley hesitated in case Wilson needed her help getting positioned in his recliner after being up on his feet so long, but once Wilson's slippered feet were propped up on the footrest, his clicker in his hand and his glasses perched on his nose, she told herself to quit stalling.

Joe stood looking outside the kitchen door, but he glanced over his shoulder at her as she entered the room, his expression closed and devoid of the many emotions she'd seen moments earlier.

"What rooms have water spots?"

"The far corner here in the kitchen. And also the bedroom above where the roof lines meet. I haven't seen any others, so hopefully the problems are confined even though the whole roof definitely needs to be replaced."

He nodded, his hand on the screen door. "I'll go check it out. Those clouds rolling in don't look good so the rest of the list and tour will have to wait."

"There are tarps in the truck, passenger side."

Ashley watched him leave the house, antsy, uneasy, wanting to help. And wondering why a baby crib bothered Joe so much.

ONCE HE'D CALMED DOWN, Joe came to the realization it wasn't seeing the crib that had upset him—it was seeing Max *in* the crib.

One minute he was standing in the doorway waiting for Ashley to return and the next, he was staring down at the baby boy, frozen and panicked because he wasn't sure if Max had closed his eyes and fallen asleep—or stopped breathing.

So much for the CPR class he'd taken in prison.

Job or no job, staying here wasn't a good idea.

"Joe?"

Ashley's voice pulled him out of his thoughts and he turned, surprised to find her balanced on the ladder instead of on the ground below.

"What can I do?"

He finished securing the tarp into place, all the while thinking there weren't many women in the world who'd climb up on top of a house in the midst of a brewing storm to help her hired help repair a roof.

"Nothing, get down!"

The wind whistled through the trees and grew stronger with every passing second. It had already sprinkled and thunder rumbled in the distance. There was such a charge to the air, Joe knew it was only a matter of time before the clouds really opened up.

He eyed the loose shingles that had already pulled away from the tar paper beneath and frowned. No way were they going to make it, but there wasn't anything he could do about them now.

"You can't do this alone," she shouted back from where she crouched near the ladder. "Let me help! It'll be faster if we work together!"

Head low, he scrambled across the roof toward her and tossed a hand up toward the sky. "Look, Mrs. Cade, I don't mean any disrespect but you'll get hurt! Go back inside and see if there are any tornado warnings!"

She blinked at him, her eyes widening even more. "And leave you up here? No! Let's fix that tarp and we can both get off this roof! Look, I'm sorry about the crib, okay? I'll get another as soon as I can, but I *can't* afford to lose the only handyman willing to work for me and what I can afford to pay him so stop being stubborn and *let me help you!*"

Joe raised his brows rose at her tone, but one glance told him the storm was nearly on them and he'd wasted precious time arguing with her.

He'd gotten the first tarp in place with no problems, but the last one over the bedroom was tricky because it needed to go on the back part of the house where all the angles V'd together. And with the wind blowing against him, he couldn't anchor the sections into place without help.

Joe locked his jaw and ignored the urge to order her inside again. So he did the next best thing and made his bossy *boss* sit on the tarp with her legs outstretched to keep her from falling while holding the tarp down.

He handed her some of the rope he'd found on the porch and showed her how to thread the rope through the grommet rings until he had enough to descend the ladder and tie the tarp to cinder blocks on the ground.

The outward facing side covered, he made several more trips up the ladder with more cinder blocks to hold down the rest, and all the while Ashley crawled along the roof on her hands and knees, her glorious rear end in the air.

Joe ignored her as best he could as he carried the last of the blocks up the ladder and joined her midway across the roof. He helped her fan out the heavy-duty blue plastic until it met the base of a windowless wall. While she held it in place, he anchored the tarp.

"Will it hold?"

"Yes—now go!"

Rain streamed down and pelted them with sharp needles of water as the wind kicked up yet another notch. Thunder rumbled directly overhead. They'd pressed their luck too far as it was, and Joe knew it. This wasn't a normal storm. Someone some-where had a tornado on their hands. He just hoped it wasn't about to descend on them.

Balance was precarious for both of them as they

made their way down the rain-slickened plastic toward the ladder. Joe held on to Ashley's arm to steady her, but found the help went both ways when his boots lost traction.

Lightning snapped, the flash illuminating the purple-darkened sky and giving their position on the roof an otherworldly quality.

"Let me go first so I can help you if you—" His boot slipped again and Joe lunged into a crouch, instantly letting go of Ashley so he wouldn't take her with him. He slid down the roof, grappled for something to stop him, then managed to grab on to a block and find a foothold almost simultaneously.

If Ashley had planned on arguing, his slide silenced her. He looked up to see her on her butt trying to edge down toward him, concern apparent in her wide-eyed stare. Joe gripped the ladder and carefully swung himself around. He descended a few rungs, then waved to her to get on. Ashley glanced up at the sky, squared her shoulders.

The woman had guts, he'd give her that.

Thunder crashed again, loud and angry and directly over their heads. The very air around them shook. The ground, the house. The ladder.

His instincts went haywire, the hairs on the back of his neck lifted and stood on end. If he'd learned nothing else during his ten-year lockup, it was to pay attention when his gut spoke to him.

He took in his position, a little over halfway down, with Ashley above him and moving much too slow.

Without time to second-guess himself, Joe reached up and grabbed her ankle, yanked her foot off the rung and pulled her toward him as hard as he could. Her scream echoed against the house. Ashley's body collided with his, and he wrapped his arms around her and held her tightly as he kicked them both away from the metal ladder.

CHAPTER FIVE

SOMEWHERE ABOVE THEM a deafening crack erupted. Sparks flew and lighting zigzagged across the sky, everywhere at once. A streak hit the metal ladder and spread out in another jagged formation, striking at least one of the large willow trees directly behind them.

Joe landed on the rain-softened earth with a grunt, Ashley on top of him, and the ground beneath them rocked from the force of the blast. Dazed, near blinded, he saw stars thanks to the flash and sudden darkness.

"Oh, my—did you *see* that?" Ashley scrambled on top of him and squeezed out what little breath he still had in his lungs. Without a doubt tomorrow he'd feel every muscle and bone, but at least there would be a tomorrow.

He didn't answer her. Couldn't answer. Tried instead to catch his breath.

Finally, painfully, he managed to inhale and the smell of burnt wood and hot metal filled his lungs. He coughed weakly.

"Are you all right?"

Ashley's hands flew to his face, angling it toward her. He registered the feel of her trembling fingers, ice cold and soft against his stubbled cheeks. Squinting he made out the fear marking her expression.

"Joe—Joe, say something."

"Missy? You okay? Both of you get on in here before you get yourself killed!"

Wilson's voice brought him out of the fog surrounding him, and Joe imagined the old man seeing them on the ground and trying to come to their aid on his walker. His *metal* walker.

"Joe?"

Inhaling as deep as his squashed lungs would allow, he groaned. "Get. Off."

"*Oh!*"

Ashley shoved herself off his chest and nearly kneed him in the groin in the process. "I'm sorry! Oh, thank God. It's a wonder I didn't kill you landing on you like that. Are you okay? Can you move?"

Did he have to?

"*Missy?*"

"Answer him," he urged roughly. "He'll come out here if you don't."

Ashley looked over her shoulder and shouted toward the back door. "Wilson, go check on Max and—and find the flashlight before we lose power!"

Joe heard the old man order them to hurry, but

thankfully the squeaky screen door remained closed. Ashley shifted beside him and pulled on him ineffectively until Joe gave in and rolled over. He got to his knees, only vaguely realizing Ashley had put his arm around her shoulders until his hand rested on the upper part of her full breast.

If only he felt like taking advantage of the moment. Joe growled out a curse and ignored his aches and pains as he got one foot under himself enough that, with Ashley's help, he was able to stand.

"Are you all right?"

"Yeah. Let's get inside."

Rain poured down from the sky in driving bucketfuls. Limbs from the downed tree were in the way and they stumbled over them in the dark, the branches snagging the wet denim of his jeans. Near the porch, tiny, rapidly growing streams gushed beside the weedy flower beds.

Another boom of thunder erupted overhead. Louder, seemingly more angry than before. The wind picked up again.

"Joe, hurry. Here comes another one."

Lightning streaked across the sky, but this time it didn't come down near them.

"Geez, I hate storms."

He acknowledged her comment with a grunt and gripped the porch rail, Ashley's arm around his waist and her cheek pressed against his chest as they climbed.

On solid footing and getting more air into his lungs than he'd had since landing, Joe paused at the top step to rest and looked out at the yard. Another lightning strike illuminated the greenery and dark bark of the trees in sharp contrast with the pale, inner flesh of the one that had fallen, split in two.

"Oh, no. Not *that* one."

He wouldn't have heard her soft exclamation had he not been standing so close. Wouldn't have seen the flicker of pain in her eyes at the sight of the destruction. To him the loss of the tree limbs would mean more work cleaning up the debris, but he wondered what the fallen willow meant to her.

"What else is going to go wrong today?"

Her voice broke on the words, and surprised at the emotional glimpse, Joe tightened his arm. He liked the feel of her. The soft yet solid way she leaned against him.

"Just so you know, I'm not crying over some stupid tree," she muttered, her words proven false by a loud sniffle. "It's just been a really, really sucky day."

Strands of her hair stuck to the stubble on his chin as he nodded. "I understand. Shock will do that to you."

Ashley nodded vigorously and her head bumped against his chest. "It's just...I'd thought as soon as Max was big enough I'd put a rope swing in that tree, but now it's gone like—like—"

Max's father?

And Josie.

Joe loosened his hold and stepped away from her. He might acknowledge being desperately in need of a woman, but he had too much pride to be a stand-in for Ashley Cade's dead husband.

Nor would he allow Ashley's son to bring back memories of a life and time he'd never again have.

Beside him Ashley wrapped her arms around her narrow waist and hugged. "There's still a big, thick branch over there," she said with a nod of her head. "I guess that one would work. I won't be able to look out the window over the sink and watch Max play, but maybe this is a sign I'm too over-protective in wanting to keep such a close eye on him." She laughed sheepishly and sniffled again.

Joe looked at the second-best tree, his thoughts trapped by the past. Overprotective? Watching over a child and wanting to protect her from harm seemed like a natural part of being a parent. At least to him.

He shook his head to clear it, determinedly putting the past behind him yet again. "Count yourself lucky. Only one tree down, and the storm's nearly over."

A wry expression spread across her face as she glanced up at him. "We fell off the roof, Joe. I wouldn't exactly call that lucky."

He liked the way his name sounded on her lips.

"We jumped off the ladder," he countered, "and if we hadn't, we'd be burnt to a crisp instead of arguing about it." He pulled his gaze away from her upturned face, damp with rain and tears and much too revealing, and looked out at the yard again.

A rough laugh escaped her. He glanced down and saw Ashley's eyes sparkle in the muted light of the stormy evening. The sight tempted him beyond measure.

A grin curved her lips as she laughed again.

"What?" he asked, wondering at her thoughts.

"Nothing, I'd just never have taken you for an optimist."

An optimist?

"Even though you're right. Things certainly could've been worse. There's absolutely no way I would've listened if you'd simply told me to jump."

Joe accepted her words with a nod and turned away, gingerly making his way to the door. He held it open for Ashley to step through only to bump into her when she stopped abruptly on the threshold. She swung around and stared up at him, her hazel eyes wide and suspicious, and all traces of humor gone while she searched his face.

"You fell off the ladder."

And he felt the results. "Yeah. So did you."

His next inhalation brought with it a whiff of musky woman, rain-soaked earth and shampoo.

The tantalizing scent teased his body to instant awareness despite his aches and pains. She was so natural in her looks and appearance. The kind of woman a man wouldn't mess up when he made love to her.

He wiped a hand over his face. *Get a grip!*

Bite Me was written across her front—or rather plastered across her breasts. Joe smothered a groan and forced himself to stare at the tiny freckle on her right cheek, Wilson's voice in his head telling him to mind his manners.

Ashley widened her stance and frowned at him. "Yeah, but—you're not going to sue me are you?"

"Now, missy, what kind of question is that to be askin'?"

Ashley exhaled in a rush and her face darkened with color. She turned toward Wilson and glared, but the old man simply glared right back.

"You shouldn't insult a man like that."

"It's a legitimate question," she argued softly. "Considering he fell off the roof—*my* roof."

"We didn't fall off the roof."

"You fell?" Wilson asked.

Joe shook his head and sidestepped around Ashley to lean against the cabinets and ease the strain on his aching body. "I jumped off the ladder and took her with me to keep us from getting struck by lightning."

Wilson's eyes widened. "You mean when that big one hit and got the tree you two were still up there? I thought you were in the garage! It's a wonder you didn't get yourselves killed!"

"We're fine, Wilson. But I want Joe to answer my question."

The old man went back to scowling. "Now, missy, ain't I taught you nothin' since you got to town? You don't go askin' a good man if he's gonna sue you. It ain't right."

"He fell off my *roof!* What if he'd been injured? Does he have insurance? Is he bonded?" She swung to face him. "*Are* you?"

"No."

"Oh, no." She moaned and shoved tendrils of wet hair out of her face. "The books said—"

"Those books don't know everything. They don't talk about the good people, just the crooked ones. Stop worryin'. Joe ain't gonna sue you."

She swung around, arms wide as she faced Wilson. "*How* do you know that? If you live in the country is there some other set of rules? If so, you people need to make a handbook and clue us outsiders in."

Joe chuckled. He couldn't help himself. The sight of Ashley in her foot-stomping upset arguing with someone so similar and like-minded as his father was entertaining to say the least.

"It's the same set of rules everywhere, people's just forgotten 'em." Wilson lifted his walker and dropped it to the floor again as if to emphasize his point. "Too sue-happy these days. Wastin' every-one's time and taxpayers' money."

Sensing no end to the argument, Joe cleared his throat. "I'm not suing anyone," he stated firmly. "I jumped, I'm not hurt and even if I was hurt I wouldn't sue." Ashley turned to face him and he stared into her intriguing eyes. He liked the way her pupils were ringed with deep amber flecks, the hazel cast more golden than brown.

"You gave me a job," he continued, softening his tone when he saw her glance into the living room where Max slept. "I took it and the potential problems that came with it. Besides, I doubt there are very many roofers out there who haven't fallen off a roof or ladder at some point in time in their career. It's part of the job."

Wilson grunted. "See?"

Thunder boomed and the house rattled. Ashley jumped in response, and then turned toward the living room with a deep sigh. "I've got to check on Max. I should've already."

"The boy's fine. He's so tuckered out he's slept through the whole storm. Even the big boom."

"Looks like another one's getting ready to roll through," Joe murmured after glancing out the door to keep from seeing Ashley's worry for her son etched across her features. He knew that kind of worry, that kind of fear, wanting to make everything okay for them, no matter how small the problem.

Lightning streaked across the sky, miles away but fierce.

"Were you hurt, missy?"

"No, I'm fine, but I can only imagine how awful Joe feels. I landed on top of him," she admitted with a wince.

Wilson's bushy brows rose. Outside, thunder snapped, lightning flashed and the light above their heads dimmed, then came back on. The wind picked up outside once again.

"Oh, great. Looks like we're going to lose power after all. I'd better change and get dinner started while I can." Ashley glanced in his direction, her frown deepening. "Thank you, Joe. I'm sorry if I offended you by asking—"

"No problem."

She nodded. "Are you sure you don't need to go to the hospital? See a doctor?"

"I'm fine," he murmured. "After a good night's sleep I'll be ready to go again. No problem."

The relieved smile she flashed him took his breath away, and he told himself to stop being a fool. She'd smiled because she hadn't lost her cheap labor. Nothing more.

Ashley turned and hurried up the stairs between the living room doorway and hall, and unable to help himself, Joe watched the sway of her hips as she climbed, her rain-soaked jeans making the sight lethal.

"Yup, I'd say havin' her fall on top would have any young man ready to go."

Joe's dumbfounded gaze jerked to Wilson's, and heat crawled up his neck when he noted the old man's censure.

"But don't be abusin' our hospitality and takin' advantage, Joe. Ashley acts tough on the outside but inside she's soft. Takes stuff to heart and tries not to show it. Don't be messin' with her like you did Hal's girl. Otherwise, you'll be answering to me. Got that, boy?"

ASHLEY DIDN'T REALIZE she hadn't shown Joe to his room until she'd stripped down for the second time that day. She groaned at the thought, sucked in her stomach and fastened the shorts at her waist. She'd never lost all the pregnancy weight and her clothes were tighter than she liked. But she was as determined to lose the extra pounds as she was to complete the renovations on her house, and those cost money she didn't have to spend on clothes she could breathe in.

She gathered up her wet jeans and T-shirt and tossed the items over the shower rod along with the others, shaking her head at the growing mound.

She left her bedroom and trudged down the back stairs to the kitchen, her feet dragging as she thought of the weeks and months of nonstop work ahead.

You wanted this, remember?

But when would she have time to put herself out there? Make friends so Max would have friends? She'd budgeted carefully and had enough cash to see her through the repairs, but little else. If she couldn't open before the tourist-vacation season began when everyone traipsed through the little town on their way south to beaches and over-crowded resort parks, she'd be forced to take an outside job. And that left her without daycare. Who would watch Max all day every day? Wilson couldn't handle Max on his own for long.

Distracted, she turned and ran into Joe. Or rather, into Joe's damp shirt that was presently molded to the incredibly wide, warm chest she'd discovered as she'd helped him onto the porch.

"Sorry, I—didn't see you."

How she could miss him was anybody's guess though.

Joe's rough hands were gentle as they gripped her upper arms to steady her, and Ashley stared up into his dark blue eyes, surprised at the sensations coursing through her. And not so surprised at all.

A deep, secret part of her wanted Joe to pull her to his chest and hold her, just for a second. One big, comforting hug that would mean nothing and yet allow her to regroup after such a trying day, month. Year.

But of course that couldn't happen. Not if she wanted to maintain a professional relationship.

"No problem."

She wet her suddenly dry lips. "I forgot to show you to your room."

"I changed in the utility room."

She forced her thoughts back to reality. "It *is* a problem. I left you standing in the kitchen after you jumped off the roof to—" His words caught up with her and she sputtered to a confused halt. "You changed?" she asked, eyeing his shirt again.

Somewhat sheepish, Joe indicated a duffel bag lying on the rug by the utility room door. "I forgot and left it on the porch earlier when I saw your kitchen flooding. My clothes are a little damp, but better than what I had on."

"You must be cold."

"Not quite."

The muttered comment brought her attention to his face and she froze at the masculine gleam she saw in his eyes. No, he didn't look cold. He looked hot. Very hot. Heat emanated from his body so much so his damp clothes ought to have steam rising from them the way he stared at her.

A tingle shot through her and Ashley suddenly realized she hadn't stepped away from him. Joe still held her, his thumbs lightly smoothing over the tender insides of her arms. Back and forth, slowly.

Swallowing, she stepped away, acutely aware of him as he looked her over from her head down to her bare feet. Her toes curled against the wide plank floors and she wished she'd taken some time recently to paint her toenails. At least treat herself to a professional haircut instead of saving money by trimming the ends herself.

Guilt niggled again. Why did she care what he thought?

"Missy, you back?" Wilson entered the kitchen from the living room. "Max is stirrin' around. I'm gonna show Joe where I put his daddy's things, but it won't take long. You fixed that chicken you bought the other day?"

She laughed wryly. "You know I haven't." Ashley headed toward the refrigerator. "One fried chicken, coming up—and chocolate pudding for dessert."

The old man winked at her, his expression softening. "You're awful good to me, missy. How'd you know what I wanted?"

Even Joe chuckled at that one.

"WE PUT ALL Teddy's things right in here."

Joe followed Wilson into a downstairs room and his nose tickled from the musty air. It appeared to be a sitting room, maybe a music room, located at the front of the large Victorian.

"Your daddy and I stacked it all along the wall there."

Pulled from his perusal of the room, Joe frowned. A lifetime reduced to lining a wall?

Wilson fumbled until he found the light switch

and turned it on. Dust-layered sheets covered the furniture, sad in their neglect, but the walls were painted a soft shade of yellow with cream trim. Thick moulding wider than any he'd ever seen lined the ceiling and floor, craftsmanship and pride in every detail. The moulding and walls needed to be washed down and repainted, the old wool carpet shampooed and cleaned. It would require a lot of elbow grease and work, but Ashley had definitely snagged a good deal.

Then again, so had Wilson.

"You need anything else, I'll be in my chair."

"Thanks, I'll be fine."

Joe waited until Wilson shuffled his way down the hall before he searched the room and found his mother's rocking chair in the farthest corner. He breathed a sigh of relief.

She'd spent every evening of her life in that chair, slowly moving back and forth as though rocking the troubles of her day away. He pictured her there now, head back, smile in place as she asked him and Jack about their day at school.

Joe walked over to the boxes closest to the chair and pulled up one of the flaps tucked down to hold the rest closed. Inside were his mother's dishes, the ones her grandmother had given her when she'd married his father.

A second box held his mother's collection of carnival glass, all carefully wrapped. He pictured his father packing them and locked his jaw, angry with himself for not being there for him. Angry that he'd been convicted, and that Jack—

He tried to pretend it didn't matter, that he understood, but he didn't. How could Jack think that he'd—

All the anger in the world wouldn't alter the past.

He inhaled and sighed, determined he wouldn't spend his life bitter over something he couldn't change. Maybe one day Jack would come back, call, something.

The third box held Christmas ornaments, some glass and fairly expensive, collected over the years. Some were faded and worn and made by him and Jack in school. A cross made from craft sticks, a candy cane from pipe cleaners. A snowman made from a gym sock. He smiled at the mix and pictured the family Christmas tree in all its glory.

A small box, taped shut instead of the flaps being crossed over each other caught his eye. A knot gripped his stomach. Joe swallowed as he removed the box of Christmas ornaments from the seat of the rocking chair where he'd set them.

Legs weak, he sat down in the creaking rocker. Surely his father hadn't— But why would he keep them?

The box on his lap, Joe carefully peeled the tape off the side, but instead of popping up after being released, the flaps stayed down. He hesitated, imagining the scent of baby lotion. He lifted one flap, then another, and pink greeted his eyes.

Joe reached inside the box and gathered his hands full of baby-soft, pink material. A couple sleeping gowns, several dresses, blankets. Tiny pink bibs and booties that would barely fit his thumb. He closed his eyes and brought them all to his face, inhaled over and over again. The scent was faint, so faint maybe he imagined it, but it didn't matter. It was there. It was Josie.

He didn't know how long he stayed in that room. The storm passed over. The light overhead flickered but didn't go off. Finally, Joe carefully placed everything back in the box and pressed the not-so-sticky tape into place.

Undecided as to what to do with it until he was shown which room would be his, he placed the box in the seat of the rocking chair. His mother would watch over Josie's things just like she watched over Josie in heaven.

CHAPTER SIX

ASHLEY COULDN'T HELP but stare at Joe. Since he'd returned from going through his father's things he hadn't said two words. And rather than being hungry from all the work he'd done, he pushed his food around his plate and looked as though he'd lost his best friend.

"Something wrong with the chicken? Is it too salty?"

"'Course it ain't too salty," Wilson answered. "The boy's just tired that's all. Ain't you, Joe?"

Joe nodded once in response.

Ashley didn't think that was it, but she wasn't about to press him for details when it was none of her business. She ate the last bite of her noodles and stood. "You're feeling the fall, aren't you?" she asked as she carried her plate to the sink. "I have some over-the-counter pain reliever if you'd like some."

"I'm fine. I'd like to turn in though," he said softly.

"Of course. I'll show you to your room." She waited while Wilson and Joe exchanged good-nights, and Joe grabbed his duffel. "Your room's upstairs," Ashley murmured as she led the way out of the kitchen and down the hall to the front stairs. At the top she turned right and entered the first door on the left. She tried to see the room through Joe's eyes, but gave up and watched for some sign of reaction instead.

She'd already repainted the white ceiling, and the walls were now a soft, robin's egg blue. Plain white curtains covered the windows and gave privacy without blocking out the light, and she'd placed a hand-stitched quilt of blue, taupe, yellow and soft burgundy at the bottom of the bed. A lighter-weight cream-colored blanket covered the sheets, ready for use when the hot days turned into cool nights.

"The bathroom is through there," she said, pointing. "And there are plenty of towels under the sink. Help yourself. Just leave them in the hamper and I'll get them when I change the sheets on the bed."

Joe remained quiet and her hand gripped the antique doorknob. "If you need something else—"

"It's fine," he murmured, his voice rough and gritty.

"Are you sure?"

Joe dropped his bag to the floor and ran his hands over his face, rubbing harshly as a gusty sigh escaped his chest. "It's the nicest room I've had in a long time, Ashley. I like it."

Relief swept through her and she smiled. "There are two closets in this room." She bit her lip and wished she could've taken the inane comment back. The man only carried a duffel. He obviously didn't need two closets and she'd sounded like an idiot suggesting it. She blamed her nervous chatter on his mood. Quiet and brooding on a man of Joe's size and appearance would make anybody agitated.

"I'll, uh, let you get settled in. If you need that ibuprofen, it's in the cabinet by the refrigerator. Help yourself."

"Thanks."

Max's cries drifted to them and Joe jerked a thumb toward the door where she stood. "Max is crying."

And that was obviously her cue to get out. She let go of the knob. "That he is. Well, I guess I'll see you in the morning."

Joe turned in time to watch as Ashley fled the room, then followed and gently closed the door. Rain hit the window in a soothing medley that matched the blue decor, but inside he was anything but soothed.

Inside he shook and couldn't seem to stop. It had started when he'd held Josie's things. He'd done his best to control his emotions during dinner, but not any longer.

He was finally out of prison. Finally on his own.

In a beautiful room in a beautiful home. Free.

And not free at all considering that outside this room, the whole town would watch his every move.

With his back to the door he slid down the length of it until he sat on the floor.

Last night he hadn't been able to sleep for excitement, fear. Wondering what would come next and now—

Everything was nice. Pretty and homey. Ashley Cade had obviously worked hard to make the room welcoming for whomever was willing to take on the job.

The thing was it was too perfect. Too good to be true. He didn't want to touch anything because he didn't want to mess it up. What would it be like to sleep on a real mattress again? On a big bed with plenty of room instead of a lumpy pallet? Soft sheets surrounding him instead of rough, scratchy ones? What would it be like to awake to the sun instead of a bell announcing roll call?

After a good ten minutes passed, a good ten minutes where he sat there to soak it all in, Joe rolled to his knees and got up to enter the bathroom. *His* bathroom.

First he'd shower without twenty other guys around. Scrub off the rain and the dirt, and hopefully, ten years of memories.

When he finished he'd lay on that pretty bed, stare at his room, and plan the life he was determined to have. Plan on how he would make up for the ten long years he'd lost.

Ashley awoke to a combination of Max crying and sunlight glaring in her face.

Right on schedule.

She turned over and hoped against hope Max would stop whimpering and go back to sleep.

How did other single mothers do this? Day after day, week after week. Year after year?

The thought brought a tug to her heart. She was tired, exhausted from too little sleep and weepy from PMS, but no matter how tired or grumpy or hormonal, she never regretted Max.

Although moments like this made her wonder if this was how her mother felt before she'd abandoned her in a bus station.

The incident was blurred by time and fear. One moment her mom, a thin shadowy figure with dark hair and a soft voice, had been there, and then she wasn't. The police were called. And at five, Ashley was placed into temporary foster care while police hunted for her mother or a relative, then delivered her to the children's home.

Had her mother had the same problems? The same fears? Had she left her to try and give her a better life, or because she simply didn't want her anymore? It was a question she'd never know the answer to.

Max's cries increased in intensity and Ashley flung back the covers and got out of bed. She hurried through the bathroom and into the nursery to find Max holding on to the bars of his crib and watching the door for her.

She smiled. "Hey, little man. What's the matter?" Ashley picked him up and snuggled his warm, stocky body close. "You're ready for breakfast, huh? You know the drill." She laid him back down and talked to him nonstop while she quickly changed his wet diaper. That done, she picked him up again and carried him with her down the hall to the stairs.

Halfway down she hesitated, wondering if she'd lost her mind or if the scent in the air could actually be coffee. From the broken coffeemaker?

On the last step, she stopped and stared at Joe. "You're up."

And he was gorgeous. The man had on jeans and a T-shirt, his chest honed with muscle. The shirt clung to him, delineating six-pack abs like those shown on TV.

She looked down at her bleach-spotted nightshirt and holey summer robe and wanted to groan—not that she needed to impress him or anything. Not that she wanted to. Still, it would've been nice to have made some sort of impression besides…this.

"I didn't know when you wanted to get started."

She bit her lip and glanced at the clock above the stove. She didn't want to start this early, that was for sure. "Oh, well, not just yet. Max is hungry and I'll have to get him settled before—"

"An hour? Two?" Joe leaned his hips against the countertop behind him, a coffee cup in his hand.

Coffee? Her gaze zeroed in on the steaming mug. It *was* coffee. "Two." She shook her head, dazed. "I can't think straight yet. Did you fix the machine?" She stepped down and hurried over to the coffeemaker, forgetting in her haste for a cup of brain power that doing so put her in such close proximity to Joe.

"A wire had come loose, that's all."

Max began to whimper again and she bounced him in her arms, her mouth watering at the smell of the hot, rich brew.

"Thanks. I don't think I could've gone another day without coffee. That was the start of my problems yesterday."

She thought she saw a smile flicker across Joe's face before he turned away and reached into an overhead cabinet. "Take care of Max while I pour you a cup."

She didn't argue. Instead she carried Max over to the countertop, which butted up against the fridge where she left his canned formula. She measured the powdered mixture into an already prepared bottle of store-bought water and shook. When it was well mixed, she turned and noted three things at once: a steaming cup of coffee waited for her on the table with the powdered

creamer and sugar beside it, a chair was pulled out
ready for her to sit down and…Joe was gone.

NO ONE WAS AT THE DESK when Joe walked through
the doors at Ridgewood, so he kept walking down
the hall and around the corner, past the cafeteria.
Several people were already sitting at tables, some
in wheelchairs, some with canes. A few looked up
as he walked by, but only one continued to stare.

"Mrs. H.," he murmured, nodding as he tried to
slip by her.

"Mr. Brody, back again?"

Joe paused, unable to keep going when Mrs. H.
had the decency to talk to him. Grouchy or not.

"Yes, ma'am. I hope to be around a lot until
he's released."

Behind the glasses, her penciled-in brows rose.
"I'm sure he'll like that. He's missed having his
boys around."

He got the hint. Joe nodded and glanced down
the hall, more weight on the foot already pointed
toward his father's room. "Yeah, well, nice seeing
you. I have to be at work soon."

A small smile curled her lips and she nodded
regally, a queen dismissing her servant. "A job
already? Very good, Mr. Brody, you've done well."
She lifted a bony hand and shooed him. "So go on
with you. We wouldn't want you to be late."

"Yes, ma'am." Joe did as ordered, and a

minute later he knocked softly on his pop's door before entering.

"Come on in, Marcie. I'm ready for my tray."

Joe shut the door behind him. "Hey, Pop."

"Joe!" Ted Brody laughed and waved him over to the bed. "Didn't think I'd see you so soon. Grab a seat. Where'd you spend the night? Did you make it to the bank and the safety deposit box before they closed?"

He shook his head. "Didn't need to. I got a job fixing up your friend's old house for room and board."

His father's head dipped several times in a nod. "I figured Wilson would help you out. Hoped so anyway. So that woman, the one who owns it now, she didn't mind hirin' you on?"

Nothing like getting to the point. Joe stared down at his hands. "She doesn't know about my record if that's what you're asking."

A sharp whistle split the air.

"I don't like it, either, but Wilson said to let her get to know me before I tell her the truth. That way she has something else to go by."

His pop nodded his agreement even though his frown deepened. "Wilson knows her so he ought to know what's best."

"I still don't like it," Joe stated honestly. "She's going to be furious when she finds out." He paused. "She, uh, has a little boy. A toddler."

His dad sent him a hard stare. "You okay?"

Joe stared down at the floor. "He's a bit older than Josie," he murmured. "But it seems like every time I look at him, I see her."

His dad reached out a hand, his grip comforting where it clasped his forearm. "You been to see her grave yet?"

Shamed, he shook his head. "No. After running into Hal yesterday I'm trying to keep a low profile. That was another one of Wilson's suggestions. To work and stay quiet and let people get used to me again."

"Don't let anybody treat you badly, Joe. Hear me? You went to prison for something you didn't do. Don't let them treat you like you're still there. Hold your head up high. Wilson's my friend, but he ain't always right."

AN HOUR AFTER FINISHING her cup of coffee, Ashley made the same trip down the stairs except this time, she'd showered and dressed both Max and herself, and she could now claim to be halfway awake.

"There's my boy," Wilson greeted from the living room. "He keep you up again?"

Ashley carried Max over and placed him on Wilson's lap as she had nearly every morning for the past few months. The awkwardness that had existed between them and Wilson when they'd first arrived was long gone.

"Not too bad. He got up a few times." Three, but who was counting? She glanced around. "Where's Joe?"

Wilson smiled when Max wrapped his baby fingers around one of his. "Haven't seen him since I've been up. Do I smell coffee?"

She smoothed her hand over Max's head and went into the kitchen. "Yeah," she said loud enough to be heard over the morning news. "Max and I came down earlier and Joe had fixed the machine." She poured Wilson a cup of coffee and doctored it with creamer and sugar before carrying it to him. After setting it on the side table where Wilson could reach it, she plucked Max up and set him on a blanket on the floor.

"There you go. You play down here while Wilson gets his fix." She dropped her hands to her hips and wondered the best way to broach the subject she wanted to discuss. With Wilson, it always paid to be direct. "So…what's going on?"

Wilson paused in the act of lifting his coffee cup to his lips. "What do you mean?"

"I mean if Joe is so talented at so many things, *why* is he willing to work for nothing?"

"Max got you up more than once last night, didn't he?"

Her gaze narrowed. "You're avoiding my question."

"He's a good boy."

She inhaled and sighed, her suspicions confirmed. "Wilson Woodrow, *what* is going on?"

Wilson took a sip of his coffee and swallowed. His expression changed from evasive to sad in a split second. "Now, missy, I don't like to tell tales—"

"Since when?"

The old man scowled. "All right, fine. Joe's had a hard time in life, but he's okay now. And that's all you need to know."

"That doesn't tell me why he's here instead of working for one of the construction companies in town."

"Some men like to work for themselves."

"And some men have problems that make them unsuitable when it comes to holding down a job," she stated pointedly.

"You heard him, he's qualified."

"I wasn't talking about qualifications and you know it."

Wilson took a couple more sips and Ashley knew he did so only to avoid her probing stare.

Finally he set the cup down and sighed. "He's a good boy, missy."

"You've said that already." Stepping closer, she sat down on the edge of the love seat and dared him not to continue. "Tell me why you don't want me to check his references. What am I going to find? Does he drink? Not show up for work?"

"You're too suspicious."

"That's not an answer." She placed her hands on her knees to shove herself to her feet. "You leave me no choice but to check him out and discover what the problem is myself."

"Don't—"

She raised a brow and crossed her arms over her chest, waiting. Wilson glared at her, his mouth pulled up into a sour, pouting expression much like Max wore on occasion.

"He lost his baby girl not long after she was born."

Ashley gaped at him. Shock overrode every thought in her head. Of all the things she'd expected Wilson to say, that wasn't it. "What?"

Wilson's wrinkled hands trembled slightly as he grasped the cup and turned his attention to where Max sat on the floor playing. "She died," he confirmed. "Joe never got over it and—he's just had a rough time, missy. He and the mother weren't married, but that doesn't keep a daddy from lovin' his baby. Anyway, Joe just…"

His words trailed off, but it didn't take much for Ashley to fill in the blanks. She knew loss. Knew what it was like to love and lose, but what about a child? How did someone cope with losing their *baby?*

"He doesn't like talkin' about it."

She wouldn't, either. How could anyone discuss such a thing without bringing the pain to the surface again and again?

"He's tryin' to move on with his life, missy. Give him a chance and don't be bringin' up that I told you."

"I—I understand," she whispered, still dazed.

Wilson ran a hand under his nose. "Parents shouldn't have to bury a child. I've been through it. But my boy was older, six. But Joe's little one, she never got to live. Never got to say her first words. There are things that don't make sense in this world, but we just have to have faith that they're in a much better place."

Ashley swallowed. She understood what Wilson said, but she wasn't sure whether she'd ever be able to take that leap of faith if it were Max they discussed.

It made sense now. Wilson's admission revealed why Joe had stared at Max so. Why he'd acted so startled, looked so haunted. He'd accepted the job as her handyman not knowing she had an infant and when he'd discovered the truth—

"Poor Joe," she whispered, feeling his pain.

"Now don't be pitying him, missy. He don't want that."

"No, but—"

"No buts about it," Wilson insisted. "You keep what I've told you to yourself. Wouldn't have said nothing except you wouldn't let it go so I wanted you to understand and give Joe a fair shot at this job without concentrating on his mistakes."

She hesitated, smoothed her hand over her hair

before she speared her fingers into her long ponytail and finger-combed the length. "I get it now. His work history is rough because of being unable to deal with his daughter's death. That's why you didn't want me to check his references."

Any reply Wilson might have made was drowned out by the squeal Max released. Her son smiled at her and held up the toy in his hand as though wanting to share. Such a small thing but so very sweet.

She smiled, teary-eyed. "How old was Joe's baby when she died?"

"Well, don't remember for sure, but younger than Max."

Max went back to mouthing the toy in his hand. Low sounds came from his throat.

Younger than Max. Her son had only recently begun making the little noises. Squeals and laughter, musical, nonsensical chatter that went on and on while he played. Joe had missed that. All of it.

She cleared her throat, overwhelmed by the stab of loss she felt for him. "I'd better fix breakfast," she murmured, hurrying from the room. Inside the kitchen she paused and leaned back against the cool refrigerator door. She'd lost her husband, but Joe had lost his daughter. *A baby.* And Wilson was right, no parent should have to suffer through that.

What if something happened to her? No matter

how long a person lived, life still seemed fleeting. Max would be all alone, and did she really want him growing up in orphanages or foster care?

No.

Imagining Wilson's scolding voice in her head to get out there and make friends, she nodded to herself. She'd put it off long enough. Used excuse after excuse to keep her distance from the townspeople.

Letting down the protective barriers wouldn't be easy, but for Max's sake she had to learn how. She had to become one of them.

HAL STEPPED INTO the police station and grabbed his messages from the box by the desk. He thumbed through them, conscious of several people looking his way as he read that Joe's father had called four times.

He crumpled the rectangular sheets in his hand and continued on into his office. He didn't have time for Ted Brody's shenanigans. His claims that his son was innocent. A baby was dead, had been dead ten long years, and no amount of wishing would bring her back.

He picked up his phone to return a call to the mayor when a knock sounded at the door. "Yeah?"

Officer Bradley stuck her head in the door. "George Thompson just called and said he saw Joe Brody walking along Old Mill Road."

"Was he sure it was him?"

Bradley shrugged. "He said he was off the road a ways, but seemed pretty confident."

Hal tossed the phone aside and stood. "I'm going to go out and take a look. If the mayor calls tell him we'll let his wife off on the ticket, but she'd better do something about the lead in her shoes. Next time she pays."

JOE SMELLED BACON when he stepped up onto the back porch. His stomach growled noisily in response and after the walk to and from the nursing home located on the outskirts of town, he craved more than the single piece of toast he'd accepted from his father's breakfast tray.

He spied Ashley through the screen door, and hunger of another kind took over.

Heat filled him. She was dressed in cut-off shorts and a dark pink tank top. Simple clothing, but with her naturally tan skin and long dark hair once again pulled back in a band she looked…incredible.

Ashley murmured something to Max and then glanced toward the door as though feeling his scrutiny. She blinked, hesitated, then smiled a little too brightly. Joe wondered at the rapidly changing expressions crossing her face.

"Breakfast is almost ready if you want to come in and wash up."

A low whine caught his attention and he glanced

beyond the porch railing where a big brown retriever mix stared at him with soulful eyes. The
canine's tail was low to the ground, but wagging
slowly back and forth. The dog took a step forward
and sniffed the air.

"Hey, buddy, what's up?" The dog's scrawny
butt twisted from side to side so hard it shook its
whole body. "She forgot to feed you, huh? The
little guy in there gets first dibs, you know that.
Hang on and I'll be back with something."

He pulled open the screen door and stepped
inside. "Your dog's hungry. Where's his food?
I'll feed him."

"He's not mine and if you feed him, he'll never
go away." She slid a frowning glance toward the
door.

Joe looked behind him to see the dog right
where he'd left him. "Looks like a nice dog. Might
make a good watchdog."

She didn't comment and Joe scowled, feeling
sorry for the mutt.

"Oh, fine—give him this, but if he hangs
around, he's your problem, not mine. I don't need
a mangy dog to feed."

Joe turned to face her, his response dying on his
lips when he noticed she'd already thrown
together a slop dish of food as though she'd seen
the animal before he'd told her. A little lunch
meat, bread, some of the bacon and biscuits. More

than she could've tossed into a bowl in the last few seconds.

He stifled his smile, remembering Wilson's comment about her pretending to be tough.

Joe ignored the look he received for his efforts and took the hard plastic plate outside. The animal dug in and Joe went back into the house to wash up. Like before, Max looked up at him with wide eyes, but he ignored the little boy and entered the utility room to wash his hands.

After spending his first night in a real bed tossing and turning and dreaming of Josie, he wasn't quite ready to face Ashley's son. Wasn't ready to stare into little eyes that reminded him of what he'd lost.

"Come sit down, boy, so we can eat!" Wilson's voice broke into his thoughts.

Unable to postpone the moment any longer, Joe dried his hands and did as ordered. He entered the kitchen and chose the seat farthest away from the highchair where Ashley's son now sat. His stomach rumbled.

"Where ya been this morning?"

"Wilson, it's none of our—"

"Ridgewood."

Wilson nodded and dug into the food Ashley ladled onto his plate. "I thought so. Sure your daddy enjoyed that."

Awkward silence filled the air, broken only by

the guttural baby sounds Max made as he picked up Cheerios in his tiny fist and tried to get them into his mouth.

"Joe?"

He jerked to attention only to belatedly realize Ashley had asked him to hold out his plate. Once again, he did as ordered, but a glance into Ashley's eyes made him frown. She looked sad.

Wilson had already begun eating, but Joe waited until Ashley had served herself before picking up his fork.

"She's a good cook, ain't she?"

Joe looked up and noted a flush rising in Ashley's cheeks. "Absolutely," he mumbled around his first bite.

"Thanks."

"Comes from cookin' all those meals at the home."

After eating with guys the last ten years, he remembered his manners and swallowed. "The home?"

Her flush deepened and she shot Wilson a quelling glance. "I'm not from around here," she murmured, breaking a biscuit in half. "I grew up in a children's home just outside Columbus."

"Oh." Joe knew he ought to say more, but he didn't know how to respond. Especially since his childhood had been next to ideal. Father, mother, friends. It wasn't until his senior year of high school that he'd screwed up so royally.

"Yup, the missy here can cook for a bunch of people with no problem. After she had to leave the home, she waitressed until she got on at a hospital as a cook. She won't have no trouble handling her guests' meals, but first she's gotta get this house of mine back to right."

Joe latched onto the change of subject. "Do you already have the supplies for the roof?"

"I didn't want to buy something and not be able to use it. I thought if you could give me a list, I'd run to the Home Depot in Baxter. The weather shows no rain for the next seven days."

"No time to waste then." Wilson wiped his mouth with the handkerchief he pulled from his pocket.

"If you're up to it," Ashley added, her golden eyes warm with concern. "You know, after falling."

He was sore as all get out, but everyone knew the best way to cure muscle soreness was to use the muscles more. "I'm fine. I'll get started as soon as I eat."

Ashley smiled and squirmed in her chair at his words. She looked excited, happy that her house was going to be a priority. His lips quirked up in response. Maybe once he proved he knew what he was doing, she'd forget about her quest for references. Give him the benefit of the doubt, as Wilson said.

He hoped so anyway.

CHAPTER SEVEN

THE NEXT FEW DAYS passed in an exhausting blur. Ashley tried to put her worry over not checking Joe's references aside and help where she could. While she ripped the shingles off, Joe repaired the moisture damage to the sheeting below. By day four her hardworking handyman was ready to begin putting on the new shingles, and she wondered how she could ever have doubted his ability.

Since she wasn't strong enough to carry the heavy bundles up the ladder, Joe had to do that himself. Every load. He'd start the morning off in a T-shirt, but as the heat of the day got worse, the shirt would come off.

And the sight of him working on her dream house was nearly more than she could handle when combined with the guilt she felt at finding him so attractive.

She glimpsed a woman's name encircled in a heart on his left shoulder and a barbed-wire tattoo on his arm.

A fashion statement? She was surprised because Joe didn't seem the type to go for fads.

"Thanks for the help getting the rest of those shingles off. Go back down now. You've been up here a while."

She had to squint her eyes behind her sunglasses because the sun was so bright, but that didn't stop her from watching a droplet of sweat snake its way down his muscled chest. "Oh, um, aren't you ready for the new shingles now?"

Joe used one gloved hand to rub the do-rag covering his hair down over his forehead to wipe the sweat away before sliding it back into place. "Yeah, but you're so tired you can't see straight, and it's getting hotter."

"I'm fine."

"You'll fall off the roof again."

"We only fell off the ladder," she grouched. How could he stand wearing long pants with the sun beating down on him? She wore shorts and a T-shirt and was roasting.

"How many times did you have to get up with Max last night?"

Her laugh lacked humor. "You're beginning to sound an awful lot like Wilson."

"Go back inside, Ashley. Cool off if you can. Rest. If you want to help me, then bring me something cold to drink. I've nearly finished off the ice water."

She tossed aside the metal bar she'd been using

to pry up the shingles and nails, and stood. "Fine, I've got plenty more to—"

She vaguely heard Joe curse, the bundle of shingles he carried slam onto the roof, and then abruptly she was in his arms, sliding down the incline toward the ground at rapid speed.

They skidded to a stop near the edge of the roof, and Ashley dazedly realized he'd saved her life once again.

"You all right?"

She ought to be asking him that question. Yet all her overly heated mind could think about at the moment was that her knees were on either side of his and she was sprawled all over the chest she'd just been admiring.

"Ashley?"

She nodded and winced when her forehead bumped his chin. The move jarred her brain. "Fine." But her head pounded and if she drank the Ohio River dry, it wouldn't be enough water to quench her thirst.

Joe rolled over and carried her with him, the touch of his hands gentle as he pushed her sweaty hair off her face. "You're too hot."

She squinted up at him—where were her sunglasses?—and liked the little lines that fanned out from his eyes. The way his body was hard all over, muscular and firm to her soft and not so toned.

"Let's get you cooled off before this turns into heat stroke."

Joe started to pull away but she stopped him by lifting her hand and curling her fingers over the bicep braced so close to her head, over the blue-tattooed skin. He smelled of hard work, sweat and the hot, burnt smell of asphalt from the shingles.

And while she knew the last thing she needed to do was think about kissing Joe, a part of her wondered. Hoped?

What? That he'd kiss her? That for a few moments she wouldn't feel as if it was her against the world? That she wasn't alone?

Joe didn't move. He leaned over her, his face concerned, and she watched, somewhat out-of-body, as her hands palmed his jaw and drew him down to her. Her lips closed over his and she sighed.

She hadn't been a virgin when she and Mac married. Not many girls remained virgins after growing up in a group home, where the right kind of male attention was hard to find. Six years her senior, her husband had been the one to make Ashley understand the difference between sex and love. But that hadn't come until later, after Mac had left the home and joined the service, leaving her to finish her schooling, graduate and find her way on her own for a while.

Joe's tongue licked at her lips, gentle and sweet as though he savored the experience, as though she wasn't the only one intrigued. But all at once a growl escaped his throat, shot straight to her core, and she shoved the memories aside and parted her mouth for him. Let him inside where he kissed her with such passion he seemed ready to combust.

She knew the feeling. It had been a long time for her. The night Max was conceived. Her husband had shipped out the next morning and she'd never seen him again. Never allowed herself to go back to the old days of seeking comfort and love from the wrong men. Nothing could fill the void unless it was the right kind of passion. The right person.

And Joe?

The kiss deepened, lingered. Warmth and texture and hot, hot need. Her body burned and it wasn't from the sun beating down on them, but from Joe. His taste, his touch.

Joe shoved himself to his knees and left her lying there on the roof, staring up at a cloudless sky and wondering what on earth she'd been thinking. She was a widow. One who'd loved her husband, mourned him and dreamed of him still.

But not as often. No, her dreams the last few nights hadn't included Mac.

"Here." Joe placed a lukewarm bottle of water into her hand. "Drink some of that and sit up slowly. As soon as you feel up to it, I'll help you down the ladder."

That was it. No mention of the kiss. No apology, either. Although if anyone should apologize it would be her so she was glad he chose to ignore the moment entirely.

Ashley didn't look at him, but did as ordered. She gingerly raised herself up on an elbow and closed her eyes when her brain beat like a drum against her skull. The water did nothing to soothe the trembling inside her, but after a moment and several more sips, she pushed herself to a sitting position and crept toward the ladder on her own.

"Don't even think about it."

"I'm fine now." Embarrassed, but fine.

A rough laugh erupted from his chest. "Haven't we been through this once already?" Joe stepped closer motioned for her to take his hand. "Come on. I'll help you down."

She didn't look at him. If he brought up the kiss, her response was simple. She'd blame it on the heat, on her dizziness. Nothing else.

Who knew, maybe it had been a figment of her imagination. He certainly didn't act like a man who'd recently had his tongue in her mouth.

Or hers in his.

Ashley reluctantly placed her hand in his and allowed Joe to pull her to her feet, allowed him to hold on to her arms when her head whirled once again and she wavered back and forth where she stood. She had to get off the roof. Go inside and cool off, check on Max and Wilson.

Get away from Joe.

JOE WAITED UNTIL the hottest part of the day to take his lunch break, then stayed outside under the shade of the willow trees to eat the sandwiches and drink the tea Ashley had left on the table for him.

The thought of her brought a rush of desire so strong he gritted his teeth. She'd looked up at him, so sexy and pretty and natural, and he hadn't been able to stop himself when she'd pulled him toward her. What a kiss, too.

He leaned his head back against the bark of the tree. She'd tasted good. Like honey and musk and the sweet tea she favored.

And he'd wanted more. So much more. But he needed a job and a roof over his head just as badly. Self-preservation made him end the kiss and distance himself from her.

The screen door opened and shut with a gentle slam. Joe watched as Ashley exited the house with long, loose strides, Max on her hip and a determined expression on her face. An overly full baby bag bounced off her thigh as she walked, but she ignored the nuisance and kept going.

She was dressed in pants that stopped at her calves, sandals and a pretty purple shirt. Her long straight hair was pulled back in her typical ponytail and if he wasn't mistaken she wore a little makeup. Her lips seemed darker than before, shinier. Her eyes bigger.

Even Max was dressed nicer than Joe had seen him before, sporting a Hawaiian-style shirt and shorts, his thick feet bare. Wherever Ashley and her son were off to, she wanted to make an impression.

Joe wondered if she knew he watched her. Or cared.

One-handed, she removed Max's car seat from the truck and carried it to the small Honda parked beneath the carport attached to the garage. A few minutes later she was gone.

He sat there a little while longer, long enough for the big brown dog to make an appearance and join him under the shade tree. When he didn't move, it flopped down beside him.

Joe patted the dog's head, gave him some water and then got up, determined to put the energy generated by the kiss into something constructive. Who knew what the future would bring—but Joe knew what it wouldn't.

"THANK YOU SO MUCH for your help. That copy machine was giving me fits and the gardening club is meeting in the diner right now. I just had to have the information about the new ivy-leafed geranium." The woman behind her called out a goodbye and then the door to the library opened and closed.

Ashley didn't turn from her perusal of the latest releases until she heard someone walk up to her.

"Can I help you?"

Inhaling deeply, she forced herself to stop imagining the pinpricks of awareness she'd felt when she'd carried Max from the house to the car, and pasted a bright smile to her face. She turned to the librarian and her smile faltered, because instead of an older woman in sensible shoes and glasses as she'd imagined, she saw a teenager in the process of blowing a bubble who didn't bother making eye contact when she began straightening the books on the shelves.

"Oh, uh, hi," she said awkwardly. "I hope so." She swallowed again and hefted Max higher. "I'm, um, here to check on classes."

"The GED class begins on Monday, seven to nine."

Ashley shifted her weight from foot to foot. "No, I—I want classes for my son."

The girl looked at Max. "Oh."

Max grinned and ducked his head shyly, one little fist shaking as though in greeting.

"We've got a couple kiddie classes," the girl stated as she walked back to the desk and searched the top until she held up a piece of paper. "Here's the list."

Ashley accepted the sheet and checked it over. "Do I need to bring anything for him?"

"No. We have apple and grape juice, cookies

and the moms usually hang around to take care of any problems."

That meant she'd be standing there with a group of strange women. "These look…nice," she said. And they did. There were puppet shows and reading hours according to age, held in the morning and early afternoon. For adults there were continuing education classes and book clubs during the evening.

"A singles book club?"

The teenager popped her gum again. "Yeah, they meet once a month."

The library door opened behind her and Ashley watched as the girl's cheeks filled with color before she lowered her lashes.

"Hi, Doctor B. This, um, lady's interested in the book club. Maybe you could tell her about it?" She spun around and practically ran down an aisle toward the back.

Ashley stared after the girl and wondered at her response, then turned and wanted to smack herself for being so oblivious. The blushing, the stammering. How could she have forgotten Max's new doctor was a hottie? Dr. Booker also had "good stock" roots—he'd taken over his grandfather's medical practice and had spent the summers of his youth visiting.

"Mrs. Cade?" He smiled. "I thought that was you. Finally getting around to checking out the town, huh?" He reached over and ruffled Max's curly hair. "Hey, Max. You get that tooth in yet?"

Max's head immediately fell to her shoulder and the doctor chuckled. "So, you're interested in the book club?"

"I don't know."

"Come on, why not?"

"I'm kind of busy. I just asked about it."

The doctor's green eyes softened with compassion. "It might be a good way of getting out there again," he murmured, reminding her that he already knew her marital history thanks to filling out Max's paperwork. "We're harmless. Single in a small town. Mostly we hang out and eat while we talk about the latest bestseller, but occasionally a couple members will hook up and wander off to do their own thing." He gave her a smile. "So how about it?"

So how about what? Getting Max into a class was one thing, but did she really want to join a bunch of small-town singles? The pressure to fit in and knowing she wouldn't—she honestly didn't know how—had her backpedaling fast. "Right now, I'm just interested in getting Max out with other kids. We might come to story hour."

And pray Max wasn't the only one to make friends.

The doctor patted Max on the back, still smiling, and earned a smile of Max's in return. "I suppose that'll work to start. I hope to see you around."

"Maybe. I'd better get going."

"Don't work too hard on that house."

Ashley managed to hold a smile tacked to her lips until she left the library. Head down, she walked to where she'd parked and unlocked the car door only to look up and see the older lady who'd been making copies in the library finish speaking to a man outside the barber shop. Three steps later she entered the diner.

Ashley's arm tightened around Max's rump. Did she dare? A singles club versus a gardening club full of older women…gee, which to choose. Weren't all old women supposed to like babies?

She licked her lips and imagined she tasted Joe.

No, no, *no*. Joe was not the answer to her problems. She had to use her head here, figure out how to insinuate herself into the town's workings like Wilson said.

She kissed Max and sighed. She really did need to know how to landscape and garden because it would have to be done before she opened for business. Decision made, she braced herself.

"Come on, Max." She locked the car door again and walked to the curb. "Let's go see if we can figure out what a geranium is."

Two minutes later Ashley endured the stares the best she could, waiting for the ladies to look their fill. Several immediately turned their heads and began to whisper.

"May we help you?" A silver-haired woman with money written all over her smiled weakly. "Are you looking for someone?"

Ashley inhaled and tried to gather her scattered nerves. "I heard the garden club was meeting and I thought I—I might sit in."

"Oh. Oh, well—"

"We don't offer babysitting," one woman snapped loudly.

So much for her theory of them liking kids.

"And we're quite a bit older than you," another added.

She stiffened at their tones. "There's an age requirement?"

A few of the dozen or so ladies exchanged glances and Ashley figured they were searching for some excuse to send her away. She wasn't one of them, they'd made that clear.

"Nonsense, dear. Rita simply means you might find us old biddies boring. We're open to one and all as our charter says." The lady to Ashley's left wore thick black frames that dwarfed her eyes, and dress in a blinding shade of purple, reminding her of the poem regarding age and purple clothes.

But she didn't want to force herself on anyone. What good would that do?

Hearing Wilson's voice in her head, she opened her mouth to say she'd remembered another appointment, some excuse that would get her out of there even if it was the coward's way out, when she caught a woman giving her a nasty nose-in-the-air glare.

"Well, dear?" the woman in purple asked. "Would you like to sit down with me? Betty's so excited about the geranium she found on the computer."

Ashley glanced around at the women's varying expressions and swallowed. Some of them obviously didn't want her there for whatever reason, but the lady in purple seemed kind, genuine.

"Thank you," she murmured, slipping into the empty seat beside her, Max on her lap. She got him settled while a matronly woman got up and began distributing copies. Sure enough, Betty ran out after giving the lady in purple hers.

"Not a problem, Betty. We'll share," the woman said quickly.

"No problem," Ashley repeated, trying to smile as Betty walked away. She turned her attention to the woman beside her, and in response the older lady scooted the sheet of paper into the middle of the table. "So," she said softly, "that's a geranium?"

CHAPTER EIGHT

WHEN JOE ENTERED the house that evening he was hungry, beyond worn out, smelled of sweat and tar—and he'd never felt better. Working outside free of supervision or armed guards had a way of making a man appreciate the little things in life.

"Dinner's almost ready. I got a late start and—" Ashley broke off with a gasp, her eyes wide.

"What's wrong?"

"You're burnt to a crisp! What were you thinking?"

She rushed toward him, the concern in her eyes softening the bite of her words. One hand held a spoon with some sort of creamy concoction dripping off the end, but her other hand was clenched at her side as though she wanted to reach out and touch him but wasn't about to.

Smart girl.

"It's fine. I've been sunburned before."

"But…this is bad. I've got burn cream. You can put it on after you take a cool shower."

"What're you sayin', missy? Don't fix nothin' for me, I'm leavin'."

Ashley turned her head toward the living room. "I know, Wilson, you told me."

Joe watched her with a frown. "He's not eating with us?" He didn't want to sit alone at the table with her and Max. It was too cozy. Too tempting.

Reminded him of the quiet aftermath following the kiss they'd shared on the roof.

"No, he's—"

"Goin' to bingo at the hall," Wilson informed him as he came into the room dressed in tan pants and a short-sleeved striped shirt. "Used to go every Friday night until I had my surgery."

"To see his girlfriend," Ashley teased.

"She ain't my girlfriend," Wilson grumbled. "Myrtle's just pretty to look at."

A car horn sounded from outside and Wilson continued on toward the kitchen door faster than Joe had ever seen him move.

"That's my ride. Saw them comin' up the drive. Two widows from Baxter." Wilson pushed the screen door open with his walker, pausing long enough to wink at Joe. "You two have fun."

Joe stared at the old man in confusion.

He waited until the car had pulled away then turned and walked over to the screen door. He groaned. Sure enough, just looking up put the side of the roof Ashley and he had slid down in perfect view. Wilson must have seem them on the roof today. But instead of ordering him to keep his distance like before, Wilson was now leaving them alone?

What had caused the change of heart?

"He was so excited about going out tonight I hated to give him a hard time. He hasn't gone anywhere except the doctor since his surgery."

Joe grunted. "I'm sure he'll be fine." Wilson had crossed the floor in such a hurry, the only danger he'd faced was going so fast he might have tumbled over the walker in his haste. "I'll go shower."

Ashley nodded, now back in front of the stove. "Take your time. Dinner won't be ready for about twenty minutes or so."

Joe headed up the stairs off the kitchen instead of walking through to the front of the house. He passed a lot of doors along the way, but paused by one in particular. The one belonging to Max.

An oak crib sat angled in the corner, a rocking chair beside it. A colorful round rug covered most of the wood floor, and ended at the base of a dresser and chest of drawers. An old-fashioned wallpaper border of antique toys wrapped around the cream-colored walls. All in all the room wasn't fancy, but he thought it suited the woman who'd decorated it. Airy and simple, warm and homey. The perfect room for a baby boy to grow and learn and live.

Scowling, Joe turned on his booted heel and continued on down the long hallway to his room.

ASHLEY HAD JUST FINISHED putting everything on the table when she remembered she hadn't given Joe the burn cream. She found it in the medicine cabinet, then peeked in on Max and saw him sleeping contentedly in his downstairs crib.

She'd leave the cream on Joe's dresser. That way he'd see it as soon as he came out of the bathroom. With that thought in mind, she rushed up the stairs to Joe's room and had just walked inside when the bathroom door opened. Joe stepped out dressed in jeans and holding his shirt in his hand.

She licked her suddenly dry lips, unable to take her gaze from him. "I—uh, sorry, I didn't mean to intrude. I thought I could leave this here before you got out," she said in a rush.

Joe didn't comment as he moved forward to take it from her. Her attention strayed and landed on the scar that trailed from his neck to his chest. With his sunburned skin, the scarred, raised flesh stood out even more than it had before.

She motioned with her hand. "Your back's really bad."

"I'll take care of it."

"Joe, about today—"

"It shouldn't have happened."

"Yeah." She hated their stilted conversation considering they'd exchanged jokes and laughter on the roof before the kiss had changed things. "So if we both agree that it won't happen again, you won't take it the wrong way if I offer to help put this on your back. Right?"

As soon as the words were out of her mouth she called herself an idiot. What was she doing?

Joe hesitated a long moment, glanced at his back in the mirror and grimaced when his sun-burned skin stretched with the act. "Thanks."

He turned for her to apply the cream, which left her having to get even closer.

She flipped the cap open and squirted some of the cream into her hands before setting the bottle on the dresser. Ashley rubbed her hands together, then paused, nerves attacking her good intentions.

A little late now, don't you think? You've already kissed him.

Afraid she'd run from the room like a coward, she inhaled and flattened her hands to his shoulders. Joe flinched.

"Oh—Sorry." She eased the pressure. "I didn't— I haven't— This is really going to hurt later."

"It'll be fine. I tan pretty easily so even though it's red now, it'll turn."

Joe's voice was husky, filled with a tension she identified all too easily. Whether she wanted to admit it or not, there was something between them. Attraction, interest. Something.

And a part of her couldn't help but feel torn. She'd loved her husband. Truly loved him. He'd been her best friend, her confidante. Her safety net when things got bad. She wasn't ready to let go of that.

So why was she reacting so strongly to Joe?

Exposed to air and the dryness of his skin, the cream disappeared and she reached for the tube once more. Joe stood still, tense, his breathing a little rough.

She smoothed her hands lower to his midback, and felt every tendon and muscle, the smooth, soft skin that hid the strength beneath. Up along his spine over the name encircled by a heart. She stared at it, only then realizing that the tattoo was in honor of his daughter. Josie. Her fingers spread the cream higher, to the base of his neck where a white scar trailed to a jagged end.

"Where did you get this?" When he didn't comment, she grabbed the tube again, keeping one hand on his back in case he thought she was finished and tried to pull away. Asking him a question while his back was turned was one thing, but staring at him face-to-face? No thanks.

"You know, I knew boys at the home who'd spent time in juvey." She smoothed her coated palms over his shoulders, down the back of his arms, hoping he might open up and volunteer some information on his own. "Some had fathers or brothers in prison. Some just liked the look." Her hand slid up again until it came to rest on the second tattoo.

Joe pulled away from her and yanked his

T-shirt on over his head. "I can be out of here in five minutes."

"Why?" she asked, confused, more than a little bit fearful of his answer.

Joe crossed the room and pulled his duffel from the closet floor. With it in hand, he turned to face her. "That's what this is about, isn't it? You know about this," he said, lifting his elbow to indicate the barbed-wire etched on his bicep, "and you want me gone."

"I'm just trying to figure out some things," she said bluntly. "Like why you got the tattoos."

A long pause followed her comment, but he didn't look away. "Don't you mean where?" he finally murmured. "I got them in prison, Ashley."

The last of her hope died. He'd just confirmed the one reality she hadn't wanted to consider. "For what?"

He didn't pause. "Drunk and disorderly, resisting arrest, assaulting a police officer and—"

"Did you learn anything?" she demanded, cutting off his litany of offenses.

Silence. Other than locking his jaw he didn't react, didn't seem to breathe.

"Joe, talk to me! You owe me that much, don't you think? Are you sorry? Will you ever do anything to go back?" she pressed. "Or are you one of those guys who's only sorry you got caught?"

He jerked his head in a negative motion. "I don't ever intend to go back."

She inhaled and sighed. She *hated* being judged. An orphan. A kid nobody wanted. Even the stupid gardening club members had given her the cold shoulder. Not all of them, no, but most. She hated it. And who was she to judge him because of stupid, past mistakes?

A mother. Max came first. Always.

Drunk and disorderly. Resisting arrest. Assaulting a police officer could mean anything from a shove to a punch, and without being told she knew these incidents had taken place after his infant daughter's death. Who wouldn't react strongly to that?

"Are we in any danger from you?" she asked point-blank. Ashley watched for a sign that he lied. A flicker of an eyelash. A smirk. Anything.

Joe's gaze never wavered from hers, if anything it softened with understanding and she tried her best to harden herself against the sight.

"Absolutely not," he rasped huskily. "I've never harmed a woman or child, and I never will."

She stared at him a long moment, still undecided. Joe stared right back. Her mind raced but no matter what questions she asked herself, she always came back to the same conclusion—she understood wanting to pick up the pieces. Wanting to leave the past behind. Understood what it was like to be thought of as different or less than desirable.

Joe had made mistakes, costly ones, and paid the price. One that would haunt him forever once people knew he'd served time. He wasn't defending his behavior, wasn't excusing it. He'd stated it bluntly and offered to leave.

What if Wilson had taken one look at her alongside the road and kept driving? Hadn't pulled over to help her, or sold her his house or given her the chance of a lifetime?

She pointed a finger at the closet, swallowing, praying she wasn't making a mistake. "Put your bag away, and come eat before dinner gets cold."

JOE FROWNED at the little face staring at him. Max grinned in response, his sparkling eyes identical to his mother's. Unable to stop himself, Joe felt his lips pull up in a smile before he caught himself and looked away.

"He doesn't bite, you know. He's curious about you, that's why he's always watching you."

Silence followed Ashley's comment. He didn't know how to respond. Didn't quite know what to make of her giving him a chance to prove himself when his thoughts were consumed with the guilt he felt at *letting* her cut him off before he'd completed the list of charges that sent him to prison.

He wondered if he'd ever know how to talk to a woman again. If he'd ever manage to casually insert into a conversation that he'd been imprisoned as a baby killer. Ashley had made it easy by bringing the tattoo question up first. Still, the most serious of all the charges stood between them.

"We never did take that tour of the house. You know, to go over all the changes I want made."

Definitely a safer subject.

"We can tonight."

"You're not going to see your dad?"

The last couple days he'd foregone his morning visits to Ridgewood to start work on the roof, then waited until late so he could arrive at the nursing home at dusk, when most of the visitors and staff had either already left or were busy.

Mrs. H. always saw him though. Gave him a nod of approval each time he passed.

"Not tonight. I'll call him later." Max banged his hand on the high chair and garnered Joe's attention once again. "Max doesn't look like you. He takes after his dad?"

Ashley stood and carried her dishes to the sink. "Yeah. Blond and light. Mac's genetics won out over mine, a good thing since he's...gone."

Joe didn't want to go there. "The girls will love him when he's older."

"I don't want to think about that yet." Ashley turned on the faucet and prepared to wash the dishes. "So...have people treated you, um, *differently* since you...you know? Got out of prison?"

He nodded, realized she couldn't see him with

her back to him and stood to walk over and stand beside her. He picked up the dish towel she'd pulled out of a cabinet drawer in preparation, and dried the glass she'd washed and placed into the second sink to drain.

"Oh, you don't have to—"

"I know." But he kept drying anyway. He remembered when his dad dried the dishes every night while his mom washed. It had been their time to talk about the day, good things and bad.

"Thanks." Ashley slid him a glance from beneath her lashes. "I guess it would be hard. Being raised here and facing everyone."

He shrugged. "What was it like for you growing up in the children's home?"

She chuckled. "That's subtle, change the subject."

A grin caught him unaware. "Whatever works." He put a glass away in the cabinet, and they shared a smile like…lovers.

In your dreams, man.

The glasses and plates washed, Ashley scrubbed a pan with a vengeance, her expression thoughtful. "Believe it or not, it was…okay. Not great but…decent." She smiled. "For as much as it could've been better, it also could've been worse."

She shrugged and started on a new pot. "I was five-six in the fifth grade and taller than most women with a body to match." She laughed softly, the sound a bit bitter. "The wives would take one look at me and give their husbands a glare. Getting adopted didn't matter though."

He frowned at the hint of hurt in her voice. "Sure about that?"

Silence. "Okay, so it did," she finally muttered. "I did get taken home one time."

"What do you mean?"

"Once the couples had gone through all the paperwork and interviews and gotten the official okay, they could take the child they were interested in adopting home over a long weekend or out for a day trip. Something where they could…bond. An older couple had gone through the process, passed all the requirements and I was one of three girls they thought they might be interested in. I got taken home first and we hit it off. They—they even took me to the pound and let me pick out a puppy so that whichever girl they chose would have a companion."

Joe didn't like where the story was headed. "What happened?"

Her hands stilled in the water, her expression carefully distant. "While I was there, the woman found out she was pregnant. Then Sunday afternoon rolled around and they took me back." She laughed softly. "They kept the dog though. One mutt was apparently enough."

One minute he stood there drying dishes and the next, Joe tossed the towel aside and pulled her against him, her soapy wet hands against his chest.

"Don't degrade yourself like that."

She stared up at him, eyes wide. "It's what the kids called me—us. We were mutts nobody wanted."

He raised his right hand and smoothed his knuckles over her face, down her sharply angled cheek and the jut of her chin.

Ashley's soft skin, the color of honey, called out to be touched. Her lips were darker than her skin tone, more tawny-colored. Full, bare of cosmetics, her mouth beckoned. Wide and kissable and infinitely tempting.

"Joe, we agreed not to make another mistake."

That they had. And despite wanting to do otherwise, he heeded the warning he heard in her tone and released her to pick up the towel again. "Sorry. But don't put yourself down like that. You're not a mutt and neither are any of the other kids out there in that situation. They're just kids."

She laughed again, the sound strained. "Yes, sir."

They both got back to work, silent for a time.

"I didn't thank you earlier," he murmured finally. "For letting me stay."

She didn't raise her head from her task. "Don't thank me too much. I can't toss you out when you're the only one willing to take on fixing my house."

Joe flinched. Yeah, there was that.

FOUR HOURS LATER Ashley learned exactly how Joe knew to do all the things he did. They'd toured the house, gone from room to room and checked out window casings, walls and ceilings. All in all, Joe said much the same as the home inspector she'd hired from Cincinnati. She'd gotten a fantastic deal.

The ceiling where the roof had leaked needed repairing, but would soon be good as new. The wiring had been updated in the early eighties, and Joe said extra support boxes might be needed if the house's nine bedrooms were ever filled to capacity, but little else.

"So you took classes?"

He nodded as he descended a ladder. "I'd always been a fixer. I got lucky because the judge who sentenced me sent me to a medium security prison instead of a max, and after I'd paid my dues, I got taken out on a work detail. One of the trucks broke down and I fixed it when nobody else could. Pretty soon that snowballed and I was allowed to transfer to a different prison where they had teachers come in. They taught us building, plumbing, electrical, you name it. Some sort of rehabilitation program."

"Good for me," she said with a laugh. "I'm glad."

Joe shot her a smile, and her heart beat faster in response. No way. Appreciating his talents and abilities for fixing up her fixer-upper was one thing, but the man himself?

She shook her head. Joe was tall and muscled and gorgeous in a rough sort of way, but he was also hard. Scarred. With a darkness behind his eyes she wasn't sure she wanted to know.

"Maybe one day you can own your own company and put all those classes to good use."

"Maybe."

The hardships of taking on such a project hit her then. Finding jobs when everyone knew his past would be next to impossible. Accusations would inevitably be made.

How did someone go about rebuilding their life after prison?

Joe grabbed the ladder and folded the frame. "This was the last room?"

"Yeah."

"Then once I get the roof done, I'll work on ceilings so you can start painting. After that, I'll work on repairing the damage to the outside of the house and then get started on remodeling the kitchen."

A weight lifted from her shoulders. "Seriously? It's doable before spring?"

Joe confirmed her words with a nod. "With two people working on it full-time, definitely."

She clapped her hands together. "I can't believe it! Come on—this calls for a celebration." She led the way back to the kitchen and retrieved an apple pie from the rack on the stove.

"Wilson will hate us," Joe commented, his tongue practically hanging out of his mouth in anticipation.

Ashley laughed. "Yeah, but it's not like he's at the

hall *playing* bingo," she countered. "They have a buffet-style dessert bar. He only goes for the sweets."

Joe chuckled as he walked to the cabinet where the plates were kept. Ashley liked his easy familiarity. Liked how he didn't expect her to wait on him.

He retrieved a couple of plates while she sliced the pie. At the table she leaned forward and plucked up the book she'd left lying there earlier.

"You ever do any landscaping? I went to the diner today and the garden club was meeting. I acted interested and one of the ladies invited me to sit down." She looked up in time to see his expression change. "What's wrong?"

A muscle spasmed along his jawline. "You didn't say anything about me did you?"

"No, why?"

Joe ran a palm over his face, his apple pie forgotten on his plate. "If you had they probably wouldn't have treated you very well."

Her mouth twisted. She remembered how hard it had been to stand there and wait while everyone looked their fill and whispered to each other as to why she'd come to their little group. The outsider.

"It probably wouldn't have mattered. All of them pretty much pretended I didn't exist except for one lady. She was nice. She didn't mind Max squirming all over the place, either." Ashley hesitated. "If you don't want me to say anything about you being here I won't."

Joe shoved himself to his feet. "Good. Wilson said—"

When he broke off, she blinked up at him. "Wilson said what? It's not like I haven't figured out Wilson knew about your past. He seems to know everything that goes on."

Joe walked away from her to stare out the window over the sink. "He thinks I might have a better time of it if I work hard, stay low and prove myself again, ease my way back into their good graces a little at a time."

"Sounds like a plan to me." She hoped for Joe's sake it worked. "You don't agree?"

"Maybe…guess I'll find out."

CHAPTER NINE

ANOTHER WEEK PASSED while Ashley mulled over Joe's response to her question. He'd looked sad, so vulnerable, that she'd wanted to reassure him and tell him time would dull everyone's memory to his ex-con status, and he'd be one of Taylorsville's "good stock" again.

A fat lot of good those kind of reassurances would be coming from someone who didn't fit in herself. How could she possibly know how long it would take for Joe to make it back into everyone's good graces? Or what it would take. If she knew, she'd be doing it herself even though a part of her rebelled and wondered why she—or Joe—should have to do anything to belong at all. They shouldn't.

Except Max deserved the best life she could give him.

That meant she couldn't stay in her big, safe house any longer. Ashley squared her shoulders and hefted Max higher on her waist. Juggling him, the book on landscaping, a diaper bag and purse plus one humongous case of nerves took some doing. But as she walked into Ridgewood Extended Care, her efforts at making sure she and Max were both immaculate and presentable were worth all the trouble she'd gone to given the welcome she received.

"Oh, my. Look at him!"

"Well, hello there!"

"What a gorgeous little boy."

Ashley forced herself to make eye contact with each and every person who greeted her, and returned the smiles shot their way as she walked to the desk and the older woman behind it.

"Mrs. Hilliard. Hi."

"Hello, Ashley. I'm glad you decided to accept my invitation."

She glanced down at Max, suddenly understanding why he always buried his head in her shoulder. "It was, um, it was very nice of you to ask me here to lunch. I appreciate it."

The older woman grabbed her cane to help her stand. "It's my pleasure. Now follow me, dear. I thought we could sit down on the couches in the cafeteria while they get things ready."

Ashley fell into step beside the woman. Mrs. Hilliard carried herself with her head held high. Although the woman was bone-thin and fragile, Ashley knew how deceptive looks could be.

She saw past Mrs. Hilliard's thin, elderly appearance to an ingrained kindness and strength she hoped one day to achieve.

Mrs. Hilliard stopped in one corner of the large cafeteria and seated herself on a couch. Ashley set the diaper bag and purse on the carpeted floor before lowering herself and Max down beside her.

Please, Max, behave.

"I, uh, read the book you loaned me and learned a lot." She grinned. "Probably more than I ever wanted to know about geraniums, too," she added, earning a smile in return from Mrs. Hilliard. "Have to admit it seems easier to hire a professional, but I honestly can't afford it."

"It isn't as daunting as it might seem, dear. All you have to figure out is your vision for things. Did you bring pictures?

"A couple," she said as she held on to Max with one hand while digging the pictures out of the diaper bag's side pocket. She straightened and handed them to her. "I bought the house about six months ago and—"

"*Willow Wood?*" Mrs. Hilliard's startled exclamation drew interested looks from several people nearby. "You're the woman who bought Willow Wood?"

Wondering if maybe Mrs. Hilliard was a friend of Mr. Thompson's from the hardware store, she hesitated. "Yeah, uh, yes, I did."

The black rims of Mrs. Hilliard's glasses rose on her wrinkled cheeks. "Oh, my dear. The rumors, are they true?" she asked. "You're turning it into a bed-and-breakfast? Oh, it will be *beautiful,* if so!"

Startled at the praise, Ashley could only nod. "Thank you."

Mrs. Hilliard looked at her expectantly and Ashley realized she hadn't answered her other questions.

"Y-yes, I hope to open my B and B in late spring or early summer."

"Oh, how exciting. Why, I remember when that house was dressed to the nines and gleaming. People from all around would make fools of themselves to get invitations to the annual Christmas party."

"I'd have loved to seen it then," she murmured. "It's kind of run-down and needs TLC now." Her mouth twisted wryly. "Maybe by next year I'll be on my feet well enough to host a Christmas open house," she added even while she wondered if anyone would come with her as the owner.

"That would be marvelous. And quite an undertaking for someone such as yourself."

She stiffened and Max looked up at her with curious eyes, his fingers in his mouth. "Such as myself?" she repeated stiffly. *Had she said something to Mrs. Hilliard about her past?*

The woman nodded. "Why, yes, dear. A single

mother with a child and a crotchety old man to care for—it must be difficult to get anything done."

The air left her lungs with a rush and tears stung her eyes. "I'm sorry, I—"

Mrs. Hilliard laid a hand on Ashley's arm. "It's quite all right, my dear. I understand. It must be very stressful."

"It's not that, it's just—" How did she compare Mrs. Hilliard's kindness to Mr. Thompson at the hardware store? To the ladies who'd pointedly ignored her after the garden club meeting had ended and their social hour began?

The older woman untucked a carefully folded tissue from beneath her long sleeve and pressed it into Ashley's hand. "Here, dear. Wipe your eyes. The landscaping will need doing soon, I'm afraid. That way when spring comes, the plants will have had a nice, long sleep and be ready to get started growing."

"Thank you." Ashley nodded, attempted to smile, and sniffled softly in a vain attempt to get control of herself. "Thank you for—Will you help me?" she blurted suddenly.

Ashley told herself the woman's answer didn't really matter. After all, why would Mrs. Hilliard help her? Loaning her a book was one thing, sketching out a drawing or two and figuring out all the different plants another. It was too much to ask. It was time consuming. It was—

"Why, yes, Ashley. I'd love to."

—something a friend would do.

JOE ENTERED the large front parlor, anxious to tell Ashley his news. Instead he leaned against the doorway and watched appreciatively as Ashley danced and sang to a tune from the radio while she painted her way down a wall.

Once again she was dressed in cutoffs and a sleeveless shirt, her toes a colorful shade of red. The sight raced through him like wildfire when he imagined those long beautiful legs wrapped around him.

He shifted against the casing.

She was his boss.

And even though he badly needed to find himself a woman, after working every day and spending every spare moment with his dad, he fell into bed too exhausted to do much more than fantasize about his employer.

Ten years of celibacy and now that he could do something about it, the only woman who appealed he couldn't have. Not without telling her the complete truth first.

Ashley shimmied, the fingers of one hand snapping as she turned to wet her roller with paint. That's when she saw him and her face flushed to a dull burgundy.

Joe grinned. "Don't stop on my account."

She shot him a glare, the corners of her lips curled up in a sheepish smile. "Hush. What's up?"

"Can't tell you."

She raised a brow.

"Didn't you just tell me to hush?" He chuckled at her expression and stepped forward, unable to help himself. He was in a good mood and she was easy to tease. "The roof's done."

She stared at him blankly. "*Done?*"

"Done. Just in time, too." He indicated one of the open windows. Outside another summer storm brewed in the distance.

"Are you serious? It's done? *Finished?*"

When he nodded she launched herself at him, paint roller in hand as she hugged him and laughed in his ear.

"I can't believe it! Joe, thank you! Thank you, thank you, thank you!" Her arms tightened even more and Joe decided to enjoy the moment while it lasted. He pressed her close until the heat of her settled against him.

Ashley's laughter ended with a gasp. She pulled away to look him in the eyes, but didn't put any more distance between them. He stared into the honey-bronze depths of her gaze and waited for her reaction. Waited for her to shove him away and stammer something about how she shouldn't have hugged him.

Instead her mouth parted and an instant later

Ashley raised herself on those sexy, red-painted toes. That was all the encouragement he needed. He pressed his mouth to hers, swept his tongue inside. She tasted hot and sweet, musky.

Joe heard her breath hitch in her throat. He grabbed the roller from her hand, uncaring of the paint coating his fingers. He tossed it to the covered floor before he pulled her closer and ground her against him, nudging her in a simulation of what he most craved.

Ashley moaned, soft and needy, the most exciting sound he'd ever heard, before her fingers speared through his short hair and she angled his head more to her liking, one voracious kiss turning into two, five.

Thunder boomed outside, sharp and loud, and the small receiver sitting on a sheet-draped piece of furniture erupted with Max's cry.

Ashley stumbled backward with wide eyes and a hand pressed to her mouth. She stared at him in horror, and it was that component of her expression that got to him, tore through the haze of desire that clouded his mind and pierced deep.

Horror. When would he learn that he just couldn't have certain things anymore?

Without a word, Joe turned on his heel and stalked out of the room, not stopping until he heard Wilson's walker behind him. He groaned, not in the mood for the old man's comments.

"You going to see your daddy?"

No, but it was a good idea. He'd waited too late the last couple of nights and found himself waking his father up when he'd gone to see him. Going early wasn't an option, either, since mornings were the best time to work given the blazing temperatures.

"Do you need something?" he asked, his voice rough and way too revealing. Maybe the old man wouldn't catch it. He hoped so anyway.

"Nope. You do though. Unless you wanna get struck by lightning on the way."

Joe turned and found Wilson pulling a set of keys from his pocket. He tossed them toward Joe. "Here. Can't have you gettin' sick runnin' around in the rain."

Joe caught the keys in one hand. "I don't have a driver's license," he reminded him.

"Didn't need one back when I started driving. Some folks out there now have one and shouldn't. I figure you'll do all right."

Wilson's trust humbled him. "Thanks."

The old man nodded, his normally mischievous gaze solemn. Understanding?

Joe continued on, out the back door, away from Ashley and her son.

Ten minutes later he pulled into the mostly empty parking lot outside the nursing home. Lunch hour was over and those who'd visited loved ones had gone back to work or home. He was glad. After the intensity of Ashley's kiss and then her response, he felt a little shaky. The last thing he needed to walk into was a center full of people unhappy to see him.

Joe left the truck and ran toward the door, the cold rain seeping into his shirt. Inside, Mrs. H. wasn't at her desk, so he continued on down the hall, trying to be as inconspicuous as possible.

"Mr. Brody."

Her voice stopped him in his tracks. "No one was at the desk, Mrs. H., so I thought I'd show myself to his room."

"Indeed. Come this way, please."

Joe frowned when she turned and led the way to the cafeteria rather than toward his father's room. He followed her, curious. After all, not many people ever disregarded an order from Mrs. H.

She stopped beside an older man who sat hunched forward in a wheelchair. "This is the young man I told you about," she stated loudly. "Joe, this is Paul. Something is wrong with his chair but his insurance won't cover the expense of fixing it. Perhaps you could help."

Joe stared. She wanted him to fix the old man's chair? Feeling more than one set of eyes watching him, he knelt beside the wheelchair and checked the battery, the cables, all the general stuff that could be wrong.

"Looks like the connector is broken. If you have

some tools around here, I might be able to get it working again."

From somewhere behind him a toolbox was produced. Joe found what he needed and spent the next ten minutes repairing the old man's chair. When he finished and the chair worked, he earned a smiling nod of approval from Mrs. H. that somehow made the experience of being under everyone's watchful supervision tolerable.

He replaced the tools into the metal box and stood. "If it gives you any more trouble, let me know and I'll have another go at it."

The old man opened his mouth. His lips moved, but no sound came out. Then his wrinkled hand lifted as though in thanks and Joe tried not to notice how badly it shook. He took the old man's hand in his. "You're welcome. Anytime."

Mrs. H. touched his arm. "Now then, Mr. Brody, let's go see how your father's doing."

Joe allowed her to escort him from the cafeteria, aware he was once again the topic of conversation.

HAL KNOCKED softly on Melissa's bedroom door, fighting the frustrated anger he felt at not being able to track Joe down. He'd had numerous people call with sightings over the last couple weeks, but by the time he made it to the area, Joe was always gone. Wherever he was staying it was close by.

He couldn't hide for long.

"You ready?"

"Yes. Come in."

He pushed open the paneled wood. "Storm's dying down so you shouldn't get too wet, but are you sure you want to go?"

"No." Melissa laughed softly. "I don't want to go at all, but since I'm having a good day, I thought I'd give Mrs. H. a hand. She said they lost their volunteer reader a while ago."

Maybe so. Still, he didn't want Mel getting her feelings hurt by some unthinking old fool who thought age gave them the right to voice any and all opinions.

Melissa set the brush down and turned. "How's it look?"

He winked at her. "Always liked blondes. Have since your mama married me and you were born."

She made a face. "I feel ridiculous in this wig, but I have to try it. Mrs. H. went to such trouble getting it for me."

Hal nodded. "It looks pretty, Mel. And no wonder she wants to help, you were one of her brightest students. She cares about you."

His daughter blinked back tears and he sighed. A distraction was needed. "Come on. Let's get you over there so you can read the latest installment of—what are you reading again?"

She laughed. "You know what I'm reading—a

romance. Something that ends happily ever after for everyone."

Hal kept his thoughts to himself. His daughter liked those books, but he knew better. Happily ever after didn't exist anywhere except on paper.

He just didn't have the heart to tell her that.

ASHLEY BOUNCED MAX in her arms, hoping, praying, his fussy cries would end soon. "Come on, Max. It can't be that bad." One look at his red, splotchy face said otherwise though.

She peered into his open, drooling mouth. The tooth was just beneath the surface and the bright red flesh of his gums looked ready to pop.

"How 'bout givin' him a popsicle?"

She turned and found Wilson frowning at them. "They have too much sugar and the diet kind have chemicals in them."

Wilson shook his head. "And you worry too much. He's hurtin', sugar don't matter if it'd help."

She couldn't argue there. Her ears hurt and her head pounded. She carried Max to the freezer in the utility room and dug down inside for the box she'd stuck in the back for an emergency.

"I knew you had some hid somewhere."

She found the ice-encrusted box and pulled. "I thought if I hid them they might last a little longer," she countered wryly. One-handed, she couldn't get the box open.

The old man clucked his tongue. "Give it here. I'll open it." He leaned against the side of the large freezer and pulled the flap up.

Max continued to cry and fuss and Ashley gave up trying to soothe him. Her nerves were stretched taut, both from Max's unending cries, the noise from the storm and—Joe's kiss.

What on earth had she expected? One minute she'd been painting away and the next, she'd thrown herself into his arms. What must he think? What excuse did she have?

She'd wanted him to kiss her.

What would Mac think?

She ignored the voice in her head and reached out to take the popsicle Wilson handed her. Max calmed down a bit while he watched her peel the paper off the treat. He'd eaten Cheerios and some other soft, pureed foods for two months now so anything she ate, he seemed to want to inspect. He opened his mouth and she inserted the tip of the orange popsicle to land gently on his gums.

"There, see? Yum."

Max pulled away, sucked his lower lip into his mouth as though trying to figure out the taste, and then opened up again.

"Thatta boy." Wilson saluted him with a purple popsicle. "So…what happened with you and Joe?"

Ashley's relieved smile quickly faltered. "What do you mean?"

Wilson stashed a second popsicle in the small basket attached to the front of his walker. "He looked like a stick of dynamite when he left, and you came in to get Max not lookin' much better. Something wrong?"

"He fixed the roof." She turned around to put the box back in the freezer.

Wilson's sudden laughter had her swiveling back toward him. "What's so funny?"

"Oh, nothin'. Just wondering if Joe got all the paint off his hands after they'd gripped your behind or if he's makin' a mess on my steering wheel."

JOE LEFT HIS FATHER'S ROOM shaking his head and laughing. His old man was in high spirits today and had every right to be now that he'd accomplished one of the requirements the physical therapist said he had to do before being released.

Between feeling good because he'd helped out Mrs. H. and being happy his pop was getting better, he'd been able to let go of what had happened at the house with Ashley. At least until he saw her next.

Which wouldn't be as often if he could help it. Maybe he should start taking his meals either outside or in his room. Sitting across the table from her three times a day was too much. He liked how she cared for Wilson. Liked how she had a goal and was determined to achieve it. Liked her. Period.

Problem was, he liked her too much.

He turned the corner, lost in thought, and walked right into a woman exiting the ladies room. "Excuse me, I—" Joe broke off, unable to speak, to move, when he stared into Melissa's panic-stricken eyes. She blanched, a frightening sight to witness since she was already so sickly pale.

His hands shot out to steady her when he saw her weave on her feet. "Melissa?" He spotted a couch five feet from where they stood and quickly led her over to it. Easing her down amongst the cushions, he asked, "Are you okay? Do you need something? Water? Juice? I'll go get a nurse."

To be so dazed at the sight of him, she reacted quickly. Her trembling hand landed on his arm. "I'm fine, just…"

He nodded his understanding. To say he was surprised to see her didn't come close to being accurate. Knocked on his ass was more like it.

She released him, her hands flying to her head. He could tell it wasn't really her hair and the sight reminded him of her illness. "Mel…I'm so sorry."

Her hands dropped, her chin raised. "Don't be. I've always known the odds were against me."

Yeah, but he knew she'd always prayed not to get sick like her mother and grandmother. "You look good."

"Don't—"

"You do," he insisted. "You're pale, but pretty as ever."

She smiled sadly at the compliment. "You look good, too." She glanced around the hallway outside the cafeteria and Joe followed her stare. If someone saw them together her father would immediately be called, and she had to know Hal was looking for him. His pop had said Hal stopped by twice that week alone in the hopes of catching him there.

"Mel, can we talk somewhere? Find an empty room or—"

She shook her head. "What's left to say, Joe?"

"Plenty—I didn't do it," he grated harshly, his tone low and revealing every ounce of fear and frustration and pain he held inside. He watched her, silently begged her to believe him. He'd done the same when he'd gone on trial, and he did it again now. "I didn't do it, Mel. I didn't hurt her."

"You were the only one with her." Tears choked her, made her voice hoarse. "You were young. Uncomfortable with her."

Joe shook his head, so angry he couldn't see straight. He hadn't hurt Josie. He hadn't—but someone had. "She woke up screaming. Loud, high-pitched."

"And you shook her."

"No."

Joe lowered his head into his hand and rubbed.

"All I know is that I didn't. Mel, I lost ten years of my life. Ten years for something *I did not do*."

Trembling fingers wiped away her tears. "You were convicted. My father arrested you. I tried to believe, to think you hadn't done something so horrible, but the doctor said she'd been hurt, her brain *damaged*." She sniffled, fresh tears replacing the ones she'd removed. "I'd heard you were back in town and when I saw you just now I thought maybe—just maybe—" Her voice broke and she paused, breathing deeply. "I'd hoped you'd own up to it, Joe. To admit that you made a mistake and stay for your dad, but let that part of our lives be over by *finally* telling the truth."

"I am. Even though it sounds like you just want to forget her."

She flinched. "What I *want* is to stop hurting."

Her head lowered and once again he stared. Watched her as she cried.

"I've tried so hard to forgive you, Joe, but when you deny everything—"

"Because it isn't true." He wondered how his life had come to this. Hissed accusations, a prison record and secrets. How screwed up could things get? "Listen to me," he murmured, careful to keep his voice low. He squatted down in front of her and pulled her hands from her face. "Mel, I didn't do it," he repeated, dipping his head to hold her gaze when she tried once more to look away. "There's another explanation—I don't know what, but there is. There has to be because I didn't hurt her and I—I want you to know that—believe it."

Joe released her and stood, managed to put four or five steps between him and Mel when he saw Mrs. H. hovering around the corner. One look revealed she'd heard every word. Every comment. And despite the redness of her eyes, she looked ready to pounce, a self-proclaimed guardian angel.

He wondered whom she guarded, whom she believed.

Then he called himself a fool for wondering at all.

HAL STARED ACROSS the desk to where Melissa sat. He'd been surprised to see her since she hadn't come to the station in quite a while. Now his anger built because she was there and giving him orders.

"You heard me, Dad. Please, lay off Joe."

He leaned back in his chair. "So the rumors are true? He's still around?"

His daughter's chin rose a notch. "Yes. I spoke with him."

Foul curses filled the air, but instead of being upset, Mel laughed.

"What?" he growled, not seeing the humor in his daughter being anywhere close to a murderer.

"I felt like saying the same thing when I saw him," she murmured, still amused, "and I didn't believe a thing he said until I heard Mom's voice in my head telling me to watch my mouth and open my mind."

"Mel, you didn't say those things because you're a better person than I am. And your mother—"

His daughter closed her eyes and rubbed her temple, stilling his comment.

"No, Dad, I'm not. I'm just tired. And I don't want the responsibility of knowing you have it in for Joe because of me."

"It's not because of you."

Blue eyes blinked at him, so like her mother's. "Josie, then. Either way, does it really matter?"

"What did he say to you?"

Before his eyes Mel's heart broke, her face, her expression, revealing a pain no mother should ever have to know. "He said he didn't do it."

"Bullsh—"

"And I believe him."

Hal stalked away from his desk. "That son of a— What right does he have to be tormenting you about this now?"

"Exactly," she said, her tone deceptively soft. The tone she used when she wanted to get someone thinking along her lines. The tone she'd learned from her mother. "He spent ten years in jail, Dad. And he still swears he didn't do it. I didn't believe him, but then once I calmed down and thought about it, I— Why would he bother lying now? It's done. There's no reason for him to deny it."

"Maybe he wants you back."

At that Melissa rose from the chair and walked toward him, put a hand on his arm. "He doesn't want me back. Ten years is a long time to think about things. We were too young. Too stupid. Too everything," she said. "We took things way too fast before we got to know one another. We both realize that, especially now."

Hal drew Melissa into his arms and held her close. "I don't like it that he's here. I haven't been able to track him, but I will. I'll find him. I don't want him around you."

"He'd never hurt me."

"He *murdered* Josie."

"Dad...what if it was a mistake?"

"You can't believe— It wasn't, Mel. He's doing this to get to you. That's all." Hal clenched his fists. "His dad's here. Taylorsville is the only home he's ever known. Maybe he's trying to convince you because he thinks you'll help him convince others." Hal felt her sigh against his chest.

"Maybe. I guess that is a possibility. So many people despise him."

With good reason. "Stay away from him, Mel. I want to know if he contacts you again." He tilted her chin up. "I mean it. I'll get a restraining order out today, and we'll haul him in if he comes near you. I should've done it already. Joe Brody hurt us once, but he's not going to do it again."

CHAPTER TEN

ASHLEY BROKE INTO her stash of coupons and ordered pizza for dinner with the excuse that in the time it would take for her to cook, she could finish putting the second coat of paint on the front parlor walls.

Once she opened the doors of her business the front parlor would be used as a general gathering area. It had a fireplace, plenty of room for several couches and chairs, a piano and a separate seating area for cards or games. Maybe even a small bookstore and gift shop.

She glanced at her watch and frowned. Joe hadn't returned from wherever he'd gone, and she told herself it didn't matter.

He was her handyman. Nothing else. She didn't want anything else from him. The goal she worked so hard for wasn't hers alone. It was her son's future, her husband's dream.

Mac might be gone, but he wasn't forgotten, nor would he ever be. He'd been a good husband, a good provider, a wonderful friend and he would've been a good father if he'd lived long enough. She wasn't ready to move on. Was she?

But if not, why was she kissing Joe?

She'd spent the majority of the early afternoon avoiding Wilson's knowing, smirking gaze. Just because he'd pointed out Joe's much larger handprints spread across her ample rear end in bright Victorian-era yellow, well, that meant nothing.

She was such a liar.

The phone rang and broke through her tormented thoughts. Ashley waited and wondered if Wilson would get it, but when it rang twice more, she set down her trim brush and hurried to the portable she'd left lying across the top of the couch.

"Willow Wood." She glanced outside and noted the big brown dog crossing the yard, head down in the rain. The poor thing was drenched.

"Ashley, it's Bryan Booker."

"Oh, hi. Is something wrong?" She pressed one finger to her ear while walking over to the radio to turn it down.

"I was just wondering if you'd given any more thought to joining the book discussion. It meets tonight and I thought I'd call with a personal invitation."

The book club? She'd forgotten all about it. "Oh…well, thank you. I'll see."

"I could come pick you up. Maybe we could go somewhere to eat?"

A date? Ashley bit her lip and closed her eyes with a silent groan. Bryan was very handsome, seemingly nice. But was she ready for a date?

She'd done more with Joe and not been on a date.

"That's— That sounds great," she murmured with a wince, "but I don't think so. If I come I'll drive myself. You understand—just in case Max get's cranky and I have to leave. I haven't read the book, either, but I appreciate the invitation," she added hurriedly. "It's very kind of you to offer."

"Well, I hope you can make it regardless. I'd like to see you, Ashley, and Max, of course."

The fact he so readily included her son warmed her opinion of him. Made her feel guilty. Dr. Booker was a good guy. What would it hurt?

"You know, I'm almost finished painting and— An evening out does sound like fun. I'll—I'll see you there," she added before she could back out.

"Great. Seven o'clock? Maybe I can win Max over and we can have dessert afterward or something?"

She'd always admired persistence. "Maybe. We'll see. I'll see you at seven. Bye." Ashley pressed the button to end the call and looked up just in time to see Joe pass outside the doorway and head upstairs toward his room.

"I ordered pizza," she called, nerves layering her tone and taking it to a higher pitch. "It'll be here soon."

"Fine."

Fine, huh? If it was fine, why had he growled at her?

And why did she feel guilty about a simple evening out with Max's doctor and his friends in the book club?

Guilty because of Joe?

THE THOUGHT OF PIZZA brought Joe out of his room a little while later. Downstairs, he found Wilson asleep in his recliner with the television blaring, but no sign of Max or Ashley.

He poured himself a glass of tea from the fridge and carried it over to where the cardboard box sat on the table. He pulled out a chair and had just sat down when the television went silent.

"She went out."

Joe didn't respond—instead he took a bite and chewed.

"Went to that singles club and took Max with her."

What kind of mother took her kid to a—

None of his business.

"That young doc asked her out. I heard 'em talkin' about it on the phone."

Wilson shouldn't be listening in on conversations.

As though reading his thoughts, the old man continued by saying, "Didn't mean to. Thought Ashley hadn't picked it up."

Joe took a big drink of the tea before he remembered she didn't sweeten it, and grimaced at the bitter taste.

"Doc's a nice fellow. Suppose he'd be good to Max and Ashley. Wonder about his hoity-toity friends. Got quite a reputation with the ladies though."

Joe glared at the foot of the recliner where Wilson's feet were propped, unable to see the rest of the old man thanks to the wall separating the two rooms.

"Pretty much ain't a man out there who wouldn't think Ashley's pretty. That's not the problem."

No, her looks would not be a problem.

"Guess if you want to lose your shot at a good life and a good woman, you can just sit there like a knot on a log and do nothin'."

Joe shoved the chair backward and stalked over to stand in the doorway of the living room. "Spit it out, old man."

"I changed my mind."

Joe raised a brow in question.

"If you're interested in the missy—and I'd say by the look of your hands on her behind today you are—that's fine. Just don't hurt her."

Joe's gaze narrowed. "Suddenly I've been approved?" He leaned against the door jamb. "What, are you afraid the doc will kick you out if they get married?"

Wilson shook a gnarled finger at him. "Don't sass me, boy. And no, I ain't afraid of that. The missy wouldn't do that anyhow. I'm just wonderin' how many chances a man like you might get if you ignore the God-given gift in front of you. I decided I won't stand in your way is all—but you'd best hurry it up."

ASHLEY COULDN'T HAVE BEEN more nervous. Her hands trembled as she unbuckled Max's car seat and if she'd eaten one antacid on the way to the library, she'd eaten five. At least they were minty.

"You came. I wasn't sure if you would."

She turned to see Bryan Booker's blond head and broad shoulders beside the open car door. "Yeah, um, hi."

His expression was warm and filled with masculine appreciation. "Come on, let me give you a hand with Max."

Grateful, she lifted the heavy diaper bag out of the front passenger seat. "Thanks. I'll get him if you'll take that." She turned back to the car and hunched down to get Max out of his seat, hurriedly finishing off the belts and straps and lifting him in her arms. She straightened and banged her head.

"Ouch!" Her face burned. What a way to make an impression.

Suddenly Bryan's hands were there, his fingers rubbing away the pain since her arms were full of her son.

"You okay?"

"Yes, fine," she murmured, embarrassed. "It only hurt for a second," she lied. The bump on her head throbbed.

Bryan lowered his hand to pat Max's back. "Hi, buddy, how're you?"

In response to Bryan's attention, Max's forehead dropped to her collarbone like a hammer on a nail. She flinched and Bryan winced with sympathy even as he chuckled in amusement. "It's a wonder you're not black-and-blue."

In that moment she gave in and smiled back. The only way to get through a night filled with one embarrassment after another was to maintain a sense of humor.

A woman walked by to go into the library and Ashley watched as the pale blonde drew Bryan's attention. He flashed the woman a smile that made the other woman blush and Ashley stood there, arms loaded with a squirming, head-butting baby and a stomach that threatened to call it a day.

Was she really up to this?

Bryan put an arm around Ashley's tense shoulders and drew her forward a step so he could shut her car door.

"Come on, let's go inside. I'll introduce you to everyone."

Ashley followed Bryan's lead and allowed him to prod her inside the library doors. The blonde had arrived ahead of them and now stood smiling shyly as she was greeted with cries of welcome and warmth. One woman came forward and pulled the blonde into her arms for a hug then led her to a chair while asking how she was feeling.

Ashley glanced away from the sight and looked up at Bryan instead, hoping for a clue to the situation. "Is she sick?" she asked quietly, careful not to be overheard.

Bryan's expression was grim. "Her name is Melissa York, and yes, she is. She has cancer."

"Oh." Ashley pressed a kiss to Max's head. "She's so young."

"Never know what'll happen, do we?"

The women greatly outnumbered the men in the room and immediately noticed Bryan's presence. Ashley wondered how much money they'd spent on teeth whitening treatments, since their smiles—bright and showing blatant interest—nearly blinded them...until they saw her. Some of the smiles fell, some of the women's gazes took on a predatory gleam and some just narrowed in what-does-she-have-that-I-don't glares.

In that moment Ashley wanted to run away, go back to her car and drive home and spend the evening working with Joe.

Then she glimpsed Melissa York and she realized she had to stay. If she didn't, she'd only waste precious time.

She'd decided to stay in Taylorsville, to establish roots for Max and herself, settle into a home and community.

This was a way to go about it.

Like it or not.

Several hours later Ashley carried her sleeping son inside the house and upstairs to his room. In short order she'd given him a bath to take care of any dirt and germs he might have picked up crawling on the library floor, changed his diaper and dressed him in lightweight pajamas.

Now she stared down at him, watching his eyes flutter and eventually close, the way his chubby arms and legs twitched as he settled into sleep.

Ashley leaned against the railing of his crib and simply stared at him. He reminded her so much of Mac. The shape of his face, his expressions. His temperament. Like father, like son, she mused with a sad smile. So full of energy and always moving while awake, out like a light when they finally exhausted themselves.

She reached out to smooth her fingertips over Max's forehead, but stilled when her eyes fastened on the silver band gleaming beneath the nearby nightlight. Heart thumping, Ashley straightened her fingers, eyes flooding with a sudden rush of tears.

How quickly things changed.

Shakily, Ashley moved the two steps it took to get to the rocking chair beside Max's crib and sank down onto the cushion, her legs no longer able to support her. The ring warmed beneath her touch and she held her hand to her heart, rocking for a long while, eyes closed. One by one the memories came to her, happy, sad. All of them special.

With every to and fro movement of the rocking chair, she remembered, smiled. Laughed softly at all she and Mac had shared. Burned pizza and card games, a scrawny Christmas tree only half lit because the lights went out on the bottom, a few rare nights out on the town hand in hand, walking, window shopping, too poor to buy anything but dreaming big dreams all the same, a soldier and a waitress against the world but totally in love.

Ashley lifted her lashes, her gaze locking on her son. *Their* son. "He's so much like you, Mac. So much like you." Her vision blurred with tears. "But…"

It wasn't right that she kissed Joe. That she was so attracted to him. That she'd gone to meet up with Bryan at the library.

Not while wearing your ring.

Sniffling, Ashley raised her hand to her mouth and kissed the band before slowly easing it off her finger. Staring down at it, she remembered how the weight of it had felt the very first time Mac had slid it on, warm from his nervous, trembling touch.

"Thank you," she whispered, lifting it to her

lips again. "For love…for *Max*. For being my hero when I needed you so badly."

She sat there a long while, rocking, crying and thinking, until finally, the tears slowed. The pain lessened. Ashley stood and carried the ring to the dresser lining the opposite wall, to the triangular keepsake box displayed on top. She placed the ring with the flag that had topped Mac's casket. Next to the medals he'd earned serving his country. Beneath the picture of him in his uniform and another of the two of them together, smiling for the camera.

"I'll never forget, Mac," she murmured, her left hand smoothing over the carefully stitched flag. "Or let Max grow up without knowing you." She inhaled deeply, tears forming again because it was so very hard to say the words aloud even though she knew they were long in coming, knew she couldn't deny the truth any longer.

"But it's time," she whispered finally. Staring into her husband's eyes, she pressed a kiss to her finger and traced it over his handsome face beside her own in the photograph. "It's time…"

JOSIE WAS CRYING. Joe walked into the nursery and searched for her in the crib but she wasn't there. Her cries rose in volume and he became frantic. Where was she? He turned, searched. Her cries grew louder and louder.

Josie!

He awoke with a start and shot up in bed, his chest heaving from the adrenaline racing through him. He looked around, unfamiliar with the room until his panic subsided.

It was only a dream.

Joe dropped back to the bed and wiped a hand over his sweaty face. A dream. Not the first and certainly not the last. Even now he still heard her cries.

You're losing it, Brody.

But it wasn't his imagination. The cries continued and Joe finally realized it was Max. Still shaking from the nightmare, he slung the sheet off his lower body and stood. He walked to the bathroom, dragged in several deep, eye-opening breaths and fought his frustration.

Max continued to cry. Was he all right? Where was Ashley?

Joe splashed cold water on his face. Still Max cried.

He left his room and walked across the large, open foyer to the second floor hallway above the kitchen.

The door to Max's room was ajar.

"I know. I'm sorry, honey. I'm just so tired I didn't wake up. Mommy didn't mean to sleep through your bellowing."

Joe smiled at the description. Bellowing was right on the money in Max's case.

Ashley got him settled on her lap in the rocking

chair, the bottle in his mouth ending his fussy whimpers. The sight hurt because it was so beautiful, so caring and loving.

"Better now? Don't give me that look, I said I was sorry." She smiled tiredly. "Ah, so you want a story now, too? So demanding," she said, humor lacing her voice. "Where were we, huh?" She leaned her head back against the rocking chair's wooden frame and sighed. "Okay…"

Joe knew he should leave, walk away, but now that he was up and the temptation of learning more about Ashley had presented itself, he wanted to stay.

Wilson's words repeated themselves in his head.

Was Ashley his second chance? His way of proving, somehow, that he hadn't hurt Josie?

Torn, he leaned a fist high against the wall outside the room. Head down, his thoughts were all over the place until he heard Ashley speak. Then he could do nothing but stay and listen.

"Your daddy was a goof," Ashley murmured. "But I loved him, Max. That man could make me smile when I was in the worst of moods. And I *hated* it," she added with a wry laugh. "Because I couldn't ever be mad at him for long. He wouldn't let me. Instead he'd do something stupid to make me laugh and keep right on until he'd teased me out of my anger.

"Since he was older, he left the home first and joined the Marines. I didn't see him again. I dated a lot of losers in that time. Then I graduated and had to move out, got a couple jobs and my own place. And one day," she said softly, "there he was. He looked so handsome in his uniform. He'd gone to the home and asked around, tracked me down. He sat at one of my tables and then stayed until my shift was over. We talked for hours just in little snatches between me running around waiting on people. From then on, every time he saved up enough money and had leave, he'd come to see me."

The chair creaked as she rocked, the rhythm soothing. Combined with the noises Max made while he sucked on his bottle, Joe felt…at home.

"At first we were still just friends, trying to figure out life. Then one night I'd had a really bad day and I wished with all my heart he was there. And then he was. It was like magic. Max, I couldn't believe it when I saw him. I actually thought I'd made him up. That weekend we realized we loved each other and we got married.

"We wanted to give our babies everything we didn't have, you know? We wanted you to live in a place where you don't have to worry about anything. A home that's warm and safe and one you can be proud of. We were going to have a family, one with a mommy *and* daddy, and brothers and sisters to fight with," she said thickly. "That was our dream." She sniffled, the chair creaking a time or two before she continued. "I want us to belong here, Max. In this big, beautiful house and this safe little town. And I'll do whatever it takes to make it happen. Even if it means doing things I don't like doing. For you, I will. I promise."

Ashley's story picked up again, but Joe couldn't stay any longer. It wasn't right. And it wasn't what he wanted to hear from her, either. She'd been happy until her husband died, had loved him. And she'd be happy and fall in love again when the right guy came along.

But he wasn't the guy. He wanted to be, ached to be, but he wasn't. She had a dream and she couldn't achieve it with him by her side. She wanted a good life for Max and that wouldn't happen with him in her life messing things up. Even if she believed him at all.

Joe retraced his steps back to his room and laid down on the bed. He stared at the ceiling for hours, searching for an answer, but one never found one. The sun broke over the horizon. Tired and aching from too much work and not a lot of rest, he got up and showered.

Another day, another project. The sooner he finished, the sooner he could leave Ashley and her dream behind for another man to have.

SHOWERS SETTLED IN over the next few days and became a consistent soft rain. Joe began the ceiling work upstairs. He ripped out and repaired the Sheetrock that had been damaged from the leaky roof, and although she'd offered her help, his gruff refusals led Ashley to distance herself with other projects she could handle on her own.

Neither of them mentioned the kiss. She supposed that was a good thing under the circumstances, but she couldn't help wondering what he'd thought—or what he'd done about the arousal he'd walked away with. Had he gone to someone else? Found a pretty girl in town and taken care of things?

Jealousy bit her hard.

It also startled.

No way. Could she actually be jealous? She'd known him a matter of weeks. Weeks, when it had taken her years of knowing Mac before she'd ever felt a smidgen more than friendship.

But she couldn't lie to herself. Or avoid the truth of Joe's past. Would he stay out of jail?

You don't know him or know he's really turned his life around.

Joe staying here was temporary and she had to remember it, kiss or no kiss.

"Ashley?"

She whirled around and found the object of her thoughts standing in the doorway of the library, his expression confused.

"What, did you need something?"

He shook his head, but still frowned. "You changed your mind?"

About him? Definitely...not. "About what?"

Joe stepped deeper into the room and indicated the trim brush in her hand. "I thought you were going to leave the bookshelves as they are."

Her eyes widened and she whirled back around only to find she'd done the unthinkable. Lost in thought, she'd finished trimming up the wall and moved on to paint over the side of the hand-carved, *stained* mahogany bookshelves.

"*No!* Oh, *no!*" She dropped the brush into the paint pan and grabbed the towel she kept tucked into the waistband of her shorts for drips. Instead of wiping the paint away, all she did was smear it around.

Ashley turned to Joe for help but found him gone. She'd nearly burst into tears at her mindless blunder when he returned with a plastic container of water and a sponge.

"Watch out."

She scrambled out of the way and Joe quickly went to work. His long, lean hands squeezed the sponge and scrubbed the wood, over and over again until the barest hint of color remained.

"Do you have a fresh towel?"

She handed him one from a nearby stack and he wiped the lower side of the bookcase down. No more paint remained that she could see.

"There. You must have really been lost in thought."

Ashley smoothed her trembling hands over her head, wet her lips. "Yeah. Yeah, I guess I was."

Joe's gaze narrowed. He stood, the action placing him so close that she could feel the heat radiating off his body.

"Did you go into town yesterday?" she blurted suddenly, the jealous witch on her shoulder determined to have her way. "To—to see your dad?"

The movement was so slight she might have imagined it, but Ashley thought she saw his lashes lower a bit, the move not as casual as it looked, but…protective?

"Yeah. Why?"

"Did you not mean to kiss me?"

"You kissed me back."

She'd hoped he'd forgotten that part.

Joe closed his eyes briefly before opening them and giving her a look she couldn't comprehend.

"Look, Ashley, I understand why you don't want me kissing you—"

"Why's that?"

He faltered. "You're my boss."

"Yeah. Yeah, I am." Did he move closer?

"And I'm an ex-con."

The air left her lungs. "It bothers me," she admitted softly. "But only because I knew guys at the home who'd get in trouble once and then they'd do it again and again, and even though they had a chance at a better life, they'd go back and screw up every time."

"That part of my life is over. I promise you that."

He said it with such conviction and strength, she couldn't help but believe him. It was exactly what she wanted him to say, too. But did believing him make her a fool when she had Max to think of, to protect?

"You think I'm lying."

"No," she said quickly. One look into his eyes told her he wasn't. "I believe you, it's just—"

"You want to be sure because of Max."

Her shoulders sagged. "I *have* to be sure because of Max," she said, inexcusably relieved that he understood.

Maybe she compared him to the juvenile delinquents she'd known growing up, but Joe wasn't like them. Not even on the most elemental levels. He'd been honest with her, and had come clean about his prison stay, worked harder than any man she'd ever known, not to achieve his dream, but to help her achieve hers.

You pay him to work for you.

But he was different, and she did him an injustice by not giving him the chance at a new life, like the one she wanted for herself.

And the attraction between them?

It was just that. Attraction, nothing else, the physical needs of their bodies calling out to one another.

Joe stepped close, so close his chest brushed hers and electricity zapped through her body.

Nothing else, huh?

He watched her, waited, gave her as much time as she needed to sort through the chaos in her mind. The next move was up to her, that much was obvious.

The scent of soap and man filled her head and added to her confusion. White powder from the gypsum board streaked across his chest, and she found her fingers following the path. Felt the warm, thick muscle beneath the material of his shirt. The beat of his heart. Joe was a flesh-and-blood man. Not perfect, but he didn't pretend to be, either. He was just…Joe.

The phone rang and she startled, then laughed. "Sorry. I'd—I'd better get that."

Joe placed a hand over hers and held it to him, his expression grim. "Ashley…there's something else you need to know."

The baby monitor crackled loudly as Wilson answered the phone, then, "Missy! It's Doc Booker. I think he wants another date!"

Joe stiffened, his expression closed. He stepped back. "I'd better get back to work."

"But—What were you going to say? What else do I need to know?"

He hesitated. "Nothing…enjoy your date with the doc." Joe scowled, walking away. "Folks consider him a good catch."

CHAPTER ELEVEN

JOE TOOK A LATE LUNCH to avoid Ashley. She'd left him a note on the table telling him to help himself to the pot roast she had warming in a Crock-pot. He ate, then ten minutes later, borrowed the keys to Wilson's beat-up old truck and headed for Ridgewood.

Inside the air-conditioned home he found Mrs. H. waiting. "Hello, Mr. Brody."

Joe laughed wryly. "You can call me Joe, Mrs. H."

She tsked at him and stood. "Perhaps I will when we're back on good terms."

He fell into step beside her. "So what'll it take?"

Mrs. H. paused, lifting her chin high as she regarded him. "For you to read to our guests," she suggested smoothly. "*Someone* frightened off our last reader."

Meaning him…and Melissa?

Joe looked over Mrs. H.'s head to find about twenty people scattered throughout the cafeteria. Some talking, some playing board games. Some just staring off into space.

"That's probably not a good—"

"Your father said earlier he'd join us today. He doesn't do that very often, but think of how proud he'd be to see you making an effort to make amends."

"Low blow, Mrs. H."

"Whatever it takes, Mr. Brody."

He stared her down, knowing without a doubt she had him. He rubbed the back of his neck, felt the grit of gypsum and frowned. "I didn't clean up because I have to go back to work. I didn't expect—"

She smiled. "You look fine. They'll be listening to your voice, Mr. Brody. And if memory serves, you have a fine voice for pubic speaking."

ASHLEY HAD FINISHED painting the library and carried Max upstairs when she heard Joe drive up to the house. She peeked out her bedroom window to watch his lazy stride, but when he left her vision she dropped the lacy sheer back into place and returned to surveying the clothes on her bed with a frown.

She'd agreed to a date—a full-fledged, kiss-him-good-night date—with Bryan Booker.

And even though she'd asked herself a million times *why* she'd agreed, she knew. She was ready. Removing her wedding band was only a part of what she'd been feeling for a while, a symbol. And now? She was ready to move on and ready to feel alive again. Ready to gain some perspective on Joe.

She hoped going out with Bryan—someone so

completely opposite Joe in every way—would allow her to do it.

Maybe this would help her decide if her interest in Joe involved his rough good looks and close proximity, or…something more. Either way, she had to find out, and a date with Dr. Booker—*Bryan*—would give her that much needed reality check.

Bryan was nice, handsome, well-educated and as far as she knew, had never broken the law or been imprisoned. She owed it to Max and herself to think with her head. That's why she'd agreed.

But unlike most women who had a closet full of dresses, she only owned one. Short and black—just the way Mac had liked them. A dress she'd bought to wear for their second wedding anniversary, but then never got the chance because his leave had been canceled.

Ashley pulled the dress from the closet and carefully unwound the knot of plastic at the hem. Soft, filmy, the dress was elegant and provocative at the same time. Wearing it for her husband was one thing, but would the dress give Bryan the wrong idea?

"What do you think, Max?" She held the dress up in front of her for Max's drooling perusal. "I thought so. But it's the only dress I have so…it's got to be the one."

Max made a happy, gurgling sound and let go

of the blankets he held on to at the side of her bed. Unable to balance, he fell on his diaper-padded rump and looked to her as though trying to decide whether or not to cry.

Ashley tossed the dress aside and clapped her hands. "Yay, good one! Yay!"

Tears forgotten, Max grinned at her and brought his hands up to clap.

"Good job, Max." She bent and picked him up. "Come on, little man. Let's go see what you've got to wear."

An hour later Max was dressed and playing in his upstairs crib. A bath had relaxed him and maybe with some luck he'd take a nap before Bryan arrived.

She pulled her hair away from her face and secured it in a twist at the back of her head, then pulled a few straight tendrils along the side of her cheeks in the hopes they would soften all the harsh angles that made up her face. Forgoing hose, she slipped into her only pair of strappy heels and frowned at her image. Dressing up for a date with Bryan felt strange yet it was funny how kissing Joe seemed right in comparison.

She looked down at her ringless finger and bit her lip. She went to the dresser in Max's room and opened the wooden box that held her wedding band.

Oh, Mac, am I doing the right thing?

A warm, contented feeling filled her. And

without a doubt, Ashley knew it was Mac's way of telling her everything would be all right. That he wanted her to be happy.

Ashley closed the box and headed toward the bathroom.

A glance at the clock said it was too late to cancel. She had to go. Bryan had mentioned he was staying at his elderly grandfather's home between Taylorsville and Baxter until an apartment above his practice could be completed, which meant to get here by the appointed time, he had to have already left.

Nervous, a little sick, she grabbed her brush.

The last thing she needed to be worrying about was Joe's reaction. They'd shared a couple of really hot kisses and enough heat between them to set the house on fire. But before she could even remotely consider Joe potential father material, she had to test the waters. Use her head and Max's best interests to make up her mind.

Whatever her feelings were for her hunky, ex-con handyman…she'd find out tonight.

TWO AND A HALF hours later, Ashley sat back against the padded booth with a moan. "No, no more. I can't eat another bite. I don't know how Wilson does this."

Bryan chuckled as he waved the ice cream and fudge covered spoon in the air between them. "Come on. You know you want it."

He'd teased her all through dinner, flirting, laughing. She'd allowed herself to flirt back, too. But more than once she'd seen the embarrassed, harassed expression on Bryan's face when the noise level from the all-girl table in the corner reached record proportions.

"Any more and you'll have to roll me out of here," she added.

"Your loss." Bryan plopped the spoon into his mouth.

Max continued to sit quietly, content to eat his Cheerios or play with his toys as he watched the waitstaff bustle by him. She was so proud of him. This was the first time he'd been inside a restaurant and while she knew his behavior could change at any moment, he'd been wonderful so far.

"I have to admit I had my doubts and considered canceling, but this date has been a lot of fun."

"Good. I'm glad you feel that way." Bryan leaned back against the bench seat. "Although you seem very contemplative for a woman having fun."

"Oh. Really?" Her laugh emerged high-pitched and telling. "Well, I guess tonight has…clued me into a few things, that's all."

"What things?"

She shrugged. "Nothing major," she hedged, uncomfortable. "Just that I need to get out more."

"With me?" Bryan suggested with a wink.

Heat filled her face, but she didn't acknowledge his question. Bryan was a nice guy. Handsome, *gorgeous*, but he wasn't the guy she'd spent the evening thinking about.

"I'm also beginning to accept the fact Wilson is right, *again*, and that settling in and becoming a part of things in Taylorsville may be easier if I open my mind and allow myself to be stared at a bit so people can get to know me and vice versa."

"Sounds good." His smile widened. "What else?"

Once again voices rose behind her and she lifted a brow in question. "Maybe you should tell me. What's the deal with the women in the corner?"

Bryan took a sip of his coffee, his eyes guarded while his face darkened. "You haven't seen the newspaper?"

"Not unless it had paint drips on it."

Bryan's smile was off-kilter and world-weary. Every one of those women in the corner wanted to be the doctor's wife and had quite happily discussed—in detail—what they'd be willing to do to achieve their goal.

And while some people might not see Bryan's handsome looks and occupation as a problem, thanks to her waitressing days she knew what it was like to get hit on constantly by people who looked at her as if she were an object rather than a person. Big boobs, a decent set of features, and no family had made her an easy target…until she set them straight.

"So you did something newsworthy to earn all the attention?"

He flushed beneath the muted lights overhead. "Not quite newsworthy," he muttered. "No, the newspaper recently came out with a contest. People had to write in and vote. Somehow I wound up winning a couple of the so-called *awards* and my life has been hell ever since."

"What kind of awards?"

He leaned forward, his gaze not quite meeting hers. "Most Eligible Bachelor, Sexiest Doctor and…Best Butt."

Ashley snickered.

He glared at her but the wry amusement in his features belied any true anger. "That's good. Laugh, twist the knife deeper."

"Bryan, oh my." She snickered again. "So everywhere you go you get…them?" she asked, rolling her eyes quickly to indicate the group nearby.

He nodded. "Young, old, married or not," he growled. "I'm shaking women out of my mattress."

"Poor baby," she crooned.

Bryan's gaze promised retribution. And friendship. She liked that since it sort of reminded her of something an older brother would do.

Definitely not boyfriend material when you think of him like that.

And that thought confirmed the decision she'd come to during the course of the evening.

"It's a hard life but someone's got to do it," she teased. "Might as well be you."

"Thanks. So much for getting sympathy from you. I'd think you'd be a little more understanding."

The women in the corner burst into laughter, drawing everyone's gaze until it was obvious they were talking about him, and the restaurant's occupants turned to stare at Bryan instead.

"Okay, I've had enough. What about you? Want to take a walk down by the river? Should be a nice breeze and I think there's a band tonight. We can spread a blanket on the ground and listen."

Ashley pulled her napkin from her lap and placed it on the table. "Sounds like fun. But if there's a band I've gotta warn you—Max and I like to dance."

Head down, he groaned. "Just my luck…in the spotlight again."

ASHLEY ASSUMED Joe and Wilson were both asleep when she carried Max into the house. She tucked her son in his crib and turned on the monitor, but was too restless and wound up to go to bed herself. She grabbed the portable receiver from her room in case Max stirred and then slipped off her heels and padded barefoot to the front hallway. At the bottom of the stairs, she unlocked the front door and headed out onto the wraparound porch, her thoughts consumed by Joe and the realization she'd made tonight.

She didn't like him. No, what she felt for Joe was much, much more. But what? Attraction and friendship didn't begin to describe her feelings. She'd acknowledge both emotions, but what should she do about them?

Should she do anything?

"Better watch where you step."

Ashley whirled at the sound of Joe's voice, her gaze searching the darkness. He sat on the aged wooden planks, one leg stretched out in front of him, one drawn up to act as a prop for his arm. In the muted light of the moon she saw the glint of his eyes but couldn't make out his expression.

"Sorry, I didn't mean to scare you."

She smiled. "No problem."

He pointed a lazy finger toward the long driveway. "The doc's got a nice car."

Ashley put her hands behind her so the chipping paint of the porch rail wouldn't snag her dress. "It was all right." The nicest ride she'd ever been in, but who cared?

Mac's death had hammered home the fact money wasn't everything.

She wet her dry lips. "Joe—"

"I'd better—"

They both stopped and stared. "You go first," he said, his tone low, rasping over her skin like a trail of well-placed kisses.

Her thoughts flew to Bryan and the sweet,

brotherly kiss he'd pressed to her cheek at the back door. She didn't want sweet kisses. Not from Joe. And while she knew it was too soon to be thinking herself in love with him, tonight had cemented the fact she felt something for him she'd never felt before.

Something she didn't want to lose.

Joe shoved himself to his feet and turned to leave.

"Don't go."

His broad shoulders squared, the breath hissed out of his throat. "If I stay I'll…"

"What?" She stepped away from the railing, toward him, and thought she saw him tense even more. "You'll what?" she pressed, laying a hand on his back. "Kiss me again?"

A long silence filled the air, broken only by the distant sound of traffic on the highway that led into town, the croak of bullfrogs in the pond just over the hill.

"What if I want you to?" she whispered. "What if I want you to kiss me?"

Joe turned just enough to glare at her over the shoulder she touched. In her bare feet she nearly met him eye to eye—nearly, but not quite. And although Mac had been taller, Joe was broader, more strongly built. Honed and hardened.

By prison.

"You deserve nice things like that car your date drove. Things I can't give you." He swore softly.

"Ashley, I can't give you *any*thing right now because I have nothing to give."

It wasn't true, but she had no doubt Joe believed what he said. She inhaled deep, deeper, trying to fortify herself against the pull she felt from him. For him. The pain she saw in his eyes.

"Give me a walk in the moonlight."

Joe's hand covering hers, the baby monitor hanging from a strap on her wrist, she led him to the three wide steps that descended onto the sloping front yard. The grass was too long from her not having mowed it this week, but it was cool against her feet.

And with every step she noticed more and more. Little things. Important things. Like how the scent of honeysuckle tinged the air. How Joe's work-roughened fingers slid against her own with every step they took. So opposite of Bryan's soft, doctor hands, Joe's were abrasive, yet just as gentle.

"Tell me about the scar," she murmured finally.

A long moment passed. "Some guy tried to cut my throat with a shiv." He laughed humorlessly. "It wasn't from some heroic act if that's what you were thinking."

She swallowed at the image his words evoked. "The one by your mouth?"

The white of his teeth flashed briefly in the darkness. "My own fault. On a work detail my grip slipped and I landed on a rock in the fall."

Her lips twisted and she sidled closer to him with a wry smile. "So I'm not the only clumsy one?"

This time his laugh was real. "No."

They strolled awhile more in silence, down the slope of the hill at the side of the house. Unintentionally, or maybe subconsciously, she'd led them near the pond and the little screened-in shed Wilson had built for his wife so she'd accompany him when he came fishing.

She looked at Joe.

Ached.

She wanted to ease the pain Joe had suffered. Ease his sorrow and loss and give him comfort.

She was lonely, tired of carrying a heavy load and needed someone to share the burden.

And now she was here in this isolated place with a man who made her body heat just thinking about him.

But this was so much more than physical need, more than lust. In her younger, not-so-bright days before she and Mac, she'd rushed to satisfy those physical needs and regretted her impulsiveness later.

With Joe it was different. She knew it was different. Special. Nothing had every felt so right. Her body seemed attuned to him. He'd saved her life, helped her daily, tolerated an old man neither of them were related to. And avoided her son because he so badly missed his daughter.

Those things—they were why she loved him.

As crazy as it sounded, she'd fallen in love with Joe and all it had taken was spending three meals a day with him. Working side by side with him. Hour after hour, day after day. They'd shared smiles and problems. Washed the dishes together. And even though it had taken years for her to recognize her love for Mac, it had only taken her weeks to love Joe.

"Ashley?"

She turned and pressed a finger to his lips, her mouth parting in sweet surprise when he immediately kissed the tip.

"I discovered something tonight," she whispered, shivering at the heated look in his eyes. "Bryan was nice—"

Joe groaned and stepped away. "I won't be a stand-in—"

"You're not." She followed him, her hands gripping the material of his shirt to hold him in place. "He was *nice,* Joe. And it was a nice, fun date, but my heart didn't race when he kissed me good night. And I didn't ache with wanting to feel his arms around me the whole time I sat across from him at dinner."

Joe tensed, the muscles of his chest hard when she moved so close her breasts rested against him. "What I feel for you... I—" She inhaled. "I don't know how to describe it yet. It's all happened so fast and I'm not even sure it's wise, but this feels—"

"Right," he growled before dipping his head to kiss her. He stopped abruptly, his mouth hovering a scarce inch over hers. "It feels right, doesn't it?"

CHAPTER TWELVE

"YES." HER GAZE never wavered, knowing exactly what he needed to hear. "I want to move on, Joe. I'm ready. But I want to be with someone who understands me. Someone who knows what it's like to be different in a town like Taylorsville. I want you."

Her heart pounded so hard she imagined her body pulsed with it, but it matched the thudding tempo of his. She felt the rapid cadence through his shirt, the heat of him, the strength of his need. "I've seen how hard you work. Harder than I've asked you to," she whispered. "Like you're trying to prove something."

She slid her hand up his chest, over his shoulder to where she clasped the back of his neck. "I know that feeling. I understand what it's like to work and strive in an effort to gain approval. To dream. Want," she breathed, finally giving in to the overwhelming need to brush her mouth against his.

It was a light, barely there kiss with just enough tongue to make his arms tighten around her.

He tasted so good.

Joe's chest rose and fell heavily. "What about Max? You need to be with someone who—"

"You're not one of the statistics, Joe. Maybe I had my doubts at first, I admit it, but now…" She shook her head. "Maybe you can't offer me fancy cars, but you can give me and Max other things. More important things." A sad smile was all she could manage. "You learn a lot becoming a widow this early. You learn what really matters. And I'll take a kind, hard-working man over material things any day."

Joe stared at her a long moment, aching, painfully aroused, but torn and shaken by her words. She believed in him. He saw it in her eyes, in the way she smiled.

He had to tell her the truth. *Wanted* to tell her, get it out into the open and pray she'd forgive him for not telling her all of it sooner. Pray she'd believe him when no one else did. For the first time in a long while, he was afraid.

"Ashley—"

She parted her lips and kissed him again. Not the brief, slight kiss of earlier, but hot and hard and sexy. One minute he could think and the next it was all he could do not to lower her to the grass but get them inside the shed. Her hands teased him, slid over his chest and arms as though she liked what she saw and couldn't get enough.

Joe broke the kiss long enough to yank his shirt

over his head. Her mouth fell to his chest, kissing, nibbling, her teeth gently biting the skin over his collarbone, a sexy, teasing nip that sharpened his craving for her.

He tossed his shirt aside and lowered his hands to her dress. Eased it up the long length of her legs.

"Zipper's on the side."

He found the pull and forced himself to slowly ease it down so as not to rip the dress off her. "I'm not going to walk away when this is over, Ashley. There will be tough times ahead, but this—" He raised his hands to her face, cradled her cheeks in his palms and forced her to look at him. "This—"

She didn't blink. "I know, Joe. Me, too."

It was enough for now. The future with all its complexities could wait. Joe drew her close and pressed a kiss to her forehead, her cheek, the wide, sweet fullness of her mouth. Ashley's hands were on his stomach, at the snap of his jeans but when he looked down, he was even more turned on by the sight of her ringless hand. She'd removed her wedding band. Pleasure filled him, hope.

"What's wrong?"

Joe gently removed the monitor still strapped to her wrist. He carefully set it on the floor beside the lounger before straightening and taking her left hand in his. He stared down at the her fingers, a frown on his face. He wasn't an honorable hero, but he'd spend his days trying to be.

I'll take care of them, Mac.

Joe lifted her left hand to his mouth and kissed where the ring used to be, lingered over the act when her lips parted with a soundless gasp.

The sound of the breeze rustling through the willows between the shed and the house faded into the background. The noise of frogs and crickets converged. But all Joe could concentrate on was Ashley's sweet, heady sighs when he slid his hands over the straps of her dress.

The fabric pooled at their feet and she stood before him in a black bra and panties. The sight alone nearly brought him to his knees.

"You are so beautiful," he whispered, running his hands up her arms, around her shoulders and down her back. He pulled her close with his hands at her hips, and she moaned his name.

The tone of her voice made him still.

"Birth—birth control," she whispered with a frown that said she was having as hard a time thinking straight as he was. "I don't have any. I wasn't planning…"

In that moment Joe was forever thankful for his prison counselor's sense of duty and humor in handing condoms to prisoners on their way out.

"My wallet." He chuckled wryly at her expression. "I'll tell you later, but no, it wasn't intended for someone else," he murmured before pressing his mouth to hers.

His hands skimmed her back, smoothed over tense muscles. And from all the sighs and moans coming from her throat, he was creating a whole other kind of tension, which was a good thing since he wouldn't last long.

He tried to slow himself down, knowing without a doubt Ashley hadn't been with anyone since her husband. The thought was humbling. Tantalizing.

Once again her fingers fiddled with the snap of his jeans, and Joe helped her, gritting his teeth as she eased the denim and briefs over the erection straining toward her.

Ashley pulled away and wet her lips before she gently but firmly shoved him to a seated position on the chaise. Joe smiled and leaned back against the musty cushion, made himself comfortable, more than ready to watch the show as Ashley gave him a shy yet sultry look while she reached behind her to unfasten her bra.

She lifted one shoulder in a shrug, repeated the action and watched him closely as the straps slid down her arms. Biting her lip, she let the scrap of material fall.

Absurdly weak, ready to explode, Joe leaned his head back on the padded lounge with a growl. If he died now, he'd die a happy, happy man.

THE EXPRESSION on Joe's face propelled Ashley to greater heights than she'd ever gone to entice a man. Joe made her feel beautiful and sexy and wanted.

"Come here."

Eager to feel his hands on her she stepped closer, but now that he was seated, the lounge didn't look big enough to hold them both. Unless she was on top, which would leave her fully exposed, vulnerable—*and in control.*

Releasing her lip, she smiled as she swung one leg over both his and let Joe guide her into a sitting position on him, just…there. She settled herself, pleased by the groan that escaped him on contact.

"I'm sorry, Ashley."

She braced her hand on his chest and leaned toward him. "For what?" she murmured, her mouth teasing his while she rocked against him.

"Ash—stop." His hands gripped her hips and held her still, his breathing ragged. "It's been too long. This is too fast. I'm not going to—aww, this is so embarrassing," he ground out between clenched teeth.

She kissed his lightly stubbled jaw and laughed, unable to help herself. Joe was in a bad way and needed release. And more than anything she wanted to give it to him. To be the one to help him since he obviously hadn't gone to someone in town like some men would have.

It was another reason she loved him.

Joe's hands slid up her waist, over her breasts. Distracting her from her thoughts. She watched his face, saw how much she turned him on. His eyes glittered as he raised his head and took her breast into his mouth. He suckled gently first, then firmly, stroking her with his tongue and mimicking the act by pressing her hips against him. She arched her back and moaned.

Then it was her turn. She slipped her hands between them, found him and encircled the hard, hot length.

His breath hissed. *"No."*

She ignored him, pressed her body against the lower length of him. Wanting him, her fingers and hand teased. Then Joe came with a groan full of self-recrimination and pleasure.

WHEN JOE CAME TO HIS SENSES Ashley still straddled his lap and watched him closely, his T-shirt in her hands. A second later, she tossed it aside and smiled a sexy little smile as though she'd conquered the world. All he knew was that she'd certainly conquered him.

He pulled her down to his chest and cradled her against him, his hands moving down her back and over her nicely rounded behind to squeeze. "You don't listen very well."

His hands smoothed back up her body to her hair where he found the clasp holding it fastened.

He released it so he could spear his fingers into the long, thick mass.

Ashley crossed her arms on top of his chest and rested her chin on the top. "You didn't like it?"

Joe chuckled and gently pulled her forward for a kiss. "Liking it obviously wasn't the problem, but I didn't do much for you."

She fingered the hair on his chest. "You needed it and I wanted to. I actually wanted to do more but…"

Her words trailed off and it didn't take long for him to catch on to what she was discreetly asking. She was afraid. And she had every right to be because this was a conversation they should've had before letting things go so far.

He kissed her again. "I'm safe, Ashley. There's a program. Some voluntary government thing. Before I was released I was given free testing."

She looked at him, her solemn gaze asking for his understanding.

"I should've said something sooner. And don't feel bad or embarrassed. I'm the one embarrassed that we even have to talk about it, but between the fights and the shiv, I wanted to know. And you had every reason to be concerned."

Some of the tension left her body. "There's no good way of bringing this into a conversation is there?" she murmured, her eyes lowering. "I didn't even think of it until…*then* and so…"

She'd pleasured him a different way. "I understand."

"With Mac's military background and my pregnancy, the stress of the funeral—they ran all kinds of tests just to be safe. They were fine," she said in a rush, as though she needed to reassure him.

"So we're both fine," he murmured, smiling gently. "Except one of us got the raw end of the deal," he teased as he tugged her hips into his. "Want to see how long it takes me to—"

Ashley's mouth covered his and she kissed him deep, her tongue stroking into his mouth, her breathing picking right back up to a pace that said she might not have found pleasure before, but she was more than ready to try again. He squeezed her hip, slid his hand to her inner thigh.

Max's whimper suddenly filled the air.

"Mmm, noooo. Oh, no." Ashley's shoulders shook. "I'm sorry."

Joe smoothed her hair away from her face before she shoved herself up, and tried to ignore the way she looked sitting on top of him now that he wasn't so trigger-happy.

"He's hungry," she said, her expression drawing a smile from him because it was obvious she was hungry, too.

She got to her feet and whirled around, searching the darkness for her black dress. Max's

whimpers turned into cries that rose in volume
with every breath.

"Here." Joe found her dress and handed it to her.
Ashley pulled it on, leaving the side unzipped. She
hurried to the door of the shed before pausing.

"Joe—"

"Go on. I'm right behind you," he said, picking
up his jeans.

She flashed him a smile and left, scurrying up the
hill away from the pond toward the house. Joe
dressed, aware the air inside the shed was scented
with the smell of sex and arousal and need. He
grabbed his T-shirt from the floor and then stretched
across the lounge chair to pick up the monitor when
Ashley's voice came over the airwaves.

Drawn, knowing he shouldn't, he sat down on
the lounge and waited for Max's story to begin.

"OH, MAX," ASHLEY'S VOICE sounded tinny and far
away. "Somehow we're going to have to work on
your timing."

Joe heard the rocking chair creak.

"Joe's a good guy, you know that? Yes, he is.
But I don't want you to worry, Max. You'll always
be my little man."

Max babbled in response and Joe smiled down
at the monitor.

"But we have to help him. Because as much as
I love Joe, you come first and if Joe can't even

bring himself to touch you because of losing his little girl—"

Joe couldn't breathe. She loved him? She *loved* him? But on the heels of that amazing realization came pain.

She knew.

He couldn't hear the rest of her words due to the rush of blood past his ears. He shook his head, noticed her bra lying on the floor next to his foot and reached down to grab it. He shoved the ends into his pocket and ignored the lacy cups that brought images to mind he couldn't be thinking about at the moment.

"Joe loved his baby, Max. He may have been young, but when he looks at you, I see the pain. He's hurting. But even though he's hurting, and even though the sight of you probably brings back a lot of memories of his baby girl, he's still here helping us. That says something, Max, don't you think? I do. I think it means a lot. I think it means he's one of the good guys."

Joe rubbed his eye with his palm. Things were such a mess and without a doubt, he knew Wilson was involved. The old man had obviously told Ashley bits and pieces, but not the whole truth. And while Ashley understood his loss and pain, that would change once she discovered the so-called truth.

She'd never understand. Would never believe

he'd kept the truth from her in the hopes she'd grow to see him as he is, rather than what people believe him to be.

She thought he'd hired on with honorable intentions, when the reality was she was the only one willing to hire him. Period.

And once she found out about Josie's death, all the love in the world wouldn't matter because she'd never look at him the same again.

Still, he had to tell her. Somehow. Before someone else did.

He owed her that.

Joe leaned back against the lounge chair, his thumb finding the switch on the side of the monitor to turn it off. He didn't have the right to listen in, to enjoy the mother-son bonding moment instead of working up the courage to tell her the truth.

He tried to picture the scene. She'd automatically smile at him as he entered the room, sweet and seductive after what had just happened, then hurt and horror would dawn on her face.

She'd hate him.

Joe shoved himself to his feet and he paced to the end of the small shack, banged his fist against a wood beam.

God above, he needed help, guidance. He didn't want to hurt her, and he had no right to let her think he was something he wasn't. No right to make love to her.

He glared at the house, the dull light trickling out of Max's bedroom window.

Over the past few weeks he'd taken care of the worst of the house repairs. The roof, the ceilings. Now he quickly made a mental list of the projects he knew Ashley couldn't handle on her own.

He'd work hard. Get those biggest projects done and come clean knowing when she kicked him out she could handle the rest of the restoration by herself. It was the only thing he could do.

The right thing to do for the woman he could love but not have.

THE FOLLOWING MORNING Joe borrowed Wilson's truck again and made a run for supplies. He planned on stopping by Ridgewood on his way home, and still get an early start on the wheelchair ramp into Ashley's house. Once that was done, the kitchen would be next. Then he'd find a place for his pop and him to live, come clean with Ashley and leave because he knew she'd want him gone.

He entered Home Depot, his mood sour, but received a only a few curious glances as he made his way to the aisle he needed.

"Hey—Joe?"

Joe spun around. A man stood a couple feet away with thick, decking spindles in both hands.

Joe braced himself for whatever was about to happen. "Yeah?" The man was around his age, maybe a little older, with a receding hairline and the thick build of a one-time athlete.

"You're Joe Brody, right?"

He nodded and backed up. "I don't want any trouble, I just came for supplies."

The guy looked down at his hands and back at him. "Aww, man, you must really be getting a hard time if you think you'll be jumped in a store." He shoved one of the spindles under the other arm and held out his free hand. "I'm Nathan Boyle. I wanted to thank you, that's all."

Come again? Joe searched his brain for recognition. "For what?"

"Helping out my granddad." His face took on a ruddy hue and he dropped his hand to his side. "I've been so busy I hadn't made it over to check his wheelchair and didn't know it had quit on him. Mrs. H. said you got it going again."

Surprised, Joe stared at him, the moment surreal.

"My grandad sure appreciated it. That's his only way of getting around, you know? Without someone pushing him." The guy tossed the spindles back onto a nearby shelf and took a couple steps closer to him, holding out his hand again. "Anyway, I wanted to say thanks. I appreciate what you did for him." His expression turned sheepish. "Hopefully you won't have to do it again, but I know who to call if I can't get it working, right?"

Joe hesitated momentarily before reaching out and shaking the man's hand. "No problem."

"So, you working anywhere?"

Joe nodded. "Yeah. Handyman stuff."

"Good. But if you ever need work, let me know. I've got my own construction business and I can always use help. I'll give you a shot if you need it."

Humbled, grateful, Joe nodded before turning away to continue on down the aisle.

CHAPTER THIRTEEN

ASHLEY FROWNED as she left the house and carried Max on her hip toward the garage. Joe was avoiding her. Last night, although wonderful, could have been better. After she'd put Max down for the second time, she'd quickly showered and left her room with the intention of going to Joe. Instead she'd found the portable receiver hanging on the bedroom doorknob.

She'd stood there, mortified when she remembered what she'd said to Max about loving Joe. Still, somehow, she'd bolstered her courage and padded to his bedroom, hoping to talk and explain her confusing emotions.

Joe wasn't there.

Nor did he come to her room during the night because she'd spent the remaining hours staring up at the ceiling and wondering where he'd gone. Knowing exactly what she'd done—said—wrong.

Stupid, stupid, stupid. Clearly he wasn't ready for that kind of declaration. What were the rules of dating? Never give up the L word too soon? Talk about the quickest way to drive a guy off.

Even though he seemed to be feeling the same way?

She walked around to the carport where she'd parked the truck, only to find it gone.

"He went to get some supplies," Wilson called from the willow trees beyond.

She hadn't seen him through the drooping foliage, but now she headed in his direction and paused once she neared the lawn chair where he sat, the stray dog lying at his feet. She ignored the dog, not wanting to get attached to something that would just leave whenever it wanted.

"Hey, Max. How are the teeth?"

"Not so bad today," she offered, distracted. "Joe's not listed on the account I set up. How can he buy supplies?"

Wilson frowned up at her, his bushy brows low to combat the sun dappling the shade above her head. "Well, now, 'cause I loaned him cash. He said he'd bring the receipt and you could pay me back. We thought it'd be easier since you weren't up yet."

"You gave him cash?"

She heard the sound of a motor and the crunch of gravel as a car drove up to the house, but when no one continued on around to the back of the house, as Joe would have had it been him, she frowned.

"I'd better go see who it is. Be right back." She

hurried to the house, through the kitchen and down the hall, smiling when Max laughed at the bumpy ride on her hip. She opened the front door in time to see two men exit a police car. Neither were smiling.

When they neared the steps, she asked, "Can I—can I help you?"

The older of the two climbed the steps, and Ashley took note of his badge and name tag. Why was the chief of police on her doorstep?

"Are you Ashley Cade?"

"Yes."

"And this is your home?"

"Yes, why?"

"Does Joe Brody live here?"

Her stomach knotted so hard she felt ill. "Yes, but he isn't home at the moment. Is something wrong?"

The chief and his officer exchanged an intense look.

"Ma'am, is the child yours?"

Her spine snapped straight and the air rushed out of her lungs. "Yes, he's mine. Why do you ask?"

The chief swore softly and stared at the windows lining the porch, his gaze moving from spot to spot as though looking to see if Joe was behind one of them.

The deputy handed an envelope to the chief and then tipped his hat before he stepped off the porch and walked back to the patrol car, obviously looking for any sign of Joe.

"No offense, ma'am. I just didn't know if you were the child's mother or simply babysitting him."

"What does that have to do with Joe?" she asked tersely.

The man held up the envelope, his expression darkening even more. "A restraining order's been issued for him."

"By who?"

The man hesitated. "By me. On behalf of my daughter."

She stared, uncomprehending. "Your daughter." All sorts of thoughts came to mind—bad thoughts, horrifying thoughts. "I don't understand. What's he done? What is going on?" Her voice revealed her growing upset.

The man stared at her a long moment as though searching for something, but when he didn't find it, he reached behind him to pull out his wallet. He flipped through a couple pictures before holding one up for her to see.

Ashley frowned. "She's a beautiful baby." The infant was dressed in a pink dress and ruffled bloomers, the bow atop her head attached to a surprisingly thick thatch of dark hair.

"She was."

Her voice shook when she weakly murmured, "Was?"

Chief York turned the picture around and stared at it himself, and when he raised his gaze back to her, he looked sad, tormented. And angry.

Very, very angry.

"The man you have living here as your *handyman*—under the same roof as your son," he continued, glancing at Max briefly, "was convicted of murdering her. Joe Brody killed my granddaughter. If I were you, I'd pack his bag and have it waiting on him when he gets back. If not, I might have to make a phone call or two about how you're not looking out for your son's best interests." He nodded at Max. "I'll do whatever it takes to keep your son safe."

AS JOE DROVE UP to the house he looked for Ashley, but saw no signs of her outside. He parked the truck close to the back porch to unload and grabbed the receipt lying on the bench seat next to him.

That's when he heard the arguing.

Ashley's voice was raised, Wilson's much calmer and more resigned.

Joe jogged for the porch steps and entered the kitchen to notice two things: the official document from the Taylorsville Police Department on the table with his name on it; and Ashley's pale angry face.

She stared at him, unblinking, shaking her head back and forth as she held up her hand. A long moment passed before she gathered herself enough to speak.

"I can't believe it. You're finally here and now that you are, I don't even know what to say to you!"

Joe stepped toward her. "What happened? Where's Max? You don't want to upset him."

Her face softened even as her eyes blazed. "Don't you dare. Don't you dare pretend you care about my son because if you did, you wouldn't be here in the first place!"

He took another step toward her only to stop when she held her hand up again.

"Stay away from me."

Give me a walk in the moonlight. He wanted to go back in time, freeze it after she'd said those words and then somehow, someway, explain.

"Ashley, don't be scared—"

"Scared? Scared is having the police show up on my doorstep claiming my handyman is a *murderer!*" Her voice shook, her hands. Her entire body. Joe wondered how she still managed to stay on her feet she trembled so badly.

"Give me a chance—"

"Every time I close my eyes I see her sweet little face. I can't get her out of my head!"

He knew the feeling. Not that he ever wanted to rid himself of Josie's memory.

"You killed her!"

"No." His hands fisted. His stomach churned.

Joe fought back the urge to puke, his thoughts on the day he'd come there looking for his father's things and saw her on the stairs with Max.

"Get out."

"Now, missy—"

"Get out!"

Joe couldn't move, his feet rooted to the spot while hurt lanced deep, stronger and more painful than the shiv slashing through his body.

She ran toward him then, fists raised, but he still didn't move because he deserved every smack and slap Ashley gave him as she tried to push him back out the door. Deserved them for not telling Ashley the truth. For not being able to save Josie.

Wilson followed them, tossed his walker aside and grabbed hold of Ashley, his old wrinkled hands smoothing down her arms as he tried to calm her down. Joe couldn't look at the old man. All he could do was stare into Ashley's pain-filled, *betrayed* expression and blame himself.

The old man nearly lost his balance when Ashley pulled away from him, her breath rushing in and out of her chest in ragged gasps. Tears trickled unheeded down her cheeks.

Once again Joe pictured her as she was last night in the shed, so beautiful, and now, so heart-broken. He'd done that to her.

"Joe, take a walk," Wilson ordered. "Go for a

drive. Come back in awhile when we've had a chance to talk things out."

"There's nothing to talk about," Ashley insisted, establishing some distance between herself and them.

Before Joe's eyes her barriers went up, and she was once again the kid from the orphanage, one of the mutts no one wanted. He saw it in her stance. Her expression. No matter what was said now, she wouldn't listen. Wouldn't believe that he wanted her and Max more than he wanted his next breath.

"*You* are leaving," she growled, her voice hoarse and thready. "You're fired, you hear me? You're done!"

Wilson frowned and he raised a hand in exasperation and motioned to Joe. "Well, don't just stand there, boy, tell her. Explain! Show her you care!"

Ashley's laugh revealed her thoughts, and he knew exactly what she was thinking, remembering. And the relief on her face that things had been interrupted before they could make love completely made his heart ache.

He stepped forward, deliberately placing himself in smacking range again. Then waited until she stopped glaring at Wilson long enough to focus on him. "I didn't hurt Josie. I swear to you, Ashley, I didn't."

Her eyes filled with tears once more. "The

police and your prison record say differently," she choked out before she turned and stomped from the room. "Get your stuff and get out of my house before I do what he asked and call him to come get you."

ASHLEY RAN UPSTAIRS and plucked Max from his crib. She held him close, Josie's image in her head. That image changed to a tiny casket and she shuddered in fear. Max protested her hold with a whimper.

"I'm sorry. I'm sorry, baby, I'm sorry. Mommy didn't know."

She paced the floor of her bedroom, unable to sit still, then peeked outside to make sure the hall was clear before hurrying down the stairs and out the door with Max in her arms.

How could she have been so stupid? She'd identified Joe as a bad boy as soon as he'd walked into her kitchen, confirmed it when she'd commented on his tattoo and he'd admitted to being in prison, and yet she'd allowed Wilson to wave away her concerns over his references and Joe to— Well, to charm her with his quiet manners and haunted good looks.

Murder.

Murder. Hal York had explained it all. But what had really shocked her beyond Joe's act of shaking his baby girl to *death,* earning a manslaughter charge, was learning Josie's mother was none other than Melissa York. There was a connection she'd never have otherwise put together. Joe and Melissa.

She moaned and used one hand to wipe away the annoying tears trickling down her cheeks. Her heart ached for the woman. To have been so young, practically a baby herself, when she'd lost her little girl. And now cancer? Sometimes life just didn't make sense.

Ashley raised her head and groaned when she discovered she'd walked to the shed. Memories bombarded her. Joe's touch, his whispered words, the revealing look on his face as he'd climaxed.

It was a conspiracy. Everyone knew about Joe, about what was going on. Everyone but her.

Joe was packing now, would be gone soon. Then what? With Joe gone the repairs on her house would stop, but who cared? Max would be safe.

From a man who said he didn't do it?

"Every criminal says they didn't do it," she mumbled to Max, moving to the dock. She sat down and placed Max on her lap, remembering how she'd lain awake last night dreaming of Joe making love to her.

"Oh, Max, didn't I learn anything from watching the delinquents going in and out of the home? They lied. They cheated. They did whatever it took to stay one step ahead of the game. Joe's no different."

Or maybe he's telling the truth.

She shook her head, glad that Max was content with simply being outdoors, since she was doing well to breathe on her own after everything she'd learned. Ashley pressed her palm to her pounding head while Max gurgled out a long line of gibberish.

Josie.

How could anyone hurt a child like that?

Something cold brushed her arm and she turned with a gasp to find the stray mutt staring at them, mouth open, its body hunched low as though unsure of its welcome.

She fought her panic and eyed the dog's big, sharp teeth, concentrated instead on its wagging tail. That was a good thing. Right?

She grabbed Max's hand when he reached out for the animal. "Max, no!" The dog's ears quirked up at her voice and his head lowered even more. "Go on. Go away!"

The dog hunched lower, its stomach nearly dragging the deck.

"I'm not in the mood for you today, dog, so go."

It whimpered pitifully.

"Go! Go on, *go!*" She turned her back to the dog and made sure Max kept his hands to himself. She didn't think the dog was harmful, but who knew? She hadn't thought Joe was harmful, either.

The dog whimpered again and its nails scratched along the planks. She glanced over her shoulder and found sad brown eyes watching her from where it lay. She turned back to the water, to the trees, and tried to find the peace this spot had always brought her before.

Before Joe. Before falling in love. Before learning she was a lousy judge of character.

Scratch, scratch.

Ashley glanced back and saw the dog crawl until it was close enough to press its cold doggy nose against her leg. When she didn't say anything, its gaze flicked to hers briefly before it released another whimper and belly-scooted another inch or two. This time it had the nerve to lay its head alongside her knee, near Max.

Seemingly satisfied, the dog didn't move, although Ashley had a hard time keeping Max from reaching for the animal with both hands.

Just as he'd reach for Joe.

The tears came again. She'd loved her husband, but she'd never felt their lovemaking as strongly as she had when she was with Joe. Never felt such pleasure at the simple act of *giving* pleasure. Never imagined falling in love with a murderer.

Still, she wouldn't be one of those needy, desperate women willing to risk everything just to keep from being alone.

I didn't hurt Josie. I swear to you, I didn't.

She kissed Max's head. "I'll protect you, bugaboo. Don't worry. Joe will be long gone when we get back."

And she'd miss him.

JOE WASN'T GONE when she got back to the house. She'd crossed the distance with her loping shadow following her, and spied Joe's large form on the back porch. Angry, she carried Max through the front door instead and was about to take him upstairs to his crib before confronting Joe when Wilson appeared.

"Don't go runnin' away again."

Her spine stiffened. "I'm not *running* any-where, Wilson."

"What are you doin' then?" the old man pressed. "We've been waitin' on you so we could talk to you."

And she recognized an ambush when she saw one. "Why is he still here?"

"Joe's workin'. He got a late start on the ramp, but he's trying to get it done before the rain hits later in the week."

Joe was still *working?* She wasn't sure what to make of that. If she could make anything of it at all. "I told him to leave. He should've been gone by now."

"Well, if you thought that you ain't as smart as I told him you were." Wilson wagged a finger at her. "Now don't go givin' me the evil eye. Ain't gonna do you no good."

"Lucky me."

The old man chuckled. "There you go. Gettin' back to your old self now that you've had some time to think things through."

The laugh erupting from her chest was anything but amused. "That's right. I've thought things through and know my ordering Joe to leave was the right decision to make, and if you don't like it," she continued, raising her voice when Wilson opened his mouth to argue, "*tough!* This is my home, Wilson. You sold it to me, *I* own it. The deed says so."

Wilson stared at her, his expression disappointed. She hated that he looked at her like that.

"Then Joe can stay with me in my rooms down here."

"No, he can't. Wilson, please—"

His brows rose even as his mouth turned down in a scowl. "You cain't tell me who can stay with me and who can't. That weren't part of our bargain. I say he's stayin'. Now, you fixin' anything for dinner?"

The gall of the man astounded her, and Ashley knew she wouldn't gain any ground with him in the mood he was in. Emotions ran too high. She ignored Wilson as best she could and stalked to the stairs.

"Now, missy—"

"Don't 'now missy' me," she said, pausing at the bottom. "I've had it up to here—" she made a slashing motion with her hand "—with all the down home, countrified, good ole boy talk about belonging and family and loyalty and—and *crap!* It's bogus, Wilson! I've cooked for you, cleaned for you, taken care of you after your hip replacement *despite* the terms of our agreement, and in return you *lie* to me?" Her voice cracked, thickened with tears she tried to control. Max picked up on her upset and began to fuss, and Ashley bounced him with a quieting murmur.

"I never lied to you. I didn't tell you about Joe's past 'cause it's done and over and he didn't do it anyway."

She stared in open-mouthed shock. "So that makes it okay? You should be on *my* side!"

"Ain't about sides, missy. It's about right and wrong. The boy didn't—"

"Don't," Joe said quietly. He walked down the hall toward them, his boots thudding gently on the wood floors. "Leave it alone, Wilson. She's angry with me so let her talk to me."

Still bouncing Max, she shook her head. "Not likely. I have nothing to say to you, you lying—"

"I never lied to you."

"Gee, where have I heard that before?" she growled with another glance at Wilson's pouting face. "You neglected to tell me a *crucial* part of your history. What's the difference between that and lying?"

"Sounds like you got more to say to him than

you think," Wilson muttered. "I'll just go on in there and sit a spell."

Ashley stared at Joe and wished she could read his mind. Then she remembered the feel of his hands on her and all she'd told him, shared with him. Her tone softened, but not her resolve. "I understand what it's like to want a second chance, Joe, but for Max's sake, it can't be here."

"I didn't hurt her." His face darkened, and his glance slid to where Wilson had disappeared, then back to her before he stepped close. Ashley fought the instinctive urge to back away.

"I'm sorry I didn't tell you. You cut me off that day in my room and I let you. I let you because I didn't want you looking at me the way you are right now. I should have told you last night, but," he closed his eyes briefly, "things were going so well I didn't want to ruin it."

"You mean you were about to get laid," she murmured, "and you didn't want to risk it not happening."

He took another step toward her and it was everything she could do to hold her ground. Not because she was afraid, but because she wanted to believe him, but knew better.

"If you'll remember I still could have been *laid*," he growled out, "after you put Max to bed. But I heard you talking to Max and I knew I couldn't let things go further without your knowing the truth. Ashley, I told you last night I wouldn't walk away from you. What we have—"

"We have *nothing*. It—everything I *thought* we had—was all a lie."

His gaze narrowed on her. "You said you loved me."

Ashley couldn't help it, she snickered, laughing at the irony of the situation. Yeah, she'd said that. She'd finally found someone who'd seemed to care for her, someone who worked hard and helped her toward her dream. She'd even gone one further and fallen in love with him and what did she have to show for it?

A murderer stood in her house.

"What if our situations were reversed, Joe? What if I were a nanny or maid or something and you hired me to work in your house only to find out—"

"It was a mistake. My mistake. I should've told you right from the beginning. I didn't and I'm sorry, but try to understand *why* I didn't."

"Because you're a murderer!"

Joe flinched at her glib tone, and Ashley felt more than a hint of shame.

"Because you didn't know me well enough to know I wasn't."

She still didn't. "All of this has made me realize I don't know you at all. I thought I did, but you've proven me very, very wrong."

Joe's face resembled stone. A muscle twitched

along his jaw, before his attention dropped to Max. Her arms tightened protectively.

"Fine. You want nothing to do with me. I get that. But until I get this house to where you can handle the rest of the restoration yourself, I'm staying...as Wilson's guest if nothing else."

She shook her head firmly. "No way. The police were here, remember? I don't want children's services showing up and claiming I'm endangering Max because you're here."

Even though he'd never been alone with Max? Had taken pains to avoid him knowing full well this conversation would take place eventually? Had Joe deliberately kept his distance, not because of Josie, but because of Max and how she'd feel right now?

Joe ran a hand over his head, his face. "Look, believe it or not no one wanted to hurt you. Wilson and I, we just wanted to give you a chance to get to know me. So you'd see I could *never* harm a child."

"The chief told me all about the evidence."

"I'll bet he did," he muttered wearily.

Ashley stared at him, lost in the depths of Joe's eyes and wondering how he could sound so sincere if he were lying.

Good liars lie well.

And honest people spoke the truth with a conviction that matched Joe's.

Wilson came back into the hall then, making her think he'd only slid around the corner and been eavesdropping the entire time. "We can go round and round if you want, missy, but it comes down to this—if you want to open by spring, you need help and Joe's it. Everything else aside, you make Joe leave and you can kiss your business and Max's future goodbye."

She silently pleaded with the old man to understand. She wasn't the bad guy, Joe was! But she saw no softening in Wilson's gaze. No, as far as sides went, Wilson was definitely on Joe's.

She swallowed, furious, disillusioned. More tired than she'd ever been in her life.

"If you didn't hurt your daughter, who did?" she asked bluntly.

Joe shook his head, his blue eyes bleak and pained. "I don't know. But I confronted Melissa the other day, which is probably why the restraining order was issued."

"You think she shook her baby to death?" She didn't know Melissa York at all, but she just couldn't imagine the woman doing something so horrible. Besides she'd read enough baby books cover to cover to know most incidents of shaken baby syndrome were almost always caused by the father, usually in his teens or early twenties, and inexperienced with child care.

Like Joe.

But Joe had never once shown signs of temper or anger when Max cried. If anyone had, it was her.

So what now?

"If you want to keep your job, you'll have to find somewhere else to live," she murmured finally, her voice hoarse.

"Now, missy—"

"I'll move into the shed," Joe readily agreed. "I've slept in worse. I need to save my cash since Pop's getting out of the nursing home soon."

She ignored the despair in his tone, ignored the shaming glance Wilson sent her. "You can take bedding and towels. One of the twin mattresses. There's already a shower," she said, trying to get the mental image of Joe using the outside shower from her head. "I'll…I'll fix your meals and all that like we agreed. It's the best compromise I can offer that will allow you to stay and still keep the chief of police from siccing children's services on me."

"It's fine."

"And Max is off—"

"Now, missy—"

"I'll keep my distance."

Ashley stared at Joe, hurt, torn, numb and yet not nearly numb enough. "Good," she said before turning her back on him and hurrying up the stairs, placing her cheek to Max's head to hide her tears. "Make sure that you do."

CHAPTER FOURTEEN

JOE HADN'T TAKEN A DAY OFF since he'd started working on the house so after watching Ashley cart Max out to her car and strap him in, he decided to go back to the nursing home and see his dad. Twenty minutes later he let himself into his father's room.

"You're back!" his dad called from the bed. "Just in time for a game of checkers. Remember when we used to play and your mother— What's wrong?"

He swung a straight-backed chair around and straddled it. "That girl found out, didn't she? You tell her or did some busybody get to her first?"

"Hal."

His father reached for the phone.

"No, Pop, forget it."

"That man don't have a lick of sense if he can't see—"

"It doesn't matter now. What were you going to say?"

His old man lifted his head to peer over his bifocals. "What's that you're holding?"

Joe laughed warily as he stared down at the book Mrs. H. had handed him on the way in, not so sure he wanted to admit what he'd agreed to do just to change the subject. "Guess I've been chosen to read the next chapter of this for the ladies out in the cafeteria." He eyed the man and woman on the cover of the book and felt his face flush. "Don't come out there this time, all right? It was hard enough reading that mystery out loud, and it was as tame as it got."

"Let me see— Have I read that?"

Joe glanced at his pop in surprise. "Huh?"

His old man waved a hand. "You know how much your mama liked those books. Had hundreds of them. When she died and you were away the house got awfully lonely. Think that might be one of hers. I read 'em all and then donated them when I moved in."

Joe opened the cover and glanced inside. Sure enough his mother's name was in the top corner. A sad smile lit his face. "I'd forgotten Ma liked these."

"Sure did." His pop winked at him. "Made for some fine nights."

Joe groaned. "That's way more than I wanted to know, Pop."

"So what happened? That girl kick you out?"

"Yeah. I'm going to stay in the screened shed by the pond." He held up the hand holding the book to stop his father's protest, but frowned at himself when the gesture reminded him of Ashley. "I volunteered to do it."

"Why?"

"Because…I don't know. I hired on for a job and I want to finish it. When it's done, I'll leave."

"You can't stay in Wilson's fishing shed all winter."

"I'm just going to get the hardest of the work done and then turn things over to her. One of your buddies here in the home—Boyle? His grandson offered me a job working construction. I'll give him a call when I'm ready to move on."

His father grumbled and fidgeted beneath his sheets. "It ain't right. Don't she know—"

"She's got a baby boy, remember? And she grew up in a home for kids. She's afraid Hal will turn her in for endangering the little boy if I'm living there."

"But you didn't—"

"I *know*," he said, cutting him off before his pop could get on a roll defending him. "But that's the way it is."

"Haven't seen that look on your face in a while."

"What do you mean?"

His dad pointed to the book. "Lovesick. You're sittin' there saying you'll move on, but you don't want to. You like this girl."

Joe tapped the book on the top of the chair as he stood. "Maybe, but it doesn't matter since there's no way to prove I didn't kill Josie."

"People get out of prison every day. They walk among us and we don't know it, how're you any different?"

Joe shook his head. He liked the fact his dad still defended him. Still believed in him. Jack hadn't. Now Ashley.

She'd grown up without having that kind of support. How could she trust in something she had never experienced?

She'd said herself that Mac had been several years older than her, which left her in the children's home struggling to survive and not believing in anything she couldn't experience firsthand.

So show her the difference. Show her you believe in her enough to ignore her lack of faith in you.

"Thanks, Pop."

"For what?"

Joe leaned over the bed and hugged him. "For always believing in me. Ashley never had that."

He'd always known his father was a smart man, but when Ted Brody grinned up at him, Joe knew he'd caught on to his line of thinking.

"Well, now, maybe it's time she did."

Joe laughed gruffly. "Maybe it is."

ASHLEY COULDN'T BELIEVE her eyes. She'd just walked into the nursing home over half an hour late for her meeting with Mrs. Hilliard only to find Joe sitting in the middle of the cafeteria reading—

she pressed a hand over her mouth to hold in her laughter—a *romance?*

Although low, his deep voice carried and she was able to make out his words. Oh, definitely a romance. She blinked, still unable to take in the sight of him surrounded by twenty or so women, a couple men, each and every one of them hanging on his every word.

"I see you've noticed our Joe," Mrs. Hilliard said as she walked up behind her.

"Our...Joe?" Could Mrs. Hilliard not know?

"Yes, he's quite a dear. Every day he comes in to see his father, came twice today, and he never minds pitching in to help us."

Joe got to a scene in the book where the hero took the heroine into his arms. His face was turning redder by the second, but other than giving one of the ladies near him a sideways glance, he mumbled his way through the kiss and into the next scene.

Ashley glanced at Mrs. Hilliard and found the other woman's gaze on her instead of him. "He...pitches in?"

Apparently that was the question Mrs. Hilliard waited for because the woman nodded, smiling. "He fixed Mr. Boyle's chair, hung a picture for Marge over there and he found one of the staff moving a bed and did it for her." Mrs. Hilliard motioned for Ashley to lean low so she could whisper in her ear. "Poor dear, the girl's pregnant and sick as a dog, but she's just hired on. Anyway, our Joe, he saw her running for the bathroom when she was halfway through moving the bed, so he finished the job for her."

"That's...nice." Not to mention considerate. Sweet, thoughtful.

For a murderer.

Stop it.

"Yes, he even allowed Carl to give him a haircut despite the man being mostly blind." Mrs. Hilliard laughed softly. "The poor man misses his barbershop so badly but lost his sight because of diabetes."

Ashley made the appropriate noises, her attention locked solely on Joe.

"With no sight, you can imagine how off Carl's cut was, so after he finished with Joe I asked another patron to trim him up and fix the damage."

"Is that right?"

Mrs. Hilliard nodded, sighing. "Our Sam, he wasn't too thrilled at the prospect, but after I'd explained what happened, he helped Joe out. Quite handsome, isn't he, dear?"

Ashley blinked. "Huh? Oh, yes. I mean, well, sure, but—"

Mrs. Hilliard patted her on the arm. "Come along, Ashley. Show me what you've brought besides young Max. Unless you'd like to stay and hear the story?"

That appealed to her way more than it should've. "No, no, that's fine." She hefted Max higher on her side. "But…maybe you could tell me more about…"

"Joe?"

She smiled, probably a little too brightly. Mrs. Hilliard didn't need to know everything. "Yeah, Joe. What else do you, uh, know about him?"

Two hours later there was no sign of Joe when Ashley carried Max back through the nursing home. She'd spent the time sharing a picnic table in the shade with Mrs. Hilliard and two other ladies from the garden club the older woman had invited to help finalize Ashley's landscape design.

Ashley was nervous at the prospect of spending the afternoon with two strangers, but Mrs. Hilliard had filled in the gaps and kept things going. It had been a fun time once Ashley took her cues from Mrs. Hilliard and asked questions to keep the ladies talking about themselves.

Genuine interest went a long way in breaking the ice and allowing her to relax and enjoy. They'd debated over boxwoods or holly bushes, variegated ivies versus plain and finally came up with a colorful sketch Ashley couldn't wait to get started on.

But once the two ladies had left early to complete some shopping, Ashley stayed because Mrs. Hilliard began to recite story after story about

Joe growing up. What good grades he'd made, how he'd always helped out.

Mrs. Hilliard's accounting of Joe's life was definitely interesting, especially when she got to the part about Joe dating Melissa York.

"Oh, dear, listen to me. I've gone on and on. Poor Max is tired and so am I, dear. Perhaps you can come visit me again soon. Maybe you'll run into Joe yourself." Her gaze turned speculative. "Unless you'd like me to introduce you now?"

Ashley managed a smile at the woman's matchmaking, aghast she'd suggest such a thing when she had to know of Joe's prison term given everything else she knew about him. And torn because Mrs. Hilliard had suggested it as though she recognized Joe as a nice guy and not the hardened, dangerous man the chief had made him out to be. Which was true?

She wanted to press for more answers, more insight, but couldn't, not without giving herself away. So instead she'd arranged to come back to visit the next week and said her goodbyes. Now she drove up behind the house and saw Joe leave the back porch and walk toward the shed. He had to have heard her car coming up the drive, seen her lights, but he didn't look back.

Guilt nagged and she shook it off. No, she had to stand firm. The chief had come right out and said he'd do whatever was necessary to keep Max safe from Joe if she wouldn't. No way would she test Hal York to see if he'd follow through with his threat.

A part of her said it was none of his business, but the other part of her knew of too many children who wouldn't have survived their home life if not for the involvement of law enforcement and case workers.

Joe sleeping in the shed was the best compromise she could offer, and she hoped the police would accept that as her doing her part as Max's parent, since Joe had no contact with Max and no reason now that they weren't…whatever.

Rubbing her temples, she got out of the car and carried a sleeping Max into the house, painfully aware of the emptiness within the walls. Joe wasn't there raiding the fridge alongside Wilson, wasn't sitting on the couch watching her while she played with Max. Wasn't there ready to discuss her dreams and goals, acting as though they were important to him as well.

Ashley sighed, then twisted the latch on the door, locking Joe out of her house.

If only she could've locked him out of her heart so easily.

FOUR DAYS LATER Ashley was ready to pull her hair out.

The morning after kicking Joe out of her house and into the shed, he'd shown up for breakfast looking as tired as she felt. She'd tossed and turned all night, her thoughts consumed by all Mrs. Hilliard had said. Now days had passed and she still wasn't any closer to a solution.

She wet her dry lips and murmured a good morning, but other than returning the greeting and shaking off the rain that had started coming down outside, Joe said nothing else.

Wilson gave her a baleful glare at the obvious tension between them, but she ignored the old man and the three of them sat around the table in uncomfortable silence like they'd done the past few mornings. Only the scrape of forks and the crunch of bacon could be heard in between Max's jabbers and squeals.

Joe practically inhaled his breakfast and stood. "I'll go sand the ceiling upstairs, then move the furniture out of the foyer. I thought you might want to get started on that while I paint the ceiling."

Which would keep them on separate floors of the house and Joe far away from Max.

You told him to stay away, remember?

Yes, but now she felt guilty. Torn because Joe had tried talking to her several times over the last couple of days and she'd simply cut him off, unwilling to listen to a word he said in defense.

"Fine."

"Fine."

"Fools."

Joe ignored Wilson and walked out of the room, but she couldn't let his comment pass. "Don't," she said immediately. "Things are bad enough without you calling us names."

Wilson grumbled to himself but Ashley didn't care. She stood and gathered up her plate, ready to get to work and concentrate on something else.

Concentrate? Yeah, right.

"I'm going out today. Don't make lunch for me."

Ashley turned to Wilson. "I—I was kind of hoping you'd give me a hand with Max since you've been gone and in your room so much."

"Nope."

"Wilson, if this is about Joe—"

"'Course it's about Joe. You're on your own, missy. 'Til you realize Joe wouldn't harm a hair on that boy's head, I ain't babysittin' so you can forget it."

So much for gratitude.

"And if the chief calls children's services?"

"If he this, if he that. Who cares?"

"*I* do!"

"Hal wouldn't take a baby away from his mama unless he's bein' neglected or abused."

"I'm not willing to chance you're wrong. He obviously hates Joe."

"That man's blind and so are you. You've let other people dictate and rule your life, tell you how to feel about yourself. It's about time you stood up for what you want." Wilson turned on his slippered heel and hurried from the room as fast as the walker could take him.

Ashley looked down at Max and found his big eyes staring at her in question. "Don't you look at me that way, too. I'm doing this for you."

Was she? Or was she doing what Wilson said and protecting herself from Joe? Things had moved fast, they'd nearly made love. Was she using Joe's past as a barrier?

It *is* a barrier.

So go talk to him. Find out what happened. Hear him out and then decide now that you've calmed down.

Her head pounded out a protest even as her feet propelled her forward.

JOE STARED AT THE BACK of Ashley's head. "What?"

"Tell me about your daughter," she repeated softly, her back to him while she spread moss-green paint on the opposite wall to where he was finishing up the second coat of paint on the ceiling.

Max was positioned in the doorway of the room, technically in the hall out of the way of the fumes. He pounded away with a rattle, his concentration intense.

Ashley had put the boy in a stationary car, so he was able to turn and play with toys lining the attached shelf, but unable to get out or into mischief.

"Well? You've tried to talk to me a couple of times and I wouldn't listen, but now…I'm ready."

"What changed?"

"Are you going to tell me about her or not?"

Joe rewet his roller and went back to work. Silence stretched between them. Finally he decided to take the tentative peace offering. At least she'd hear his side this way.

"Her name was Josie," he murmured. "Anna Josephine, but we called her Josie."

"Pretty name."

He didn't comment. "She was tiny, a preemie. Melissa had just lost her mom and was having a hard time dealing with it so her blood pressure was all over the place. She went into premature labor.

"Even though she was a preemie, Josie looked like an angel. She wasn't red or cone-headed or anything. She was small, barely three pounds." He grinned. "Fifteen inches long." Joe paused, his thoughts in the past, so proud when Mel had placed Josie in his arms. "I could hold her in my hand with her head on my fingers and her feet only came my wrist."

"But she was okay?"

Ashley's voice prodded him on. Looking down at the paint-spattered plastic, he nodded. "Yeah, everybody was afraid her lungs weren't developed enough, but the doc said they were fine."

"Dr. Booker?"

He shook his head. "No, he's new. This was one of the old docs, Peters. Don't know where he's at now. He was the old Doc Booker's competition."

"Did you like being a dad?"

Joe glanced at Ashley, expecting to find some sort of criticism in her expression, but instead he found curiosity, concern. "I loved it." He went back to work because it was easier to talk about Josie when he didn't just stand there and think.

"Mel and I, with everything going on with her mom's passing, she decided to break up with me. I'd asked her to marry me when we found out about the pregnancy, but she refused."

"That must have been hard."

Joe nodded. "It was, but now I see her side of things. She was overwhelmed, confused. We'd dated for a while, necked, but never gone all the way until her mom was on the brink. She passed away and now I see that's why Mel slept with me. The fact she got pregnant only made things worse for her."

He tossed the roller into the pan and stalked over to the open window. Rain continued to pour outside and the walls were closing in on him.

"A day hasn't passed that I haven't asked myself what went wrong." He shrugged. "But once the docs said it was shaken baby syndrome, and almost always the father, that was it. The thing is, other than the brain damage the autopsy showed, Josie had no bruises, no marks at all. Nothing to judge the size of a person's fingers. Everything was perfect and matched the exam she'd had at the doctor's office a few days earlier. Josie was completely healthy until—" He broke off, cursed softly then regretted the word. He glanced at Max before turning back to the window and scrubbing a hand over his face to wipe away the tears burning his lids.

Ashley touched his arm and turned him to face her. Shaking, she raised a hand to his cheek. "Oh, Joe."

"Mel asked me to come over," he murmured, inhaling the sweet scent of Ashley's hair and drawing strength from it. "She said Josie had cried off and on all day and she couldn't take it anymore. That she needed a break and thought I'd like to see her."

"Didn't she call the doctor?"

"She said she couldn't call every time she cried, and that she thought Josie had picked up on her frustration. She asked me to come over and watch her so she could get out of the house for a while."

He pulled away, needing some distance to get it all out. "I went. Mel and I had been fighting a lot because she said since we'd broken up I shouldn't be hanging out there all the time. She said it looked bad and people would talk even more." His laugh was rough. "I thought I was doing the right thing. That if I went over as much as I could, I could help with Josie and maybe get Mel to see she didn't have to do things on her own. That I wanted to be a part of Josie's life."

Joe forced himself to turn and stalk across the room to the other window, away from Ashley. Farther away from Max. "Josie was asleep when I got there and even though the timing was lousy, I asked Mel to marry me. She turned me down again and left. Josie woke up crying. She didn't have a temperature, didn't want to eat, nothing. So I walked her, rubbed her back, her belly. Nothing worked."

He smiled sadly. "Part of the prosecution's so-called proof was that I was angry with Mel because she'd turned me down. They said I took my upset out on my little girl." He stared at the floor. No matter how many times he'd told the story, to his dad, to Mel, to Hal and the judge, it never got any easier.

"Then she stopped crying." He shook his head but couldn't get the image out of his mind, the feel of her in his arms. "Just like that, she stopped." He leaned his head against the cool glass. "She opened her eyes, looked at me, then closed her eyes again like she'd gone to sleep." The lump in his throat grew larger. "She stopped breathing, shook. She died and I just sat there and watched it happen. I didn't know what to do…I couldn't save her."

"Joe—"

He turned bleak eyes toward her and Ashley felt his pain, his overwhelming heartache. Felt it dig deep into her mother's soul.

"I didn't know what to do. I wasted precious seconds thinking I'd missed something, waiting on her to breathe again. Finally I realized she wasn't and called the ambulance but it was too late. She died in my arms."

Ashley didn't know what to say. What could you say to someone who'd experienced what he had? The chief had been adamant that Joe had killed his granddaughter, but now after hearing Joe's side of things, after witnessing for herself the horror and the pain Joe had endured—

She wasn't so sure. But neither was she convinced, considering he'd spent ten years behind bars for Josie's death. She was so confused.

"You'd better go take care of him."

Only then did Max's fussy whimpers reach her ears. She turned toward Max, hoping he'd hush so they could still talk. "Joe—"

"Take care of your son, Ashley. I'll finish things up here."

TWO DAYS LATER it was still raining, Ashley was beyond exhausted, and she was getting more frustrated by the second. Wilson got up and left every morning with one excuse or another, which severely limited her time and focus on the house.

Joe continued to avoid Max. When they did happen to cross paths, Joe circled around him or exited the room, didn't talk to him or acknowledge him even though Max stared at Joe more often than not during his nonstop gibberish sessions.

Max wasn't used to being ignored, and he got upset by the fact Joe didn't pay him any attention.

Upset enough that now every time Max got tired of his exercise ring and she placed him on the floor, he was off like a shot, crawling across the room as though setting out to find Joe and figure out why he wanted nothing to do with him.

She usually caught Max in plenty of time before Joe noticed, but now she looked up from what she was doing to find Joe staring at Max with an expression nothing short of heartbreaking.

All because Max had used Joe's leg to pull himself up and now stood with his head tilted all the way back as he stared up at Joe's face. Max wobbled and held on, wrinkled his little nose and grinned, proudly displaying the tooth that had finally managed to break through. But just when Joe started to smile he caught himself and turned back to his work.

Ashley hurried over and plucked Max from the floor. "Sorry."

"No problem."

"Da."

Ashley froze and stared at Max. No way. "Did he just say— Max, did you just say—"

"Da-da-da-da-da-da."

Ashley laughed, amazed that her baby had said his first word—words!—and looked up to share her excitement only to see Joe stalk from the room.

She stared down at her son, her smile fading fast. "Oh, Max," she murmured, hugging him close. "He didn't do it, did he?" She kissed his cheek and sighed, smoothed a hand over his fine hair and kissed him again. "What happened to Josie?"

CHAPTER FIFTEEN

JOE CURSED AS HIS eyes opened and he realized a shadow loomed over him. Of all times for his senses to fail him.

He lunged up off the lounge chair where he'd slept, grabbed the person and twisted so that he'd land with him on top, belatedly recognizing the person was Ashley. He shifted again but it was too late, half his body crashed down on top her.

"Oof!"

He shoved himself to an elbow and pushed the hair off her face. "What are you— Don't ever sneak up on me like that."

Wide eyes stared up at him and each breath that panted out of her chest hit his mouth with the scent of mint and woman. "I'm sorry. I didn't think—"

He closed his thoughts off from where her nearness led them. "What are you doing here?"

Her expression firmed at his tone. After Max used his leg for a pulley, he supposed she had every right to be angry with him since he hadn't managed to stay away from her son, but he'd done the next best thing and stayed away from both of them the rest of the day. Now she was here?

"Stupid man, don't you know enough to come in out of danger?"

He stared.

"The rain! The pond's overflowing and the shed is built over the water!"

Joe leaned over the side of the lounge to look at the floor and did indeed see water just beginning to come through the cracks. "So you came down here to—"

"Tell you to come to the house."

He shoved himself to his feet. "I'll be fine."

"You're not staying here."

"The pond has a spillway on the other side, it won't get any higher than it is now."

"Says who?"

"*Me.*"

Somehow they'd wound up shouting at each other. Joe stared down at her sprawled form, all too conscious of her long bare legs stretched out and parted before him.

"Go back to the house." He reluctantly held out a hand to help her up.

"Not without you," she challenged. Ashley ignored him and pushed herself to her elbows, onto her feet. "Come on, this is stupid."

"What about children's services?"

"This is an emergency—and we can talk inside.

Come on!" She pressed her hands to his bare chest and shoved firmly.

Joe reached for his jeans and pulled them on. She waited, watched while he grabbed his duffel and followed her out to the hill leading up to the house. Ashley's feet slipped and he grasped her elbow to steady her on the incline.

At the top they ran, slipped and slid across the wet grass to the front porch. Finally they made it and Ashley laughed as she ran up the steps. Joe looked up in time to see her nicely rounded rump at eye level, and that's when he noticed she wore a T-shirt and nothing else. A *wet* T-shirt.

He groaned.

"I know. How can it be so hot and the rain be so cold?" She swung around to face him and her mouth parted with a gasp.

Joe tried to hide his need for her but he figured at this point, why bother. She knew all there was to know about him.

"Oh, Joe."

That was all she said before she stepped close and pressed her body to his. Her hands cupped his face and since she was a step above him, she stared straight into his eyes, searching.

He knew what she searched for.

"I swear to you, I didn't. Ashley, I'd trade my life in a heartbeat if I could. I didn't hurt her. I didn't kill her."

She nodded once before she kissed him. Joe dropped his duffel to the porch floor and filled his hands with cold, wet material and hot, willing woman.

Ashley moaned against his lips. "Inside," she murmured, licking the corner of his mouth with a sexy little stroke that set his body on fire.

Ashley pushed him away but grabbed hold of his hand and opened the door. Joe stooped and lifted his duffel, then stared at her in dawning wonder.

She believed him.

Inside her room, Joe had barely closed the door when Ashley grabbed the long T-shirt and pulled it over her head.

He groaned and reached for her.

"Oh, no. This time you've gotta wait," she murmured. "This time is for both of us."

Warmth filled him and in that moment he knew he'd spend the rest of his life proving to her and Max how much he loved them.

Ashley smiled and curled a finger for him to come to her, backing toward her bed.

"Ashley—"

"Don't," she whispered. "We have plenty of time to talk and figure things out. And we will," she promised huskily. "Later."

His heart thudded hard against his chest. "Whatever you say, boss."

Her breasts jiggled as she laughed. "I think I

like the sound of that." Her head tilted to one side. "But in the meantime one of us is overdressed."

Joe lifted a hand to the snap of his jeans.

"I knew I shouldn't have let you put those on," Ashley said while she watched Joe ease the zipper over his straining erection. Their cold run to the house had done nothing to suppress the heat inside her. Heat generated by the images bombarding her head with every step she'd taken with Joe at her side.

The future would have to be faced, the police chief dealt with. But for now she had Joe and she wasn't letting him go.

His jeans and briefs hit the floor. "Now who's overdressed?"

She liked this side of him. This teasing, masculine side that turned her on and gave her the shivers at the same time.

Her hair was wet from the rain and she felt a drop of water slide over her collarbone to the tip of her breast. And thanks to the light she'd left on to read the latest home repair book she'd picked up at the library, she knew Joe saw it as well.

"You are beautiful."

She felt beautiful the way he looked at her. In Joe's eyes she was just the way she was meant to be.

"So are you." His body was lined with muscle, hardened, seasoned by years of having to defend himself against other inmates. She shoved those thoughts away, unable to think about all that could have happened.

Joe closed the distance between them and just when her breasts met his chest, she lowered her head and kissed the tattoo on his arm. "Turn around."

"Things won't work that way," he teased, the words rumbling out of his chest.

Still, he did as she asked and she got an eyeful of taut backside and corded muscles. She smoothed her hands up his arms, trailed her fingers to his shoulders, in to his neck and down his spine. She rose to her tiptoes and pressed another kiss to his skin, this one to the tattoo of Josie's name.

"Ashley." His voice broke, husky, filled with too much emotion and needing an outlet. Joe turned so fast she gasped, and even though she stood mere inches from the bed, he swept her into his arms to lower her to the surface. Then Joe's mouth covered hers, his tongue delved deep and she immediately discovered a difference between this kiss and the ones they'd shared before she'd found out the truth.

Joe's hesitation was gone. Her acceptance of him, of his past, had unleashed something inside him, a fierceness, a tenderness.

His lips left hers to explore and they followed the same path as the droplet of water earlier. Rough, callused hands rasped over her skin, teased, dipped into curves, his fingers stroking and squeezing until she had a hard time catching her breath because over and over he'd find some erotically tender spot and the air would rush from her lungs again.

His head dipped lower, his hands smoothed over her legs and parted them even more as his lips grazed her stomach, her inner thigh. She closed her eyes when he found her. Kissed her with a passion long denied and within moments she flew with a hoarse moan of surrender.

She loved him, loved him.

"I love you, too, babe."

She hadn't realized she'd said the words aloud until Joe's husky murmur slid over her skin. Until he kept repeating the words while he hastily donned the condom pulled from his wallet and settled himself between her legs. He kissed her and she sighed, knowing everything, no matter how difficult, would be all right. It had to be. Wilson's faith in the power above had rubbed off on her. They'd find a way.

Ashley sucked in a breath as Joe pressed deep. It had been so long. Not since the night of Max's conception. Joe paused, his arms straining. He held himself still when he obviously wanted to move.

She smoothed her fingertips over his face. "Don't stop."

"I don't want to hurt you."

She smiled through the tears stinging her eyes, raised her head to press her lips to his the same time she lifted her legs and curled them around his hips. She pressed him down, deep inside her, and moaned when she felt Joe's strength.

The care he took with her, his gentleness, made it all too clear how wrong she'd been.

Her climax caught her by surprise. She gasped, her body tense. Maybe it was because it had been so long. Maybe it was Joe. Maybe it was the love they shared, more powerful than any she'd ever known.

Joe caught her moan with his mouth, his hard body pumping into hers, once, twice, then harder and faster until he groaned out his own release.

JOE AWOKE WITH A START and wondered where he was. An instant later he felt Ashley's body tucked up against his and smiled. After making love for the first time, they'd showered and then made love twice more.

Max whimpered, and Joe recognized the sound from the monitor as the same that had woken him. He glanced at Ashley and saw her sleeping deeply, her mouth parted slightly.

The soft shadows beneath her eyes had him getting out of bed and ignoring the voice in his head telling him not to push too hard, too soon, and chance screwing things up.

Still, he padded into Max's bedroom, the night-light allowing him to see replicas of Ashley's eyes staring up at him. "Hey, buddy. You hungry?"

Max rolled onto his rump and pushed himself up to a sitting position.

"You're not going to scream if I touch you, are you?" Joe braced his forearms on the crib, his hands out, and waited to see what Max would do. If he didn't want him to pick him up, fine. Either way the choice was up to Max.

Tiny hands, their strength unimaginable, latched on to his fingers. Max pulled himself up and took a step toward him in the crib. Joe smiled and carefully lifted Max into his arms.

"Okay, it'll be us guys then. We'll let your mama sleep."

Slowly so he didn't frighten Max, Joe made his way down the stairs to the kitchen. He'd watched Ashley make Max's bottles countless times so he did the same now, holding Max in one arm while he measured the powder into a prepared bottle of water.

Hesitant, he nearly panicked when Max whimpered and reached for the bottle before it was ready. Joe shook it harder to get the mixture to dissolve and Max glanced up at him, then laughed his little baby laugh at the jostling.

"You like that, huh?" He shook the bottle a bit more to hear the sound again. "Okay, it looks ready. Here, try it out."

Max took the bottle in both hands and leaned his head against Joe's chest while he drank. Legs weak from the whole process, Joe headed back upstairs. He entered Ashley's bedroom long enough to turn the monitor off, and then carried Max through the bathroom and back into the nursery.

Joe eased himself down into the rocking chair with a sigh. "You keep staring at me. Am I doing something wrong?"

He got a blink in response.

"You want a story, don't you?" He shook his head. "Sorry, buddy, I don't know any."

Another blink. Max pulled the bottle from his mouth and stared up at him, a pout forming on his lips. Joe gently bounced the baby boy in his arms. "Okay, okay, I get it. You gotta have a story 'cause your mama always tells you one."

As though understanding or at least willing to give him another chance, Max put the bottle back in his mouth with a sigh.

"Once upon a time," Joe began uncomfortably. "That's how they're supposed to start right? Okay, so…once upon a time, there was an unbelievably beautiful woman with a son named Max…"

ASHLEY STRUGGLED THROUGH the fog of sleep and turned on her side. That's when she noticed her body was sore and achy in a pleasant way—and Joe wasn't in her bed.

Max.

She sat up so fast her head spun. Had he really slept through the night for the first time ever?

She shoved the sheet aside and grabbed her nightshirt from the floor only to discard it with a wrinkled nose. It was still damp and cold—no way was she putting that on.

She grabbed the sheet from the bed and wrapped it around her, tucking the end between her breasts. She'd check on Max then hop in the shower. Get dressed and go find Joe. Humming one of her favorite country love songs, she entered Max's room only to stop in her tracks.

Joe sat sprawled in the rocking chair dressed only in his damp jeans. Max was held firmly against Joe's bare shoulder, both sleeping soundly, an empty bottle on the floor by Joe's feet.

She stared at them, her hand over her mouth to muffle her gasp. How could she have ever thought Joe would harm a baby? Even now, in sleep, Joe was protective of Max. Tender. His arms firm and guarding.

Just like he'd protected her from the lightning. Risked himself in their fall. Volunteered to stay in the shed.

One after another the images came. Joe at the nursing home reading to those whose eyesight wouldn't allow them to read for themselves. Joe fixing a wheelchair and hanging a picture, moving a hospital bed for a woman who didn't want to lose her job. All thoughtful, wonderful, considerate things. Things an uncaring, selfish, mean-spirited person wasn't capable of doing on a regular basis. Things he could've blown off but didn't.

She must have made some sound because Joe awoke, but unlike the way he'd startled awake in the shed, this time he merely opened his eyes and smiled a sexy, sleepy smile as he pressed his bare foot to the floor and set the rocker in motion.

Then he saw her. His face darkened, he stiffened, the rocker stopped. "Ashley, I—"

Joe shifted in the chair as though to stand and Ashley quickly stepped forward and placed her hand on his shoulder before leaning over him and pressing a kiss to his lips. "Would you mind holding him long enough for me to shower?"

She let the impact of her words sink in, knowing it would take Joe a while before he understood that she trusted him with Max. Joe had spent the last ten years fighting to protect himself, and that wouldn't change overnight. Nor would it be easy to face a town that already thought them different. But together they could and would stand strong. Lean on each other.

He blinked at her as though unsure he'd heard her correctly and she kissed him again. "I won't be long, but if he wakes up and cries just bring him in." She smiled tenderly at the raw emotion she saw reflected in his eyes. "I love you, Joe. Me and Max both. Enjoy the snuggling."

TWO HOURS LATER Joe was still shaking his head at how fast things had changed. When he'd opened his eyes to find Ashley standing beside the rocking chair, he'd expected her to be angry, upset at least. Instead she'd given him a kiss that broke through the last of his reserves, and made him hopeful.

"So what do you think? You like it?"

He turned to find her holding a paint stick up for his perusal, the light brownish color pooling off the end. "It looks good."

"Uh-huh, you couldn't care less, could you?" she asked, her tone amused.

He winked at her, but didn't respond. At the moment the only thing he wanted to do was take her back upstairs to bed and hear her say a million more times that she loved him. He'd never hear it enough, never feel it as much as when he was in her arms.

Max played on a blanket on the floor, mouthing every toy he picked up and staring at him with his mama's eyes. Ashley had still been in the shower when Max had awakened and Joe knew he'd never forget the moment Max lifted his lashes and yawned sleepily before smiling up at him.

Whether she knew it or not, Ashley had given him the most precious gift imaginable by trusting him with her son. He was still afraid of doing something wrong, still afraid of someone saying something to Ashley that would make her doubt him. But regardless of the future, Ashley and Max were worth whatever risk he took with his heart.

"Okay. The paint's mixed but I forgot to get a clean pan. Can you keep an eye on him while I find one?"

He nodded. "No problem," he murmured, still working his way along the wall with the double-sided tape.

Ashley flashed him a smile of thanks before she left the room, and he watched the sway of her hips with an appreciative leer. "Max, you've got one hot mama."

The boy gurgled out a response and picked up another toy. Chuckling, Joe turned his attention back to the wall and shifted so he could flatten the tape along another couple feet.

He glanced over his shoulder at Max and found him turned around on his rump, facing the door as though looking for his mom. "She'll be right back, sport. Just hang on a second."

Joe fingered the tape in a couple spots to press it down and then glanced at Max again. "Hey, Max?"

The baby boy ignored him and didn't turn but just when Joe was about to move farther along the wall, he noted Max's head had taken on a reddish color.

"Max?"

The boy turned then, his little eyes watery and wide, his face going from red to blue in the space of a heartbeat. The air rushed from Joe's lungs and in a split second he held Josie, watched as she couldn't breathe anymore, and panicked because he didn't know what to do.

Right then and there *his* heart stopped, but with a rush of adrenaline he tossed the tape aside and scrambled across the floor.

This time he knew CPR.

This time, he knew what to do.

This time a baby wouldn't die.

ASHLEY HEARD Joe's shout in the utility room and took off running, but the sight that met her eyes when she made it through the kitchen and down the long, long hall was one she'd never forget.

Joe hunched over Max, his face white as a sheet and his hands around her baby's neck. Max strained weakly away.

"What are you doing?" She rushed toward them and tried to shove Joe out of the way to see what was wrong with Max, but Joe shrugged her off with superhuman strength. "Joe! Let me—*get away!*"

Joe ignored her prying hands, ignored the accidental scrape of her nails when she tried to get Max from him. Then suddenly Max gagged, coughed, inhaled deeply and screamed for all he was worth. Ashley tore at Joe to get to her son.

Joe finally let him go and she pulled Max away and held him tight, rocking him back and forth and trying to calm him down. Joe got up and quickly staggered out of the room.

"Max, oh, God, Max, what happened? What happened?"

Max quieted some, enough that Ashley was able to really see him. A trickle of blood mingled with the slobber at his mouth and she gasped. "Max?"

That's when she saw it. Lying on the floor where Joe had knelt with Max was one of the plastic outlet plugs she'd been installing throughout the room for Max's protection. It was covered in water. And blood.

"Joe?"

No answer. Shaken beyond measure Ashley picked Max up and ran from the room, grabbing her purse on her way out the kitchen door. She'd find Joe later. Thank him for saving her son and make sure he was okay.

The scene must have made him think of Josie. Had to have brought back the nightmare. He'd need time. Distance.

And she couldn't do anything about that now. She had to get Max to the doctor.

Five minutes later she'd broken every speed limit between her house and town and arrived at Bryan's office. She carried Max inside, past the patients waiting and the screeching receptionist who demanded she stop, down the hall to the exam rooms.

Bryan left his office once he heard the commotion. "Hey, you aren't due in for a couple more hours," he said, referring to Max's appointment later that afternoon. He stilled when he got a good look at her face. "Ashley, what's wrong?"

"We have to see you *now*."

Bryan tossed the chart aside and indicated the room behind him. "This one's open, come on."

She ignored the receptionist hovering behind her and carried Max into the exam room, Bryan following.

"What happened?"

"He choked on this," she said, pulling the two-pronged plastic outlet cover from her pocket. "I heard Joe shout and I ran as fast as I could and Joe was hunched over him and—"

"Joe?"

She nodded and tried to breathe. Now that the crisis was over, now that her son was safe and with Bryan, she was rapidly falling apart. The shaking she'd held in check breaking free. "Joe B-Brody."

Bryan gave her a quick glance she interpreted easily. "He's—I hired him as my handyman. Joe isn't what people say he is, though. He's not, Bryan."

Bryan took Max into his arms and laid her son on the exam table, his stethoscope in his ears. "What was Joe doing to Max when you saw him?"

"He— I don't know. He had his fingers around Max's head and—and in his mouth." She ran her hands through her hair and tried to calm down. "I freaked. Max wasn't moving and Joe wouldn't let me near him—"

"Was Max crying?"

"No."

"Not at all?"

"*No.* There—there was blood at the side of his mouth after Joe let me have him though."

Bryan frowned at her comments, but then smiled down at Max. "Hey, little man, can I see your throat? You've got to open up, okay?" Gently but firmly Bryan inserted a tongue depressor past Max's lips to shine a light inside. "Looks like it scraped the top of his mouth and the back of his throat. He's cried since then?"

She nodded. "At the house. After— He started screaming. That's when Joe gave him to me."

Bryan felt Max's neck and throat, listened to his heart again, checked his pupils and took his temperature with an ear thermometer before picking him up off the table and turning to face her. "Looks to me like Max is fine."

Ashley pressed her hands to her cheeks and sobbed. "Are you sure?"

"I'm sure. You on the other hand…" Bryan's expression softened even more. "Ashley, Max is fine. He choked, and as scary as it was, he's all right now."

She inhaled, over and over again. Tried to pull herself together.

"Hey, don't hyperventilate on me."

"It's just—I just—"

Bryan pulled her against his chest, one arm around her and the other holding Max. "I know. It's scary when it happens to you but scary as hell when it happens to someone you love." He patted her back soothingly before drawing away to look into her eyes. "Joe's the guy you were thinking about the other night, isn't he?"

She wiped the tears from her cheek with a hand that wouldn't stop trembling. "I'm sorry. Yes, he was—*is*—but I know he wasn't trying to hurt him," she added firmly, afraid Bryan might say something to the police chief.

Bryan's mouth twisted into a smile. "You don't have to convince me, Ashley. I'm holding Max, remember? Despite Joe's past, looks to me like he saved Max's life by getting his air passage cleared."

More tears leaked out. "Oh, thank you, God."

"Where's Joe now? Did he drive you?"

She shook her head. "After he gave Max to me, he left and I know he thinks I think the worst but honestly, I just wanted to get to Max. To hold him because I knew something was wrong. I didn't think he was hurting him. He wouldn't hurt him, Bryan, but I know he probably thinks—"

Bryan rubbed her back again. "Calm down,

Ashley. You can explain it all to Joe as soon as I give Max his shots and drive you home."

Ashley took Max from Bryan and held him close, kissed him repeatedly. Bounced him and patted him, unable to keep from touching him. "Are you sure he should get them today? After all this?"

Bryan flashed her a tolerant smile. "He's *fine*. You're welcome to reschedule if you like, but it is good to stay on track with these things. Max is healthy, high in his percentile for weight and height. And you didn't have any history of gestational problems so we don't have to worry about any of the weird complications cropping up like they can with a preemie or sick child."

She searched her mind for what she'd read in her baby books, but drew a blank after the trauma of the day. "Tell me again what his weight and percentile ranges have to do with the shots?"

Bryan settled his hips against the exam table behind him, patient tolerance etched into his features as though he'd heard the question a million times before. "If a baby is underweight sometimes it's best to wait and give the inoculations when they're bigger and stronger. If a child is really small due to premature birth, or a candidate for the side effects for other reasons like severe illness, I like to break them down into smaller, more manageable doses. But Max doesn't have to worry about that, do you, big guy?"

Ashley stilled when Joe's voice filled her head.

Josie had been underweight. Tiny, according to Joe. And she'd been to the doctor days before. For shots?

"What about the preemies?"

Bryan's smile turned into a frown. "What about them?"

"Could they be in more danger from the shots? For the complications? What are the complications exactly?"

"Ashley, the reactions are very, *very* rare, and Max wasn't a preemie. But, to answer your question, some vaccines can lead an already ill child to have blood vessel irregularities, which means the brain may not receive enough blood."

"Can that cause seizures?"

Bryan shook his head back and forth as though he debated whether or not to answer. "If the dosage was full strength and too much for the size of the child or if—"

"So it's possible?"

"Yes," he finally confirmed with a reluctant nod. "But it's rare. Now, tell me why you—"

"What about other problems? Overwhelming stress? Blood pressure problems with the mom, problems delivering? Could all those things add up to increase the probability that the baby might react?"

Joe swore he didn't hurt Josie, and she believed him with her heart and soul. But Joe also believed Melissa was innocent which meant—

"That would certainly add into the equation, yes, but—"

She blinked up at him, afraid to get her hopes up too high. "Bryan, did you know Melissa York and Joe had a baby girl that died?"

He pinched the bridge of his nose with a sigh. "I was afraid that's where you were going with this."

She looked at him, stared into Bryan's eyes and hoped the compassion she sensed within him ran deeper than any river on earth. "He saved Max's life, Bryan. And he *swears* to me he didn't do it. And yes, I believe him because after all these years, after going to prison for it, why would he bother to lie about her death now?"

Bryan's disbelief was evident in his eyes, his expression.

"Bryan, something happened to that baby. Something Joe didn't do. Please, I need you to look into this for me," she begged.

He shook his head. "Ashley, the odds alone—"

"*Please.* If you won't do it for me, do it for— for science. For your patients. Especially for Josie. For *Max.* Check into this. You told me you spent your residency in a big hospital back east. They would have up to date information on this, wouldn't they?"

"Yes, but—"

"Please, Bryan."

He stared at her a long moment. "I do have a

buddy who's a pediatric specialist. If I remember correctly, he's gone to court on a case like this once. If anyone would know more about this, he would."

THAT EVENING Hal frowned when he pulled up his drive and found Dr. Booker's Mercedes parked by his door. He shifted the cruiser into Park and got out, his heart thumping wildly as he ran up the walk. A neighbor had called him when she'd seen the doc's car and now he entered his house, glad she had.

Melissa was hysterical.

"What's going on? What's happened?"

Mel raised her head from a woman's shoulder and Hal frowned when he recognized her. "What are you doing here?"

"She came with me," Dr. Booker murmured. He stepped from the kitchen carrying a glass of water and pressed it into Melissa's hand. "Drink this."

Hal moved forward only to have to stop and go around the baby boy crawling across the floor. "*What* is going on?"

Melissa finally found her voice. "I can't believe it. All this time. Oh, he's got to hate me." Melissa put her head in her hand and cried some more.

"Mel, what—"

The doc straightened. "We came to talk to Melissa about Josie."

Hal curled his hands into fists and glared at Ashley Cade. "What have you said—"

"He didn't do it," Melissa choked out. "Dr. Booker doesn't think Joe hurt her."

Hal shifted his gaze to the doc. "He did."

"There are multiple factors that indicate something else might have happened," Bryan said.

"The lack of bruises," he snapped. "Josie didn't weigh anything. He didn't have to grip her hard and that's why he didn't bruise her."

"Chief, there's reason to believe it could have been from something else."

"What *else* could explain a man shaking his baby to death?"

Booker inhaled. "I checked with a colleague of mine back east. He's one of the best pediatric specialists in the States. We went over every aspect of Josie's file as well as Melissa's records."

Hal stiffened. "How did you get those?"

"Melissa used to be a patient of my grandfather's before her diagnosis. I had copies of her records in my office. But the point is," he continued, "we went over everything and after talking with Melissa, we've drawn a different conclusion—that Joe didn't kill her."

"Then how did she—" Hal stopped, unable to go on, unable to take it all in. It wasn't possible.

Joe was guilty.

"Swelling of the brain caused by an accidental

overdose of an inoculation given too early to a baby too small. Vaccinations for children are safe so long as the children are healthy, but if they're not—"

"The baby was fine."

"Josie was under distress first during Melissa's pregnancy, then during premature birth. I, uh, took the liberty of checking Melissa's hospital chart. Her blood pressure was much too high during her pregnancy and extraordinarily high when she was sent to labor and delivery. The baby's heartbeat was erratic and stopped *twice* during labor. That's why her doctor performed a caesarian."

Hal felt his knees grow weak. Could it be possible? "Nobody ever told us her heart stopped."

"My guess is that they didn't tell either of you about the problems because Josie's tests came back within the normal ranges. Sometimes the effects of lack of oxygen don't show up for years, sometimes not until the children are in school. When her tests came back fine, I'm sure they felt there wasn't any need to frighten you any further than you already were under the circumstances."

Hal looked at his daughter. The little boy had crawled across the room to where his mother sat comforting Mel and now he used Mel's pant legs to pull himself up. Even though she cried, Mel smiled at the baby.

"Keep going," he ordered.

"Because of the multiple complications,

Josie's vaccinations should have been more closely monitored."

That got his attention. "You're saying they weren't? Who was the doctor?"

"Dr. Peters," Melissa whispered, her voice hoarse. "He's in Florida now with his daughter. He has Alzheimer's, remember?"

Peters. The man had been older than the hills and thought of as a quack, but in small towns where doctors and money were typically scarce, the people took what they could get and prayed for the best.

Booker cleared his throat. "I was talking to Ashley today about shots for her son when she asked specific questions based on some things Joe had said to her. She asked me to follow through and I did. Josie received full-strength vaccinations three days before she died."

"It's my fault."

Melissa's comment had Booker lowering himself onto his knees in front of her. "It's no one's fault. The doctor should've known better, yes, *but* odds of something like that happening are astronomical. *No one* could have predicted such severe complications, not even Peters."

"But if I'd paid more attention to the dosage…"

"You aren't a doctor or a nurse," Ashley murmured.

"And this scientific information wasn't available until the last few years, Melissa. Ten years ago no one knew it was a possibility."

"I certainly wouldn't have known if it were me," Ashley continued. "Melissa, you're not to blame. That's not why we're here. We wanted to confirm Josie's behavior before you left her with Joe that day, that's all."

"But you're saying that killed her?" Hal questioned, still unsure. "Not Joe?"

Dr. Booker stood and stared him straight in the eyes. "In my professional opinion and given the lack of bruises or other abuse common in Shaken Baby Syndrome, yes. I can get a statement from the doctor I contacted if you'd like, confirming what I've told you. For some babies, the mistake wouldn't have mattered, but with Josie and with all the other complications…it was too much. The type of reaction she had mimics the brain damage done by Shaken Baby Syndrome. The blood vessels swell and burst, seizures, brain damage—exactly what would have happened if she'd been violently shaken."

Melissa's sobs filled the room. "Joe always said he didn't do it. *Always*. But no one believed him. *I* didn't believe him." Her sobs increased again. "What have we done? Ten years of his life were taken away for nothing!"

The enormity of it hit him then and Hal fell back into a chair. Dazed, sick. Mel was right. For ten years he'd blamed Joe. Watched an innocent kid be sentenced to a life most men wouldn't have survived.

He lowered his head into his hands and closed his eyes, but quickly opened them again when Ashley Cade's baby boy pulled on his legs and smiled up at him, one small white tooth shining.

"Bryan, I'm sorry, but I have to go. I have to find Joe and let him know Max is all right—I have to tell him about Josie. I know what happened today brought back memories for him, and I've been gone way too long as it is."

Hal stood, torn. "What happened today?"

Ashley Cade glanced at Booker before her chin raised. "Max choked on an outlet cover. He couldn't breathe and could've died, but Joe saved him."

He looked down at the baby boy, staggered by the events of the last few minutes. "Doc, can you stay here with Melissa? I'll drive Ms. Cade to— I…I have some things to say to Joe myself."

Booker nodded. "No problem."

Hal walked over to his daughter and drew her to her feet. "I love you, Mel." He kissed her on the cheek, her tears wetting his lips. "You heard the doc. It's not your fault."

"But, Dad—"

He forced a smile to his lips. "God's will be done, Mel. God's will be done. Josie's in heaven with your mama, keeping her company until we get there."

JOE SQUATTED DOWN next to Josie's grave and placed the bouquet of wildflowers at the base of her headstone. He was on his way to Baxter, but knew he couldn't pass the cemetery without stopping.

"Josie, I—" Tears clogged his throat and he swallowed them back. "I'm so sorry, baby girl. I'm so sorry I didn't know what to do for you." He fingered the lettering of her name, the tiny angel carved into the stone so similar to the one on her crib. "And I'm sorry it's taken me so long to come see you." A shudder racked him before he regained control. "I didn't want to see you like this, you know? I always want to think of you as awake and smiling and—" Joe ran a shaking hand over his face, his eyes. "I love you, sweetheart. I love you. I'm so sorry."

Unable to stare at her name a moment longer, Joe shoved himself up and grabbed hold of his duffel. "You stay with your grandmas and keep them smiling, okay?" He turned on his heel and stalked away. Head down, his duffel over his shoulder, he left the cemetery.

He'd already walked to Ridgewood and said goodbye to his pop. His old man hadn't wanted him to go, and he'd spent more time there than he should have, arguing with his pop about his leaving. Afraid he wouldn't come back like Jack, his father wanted Joe to check him out of the home early. But with no transportation and very little money, he couldn't do it—wouldn't do it and risk his father's health.

Joe kicked a rock in the road. For one brief moment in time, he'd been happy. Unbelievably so. And he realized it was more than some people ever experience in a lifetime so he should consider himself lucky and let it be enough.

But it wasn't.

She hadn't believed him.

His footsteps faltered, staggered, before he pulled himself together and kept walking. He'd be lucky to make it to Baxter before dark. Fatigue ate at him, dragged him down. The first stirrings of hunger after a day spent sick to his stomach with regrets.

After making love all night, letting him hold Max while she showered, Ashley had still believed the worst. And maybe she should have.

Lord above, he'd panicked. He'd stared at Max in horror when the boy's face turned three shades of purple, and all the while he'd tried to get the piece of plastic out of his throat, he'd kept picturing Josie. Over and over. Dying in his arms.

Don't go.

The whisper came to him from nowhere. A woman's voice. Joe turned, but saw nothing. No one. He shifted the duffel on his shoulder and wondered if he'd lost his mind.

He began walking again, picking up his pace. He didn't want to go anywhere. He wanted to stand

and fight, wanted to somehow make Ashley believe in him. Wanted to make the whole town know he wasn't a baby killer, but that was an impossible task and sometimes a guy had to know when to cut his losses and go.

The Lord's unfailing love surrounds the man who trusts in Him.

The line from his mother's favorite Psalm came to him then as though sent directly from her, something he couldn't ignore.

Inhaling deeply, Joe paused there by the side of the road, his feet seemingly unable to move, the sound of crickets and bullfrogs in his ears, honeysuckle in the air.

He didn't want to go. He wanted to stay. To spend his life with Ashley, but to do that he had to go back and face her. Not take the coward's way out.

Somehow he had to convince her he hadn't been trying to hurt Max. Somehow he had to show her how much he loved them both.

A siren wound into a squawk behind him, but then went silent. Fear spiraled through him at the thought of going back to prison before he could say the things he needed to say, but the verse echoed through his head again.

Joe dropped the duffel, raised his hands. A door slammed behind him and he slowly turned to face the car. He hadn't made the complete circle when Ashley slammed into him, her scent surrounding him even as her arms wound around his neck and she pressed her mouth to his, her tears wet on his face.

"What are you *doing?* I went to the house and you weren't there. You weren't at the shed, weren't at Ridgewood. Joe, you said you wouldn't walk away!"

He blinked, trembled...hoped.

"You thought I hurt Max."

"*No!* Joe, I knew you weren't hurting him. I believe you, Joe, I swear I do. I panicked. Something was wrong with my baby. I heard you shout and saw you—I freaked. I had to get to him, I had to help him and hold him. I admit I wasn't thinking straight, but I certainly didn't think you were trying to *hurt* him." She framed his face with her hands, her expression furious, reminding him of the first time he'd seen her in Thompson's hardware store. "I *love* you, Joe Brody. I believe in you and I know it might take a while for you to believe in me, but don't you *dare* walk away from us after telling me you love—"

Joe smothered her words with his mouth.

"Joe, *umph!* S-stop— You—"

He didn't want to stop. If Hal was going to drag him to jail on some trumped up charge, he wanted Ashley's taste to remember, to hold with him always.

"If you'd let her up for air she'd be able to tell you we have something to say, Joe."

The chief's tone got through the haze surrounding him. Joe looked up to see Melissa's father leave the cruiser running and walk toward them.

In the back seat, Max was tucked firmly in his carseat, sound asleep.

Ashley slowly pulled away from him but stayed within arm's reach, a hand at his waist. Her gaze slid between the two of them and she licked her lips nervously. "First…I need to explain something to you. Something very important."

And there on the road, outside the cemetery where Josie was buried, Joe learned the truth he'd always known. He staggered but Ashley was there, her arms firm while she held him close with support and love.

Silence surrounded them, broken by the sound of the idling vehicle, crickets and birds. Ashley's soft, husky voice telling him everything would be all right.

"I don't know what to say, Joe," Hal murmured finally. "'I'm sorry' isn't enough, and it never will be enough, but Lord knows I am." Hal's voice broke and the larger-than-life chief battled to hold on to his composure. "If I could go back in time—"

"We can't," Joe informed him gruffly. Rage, the senseless loss, bombarded him at once. "We'd all change the past if we could."

Hal nodded, his head down. "I'll do what I can to help you," he continued. "Set things as right as I can. Try to make up for…everything."

Joe accepted the offer with a tense nod, knowing it would do no good to voice the responses in his head. He was willing, desperate, for the past to finally be over. And now that it seemed it might possibly be, he was also afraid he'd wake up. Afraid he'd dreamed the whole thing.

Believe.

Ashley stiffened, lifted her head from his shoulder and looked around them curiously. "Did you hear something?"

Joe kissed the top of her head and took in the many rows of headstones, the one where the wild-flowers lay already wilting. He blinked, barely breathed, narrowed his gaze when he thought he saw a little girl holding hands with two women. Two women who looked amazingly like his mother and Melissa's.

"Joe?"

He didn't look away until the image faded into nothingness. Then he swallowed, felt a peaceful-ness he hadn't ever had before.

"Joe?" Ashley said again. "Are you ready to go home now?"

He pulled her close, hugged her too tight and buried his nose in her hair. "Yeah," he whispered, inhaling the scent of her. "I'm home."

EPILOGUE

ASHLEY WAS EXTREMELY conscious of Joe's proud
gaze when she and the mayor of Taylorsville cut
the ribbon marking the official opening of Willow
Wood Bed & Breakfast. Max squirmed in Joe's
arms to get down and she watched with a wince as
he took off running and immediately stumbled.

Big tears filled her son's eyes, and her heart
tugged with love as Max turned to Joe for help.
Several murmurs of approval sounded around her
as Joe righted Max, brushed off his tiny hands and
then had Max smiling soon after.

She sighed. Things just kept getting better.

Since the choking incident, she hadn't worried
as much about being accepted or forcing herself on
people. Partly because she'd realized the best way
to go about things wasn't to put herself in uncomfortable situations, but to simply be herself. Instead
of a stranger, she was now a neighbor, a friend.
When she went to the store, people greeted her by
name—the same at the library, the gas station, the
post office. Once she'd gotten over her fear of

being rejected and placed her concentration solely on being a good, friendly person, things had changed. She had changed.

All she'd had to do was take the first step. Smile, pitch in to help someone in need. Little things that meant more than she'd ever dreamed they could. Maybe in the beginning her reasons for helping were selfish, but now, well, now she couldn't imagine not helping out the people who brought such happiness to her life.

Bryan, Melissa, Hal and Mrs. Hilliard had also seen to it she and Joe were invited to a multitude of gatherings. Even Mr. Thompson had come around, and as though sensing her perusal, he lifted an obliging hand in greeting where he stood talking to the mayor.

Smiling at the turnaround and still amused at his earlier begrudging praise on how nice her house looked, Ashley swung around to find her fiancé only to discover him closer than she'd thought. In a blink she stood nose to chest with Joe just like that first night after the storm.

Her smile widened and as a result, Joe bent his head and kissed her, a hot, sensual caress that made her knees weak each and every time it happened.

"Wow," she whispered when he lifted his head. "Trying to boost my confidence over the ribbon-cutting or convince me to sneak inside?"

Joe's chest rumbled beneath her ear while he

hugged her close. "I think it's a great turnout. Exactly what I predicted each of the hundred times you asked," he teased. They both looked around at their guests, the evening twilight giving the party a special warmth. "But there's one thing that could make it even better."

She blushed. "Joe, I was kidding. We can't sneak inside now."

"Sure about that?"

Ashley leaned against him, loved the strength of him surrounding her. She'd been on her own for so long. But not anymore. She had a family now.

"We've worked too hard getting ready for this," she chided, smiling. No matter how badly she'd like to join him inside behind a locked door, she wanted to savor every moment of the evening.

"So let's stay outside and make this really special."

She glanced up at him in question.

"We've already bought the rings. You've got a dress." He nodded over her shoulder. "The mayor's here." He paused. "And I sort of took it upon myself to have him bring a license with him."

Her mouth parted. "You mean...*now?*"

"Why not?" He took her hands in his. "You asked me to give you a walk in the moonlight once, now I'm asking you to marry me in the moonlight. Tonight."

She gave him a teary smile. "On the porch steps with all the flowers blooming around us?"

Her soon-to-be husband laughed as he squeezed her. "Wherever you like."

Excitement rose amongst their guests and now that she paid attention, she realized quite a few already knew what Joe asked. Small towns were like that. People always knew what you were thinking before you thought it. Asking questions that would have offended her at one time, but now made her feel welcome. Cared about.

"Well, Joe?" Hal York's voice echoed throughout the yard.

Ashley glanced around at their guests, at their expectant, encouraging faces. Hal and Melissa York. Bryan. Joe's father, Ted, and Wilson. Mrs. Hilliard and the whole gardening club, their families. Taylorsville city officials. Even Nam—short for Not A Mutt—lurked in the shadows with his shiny new dog tags listing Willow Wood as his home. The only person missing was Jack. A flicker of protective anger seared her before she squelched it. Joe's brother would come home one day. And when he did, she'd be ready for him.

"Is that a yes?"

Her arms tightened around Joe's neck, her gaze locked on his. She might not be from Taylorsville, but she lived there now and she'd protect her family no matter what. "Yes."

"Do I still get to give you away, missy?"

"I get to stand up with Joe," Ted added.

Ashley tilted her head back and laughed, happier than she'd ever been in her life. "And Max is the ring bearer," she said softly. She bit her lip nervously, one small detail left. "Mrs. H., would you be my Matron of Honor?"

The older woman eagerly stepped forward while the ladies in the gardening club flew into motion and set about making a bouquet from the various plants blooming around the yard.

Ashley watched as everyone pitched in, rearranging chairs, gathering up potted plants and adding them to the stairs where she and Joe would stand. Wilson hurried inside to get a tie.

A shiver raced through her. She'd found home.

"Look okay to you?"

She stared up at Joe, fingered his lips and smiled when heat flared in his eyes despite their audience. "It looks absolutely perfect."

And exactly how she'd pictured a home to be.